PUREHEART

A Time Warden Chronicle

Thomas W. Everson

Welcome to Salvoa, an Earth-like planet with humans living their lives. This is a work of fiction. Any presumed likenesses of names, characters, businesses, governments, or places is all just coincidence.

ISBN-13: 978-0-9864120-7-3

<u>Dedication</u>

Thank you to my wife, my friends, and my coworkers who have been supportive and been my morale boosters. Your enthusiasm for my stories is exactly why I write.

Contents

Acknowledgements

Thank you to my beta readers, Brandi M. (my wife), Lillie B., & D.P. I take your feedback seriously because I want to do my best job at entertaining people. The stories are what they are because of you.

Thank you to Jake Murray, my cover artist, who always provides nothing but the very best artwork. His ability to take what I write and turn it into an image is unparalleled. Pureheart needed the feeling of "care" embodied in the imagery, and I knew in Jake's hands, that's exactly what I'd get.

Thank you to Tim Marquitz, my editor, for providing the professional sounding board I need to make sure things flow right. I am a better writer because of not only the technical corrections he provides, but also the outside perspective he brings.

Prologue:
Story of the Reset

"I need details. All the stuff you know. All of the people we met. I know you've been to see them! Start with Emma!" *she* begs, tying her brunette hair up with a red ribbon.

He laughs and leans back in the wood chair at the head of the kitchen table. He pulls on his white shirt to unwrinkle it.

He thinks fondly of the times their group had at the table together, before the timeline reset. Emma was the little sister he never had, figuratively and literally. She holds a special place in his heart, so, of course he was keeping tabs on her in her new timeline.

"Once upon a time Emma's parents, Phyllip and Gwendy Pureheart, were destined to perish. A train derailment would have left her orphaned. However, they never got on. Instead, a *mysterious couple* on the street offered them tickets to a United Fighting Arts match under the guise that they'd purchased them for friends, but the friends backed out."

"Mysterious nothing. You and Auntie intervened, didn't you?"

He shrugs, smiles, and continues.

'We purchased two sets, but our friends can't make it, and we don't want them to go to waste,' he told them. 'Would you like to go with us?'

"They accepted, and the four of them went to the UFA tower."

"In between rounds, the owner of the establishment, Trevor Lindali, called for a volunteer from the audience. He had a challenge. Last one round in the ring with one of his biggest fighters and win ten thousand credits. With Gwendy's approval, Phyllip volunteered and went toe-to-toe with Driesen, "The Behemoth." Not only did Phyllip last the round, but he landed some good hits, too.

"When it was all said and done, Trevor declared Driesen the winner, but on top of the credits, he offered Phyllip a full-time position as a UFA fighter. After a thoughtful discussion about their future, Gwendy gave him permission."

'We'll be able to afford to send her to a good school,' Phyllip said, beaming. Gwendy smiled.

"Once upon a time, Emma's story would have been much different, but that timeline no longer exists. Her biggest worry now was simply to live her life," he says.

"And then?" she questions.

"And then what?"

"That can't be it. Auntie has been chronicling all of your adventures for something. What is it?"

"Ohhh, you want a full story?" He laughs.

She smacks him in the arm. "Yes!"

"Okay. Just keep in mind, though this is in the future, these events are set. Emma has a new destiny to fulfill."

"Get on with it!"

♥

Chapter 1
Decision of Life

Emma leapt out of bed at the sound of her alarm. It was Celebration Day, the day where she would make the most important decision of her life to date. All the previous school year she'd been tested on her strengths and weaknesses academically, as well as evaluated on personal tastes and extracurricular activities. It would all culminate in a choice of career paths and what classes she would be enrolled in at her new school.

She and Gwendy had argued over her dressing up versus wearing her casual overalls for this momentous day. They'd come to an amicable agreement they would have a tailor create a nice pair of overalls, one that both fit Emma's tastes of comfort and her mother's sense of style.

After a quick shower, Emma changed into them and a clean white shirt. Gwendy came in and smiled.

"Would you like me to do your makeup for you?" her mother asked.

"No thanks, Mom! But could you do a high braid for me?"

"Of course, honey."

While her mother braided her long, blonde hair, Emma wondered what her test results would be. What career options would she be given? Gwendy finished and rubbed her daughter's shoulders thoughtfully.

"Hurry up and come eat breakfast," she said and left Emma to finish.

In contrast to her norm, she applied light makeup and likened her image in the mirror to an alien. Neither she nor her best friend Rina cared too much about appearances. It's one reason they got along so well.

Skipping out to the living area, she joined in the morning family routine. Phyllip had breakfast cooking. Gwendy set the table. Emma poured their drinks. With the pancakes and bacon laid out and their juice poured, they sat to eat.

"So, are you nervous?" Phyllip asked.

"No. I've been pushing social and humanitarian studies hard. I think I'll be able to get into a career field where I can help others."

"If you're given the Caregiver Path as a choice, you could become a nurse or doctor and might be able to get a job bandaging your father up after his fights. He certainly doesn't dodge well," Gwendy said and let out a little snort of laughter.

Phyllip grabbed his chest, feigning being wounded by her words. "Maybe you could be a mental health specialist because I need therapy from all the thrashings your mother gives me."

Gwendy smacked him playfully, and he smiled big. Emma giggled.

"Maybe I'll be an infirm assistant. You *are* getting older," Emma jabbed in between bites.

"Might as well put me in the grave now," he joked, and they laughed.

With her breakfast wolfed down, Emma cleaned up and checked the clock. There were still two minutes before Rina would ring the doorbell. She grabbed a light jacket and kissed her parents on their cheeks.

"Good luck, honey!" Gwendy said. "We'll be right behind you and watching from the other side of the colosseum stands."

"I can't wait to hear what you pick," Phyllip added.

The doorbell rang, and she answered it. Rina, also slightly more dressed up than normal, tapped her boot impatiently. Emma threw her arms around her friend in a bear hug. Rina hugged back.

"Come on, slowpoke! We're going to miss the train," Rina chided.

"Not if we run we won't." Emma bolted down the hall.

She reached the elevator and smashed the button several times. Thankfully, it hadn't been called to any other floor, and the doors sprang open. Rina was only halfway there. Emma ducked in, but not before giving her a cheeky look. She pressed the thirtieth floor button and let the doors start closing before her friend had reached the elevator.

"Hey!" Rina yelled out.

Emma giggled and pressed the 'Open' button.

"Now who's the slowpoke?" Emma taunted.

Rina hopped in, giving Emma a playful poke in the arm. They laughed and talked as the elevator headed to the roof.

"Do you think we'll have any classes together?" Rina asked.

"Hopefully, at least core classes."

The elevator opened to chilly air, and they walked to where a group was gathered to wait for a train. Passing the ticket booth, both girls flashed their permanent passes. A slight breeze crossed the building tops, taking with it some clouds. She heard the train coming and turned around.

It pulled up, and Rina's face paled. Emma grabbed her hand and held tight.

"It's okay to be nervous," she said.

Rina smiled, and they boarded the train hand-in-hand. They sat on a bench seat facing the windows and watched the metropolis of Chas whiz by. The train stopped several more times before dropping to ground level. The campus of their new school was enormous, with multiple buildings and a colosseum. It intimidated Emma a little, but she didn't let Rina notice. They exited and followed the other kids.

With forty-five minutes to spare, they had time to get to the colosseum and find seats for the ceremony. Emma led, pulling Rina along to where all the other kids gathered. Banners hung over several doorways to direct students in. Greeters were stationed at each entrance and, when it was their turn, Emma and Rina were greeted.

"Welcome to Celebration Day at Chas Elite Academy! Please, find your section by the first letter of your surname and take a seat! The ceremony will start soon!"

The inside of the colosseum was decorated with bright-colored balloons and streamers. A cloth banner spanned the length of a dead-center stage, which had the words 'Celebration Day' embroidered in gold. Behind the stage were tables, food, drinks, and a wait staff prepared to serve them after the ceremony.

Emma's heart leapt to her throat, and she felt instantly cold when she and Rina separated. She joined a group she didn't recognize. It was hard to be her exuberant self because she didn't know them.

Looking across to the other side of the colosseum, she tried to find her parents as adults were funneling in. It was far, and the mass of people just looked like a multicolored blob to her. When the groups coming through the doors slowed to a trickle her focus shifted to the stage. Administrators took positions on a stage, and one of them spoke into a microphone.

"Today is more than choosing your career path. It's a celebration of moving from childhood to adulthood. Today, you shape your destinies in how you will not only better yourself but build the future. You will affect lives and contribute to society. Honor to you, the next generation, and choose well."

Emma had poured over the career path list a year ago. There were so many paths and specialties off the parent paths. Many sounded appealing, but she really wanted something that would help people. When taking her evaluations, she purposely picked the selfless answers, not only because she wanted that path, but because she genuinely felt it was her calling.

One by one, students were called up in grand announcements, and they chose their paths. When chosen, the administrators clapped, and the crowd followed. The rest of their lives would revolve around the choice as, once you'd chosen a path, it was quite difficult to change afterward.

She'd heard her father's story a hundred times, as he loved to tell her all about the fateful night his and her mother's lives were changed. How he'd gone from a waste manager to a guild fighter.

Her mind had wandered some, and when she came back to reality, it was Rina's turn to head to the stage. She held her breath for her friend.

"Marina Gladia, step down and embrace your destiny!"

Holding her head high, Rina descended to the stage. Once with the administrators, she shook hands with everyone and, at the end of the line, she stood in front of the podium that held her three options.

Emma knew her friend wouldn't be following the Caregiver path, but she didn't know what other choices would be offered until she talked to her after the ceremony. When Rina chose, Emma was the first to leap up and cheer. She yelled as loud as she could for her and clapped so hard it hurt.

Through the rest, Emma's heart beat harder and faster. Those leading up to her were called and, finally, it was her turn.

"Emma Pureheart, step down and embrace your destiny!"

She stood slowly, and then made her way down the steps. One foot in front of another, she did her best to not trip. Her head swam, and she grabbed the rail. At ground level, she'd managed to stay upright and not embarrass herself. In her daze, she nearly passed the first administrator who offered their handshake in congratulations.

She shook the first's hand with fervor, and they offered a word, "Miss Pureheart, choose wisely."

On to the next, the cycle repeated.

"Miss Pureheart, do great things."

"Miss Pureheart, change the world."

She was sure every other individual received similar words of encouragement, but the confidence in their voices gave her a sense of importance. At the end of the line was the final administrator. She seemed to beam with pride at Emma, though a total stranger.

"Miss Pureheart, before you are three choices. This is your calling to be something greater than the individual. From here, you become part of our ever growing society."

Back to reality, the anxiety returned. She stepped up to the podium where three cards were laid out, face down. Turning each one over revealed her three path choices: Social Engineer, Educator, Caregiver. All of them fell under her want to make a difference in peoples' lives. A social engineer would require a steep climb to start making a difference, while educator and caregiver would be immediate.

It felt like she stood there for an eternity, weighing the differences, the pros, and the cons. Her muscles locked up from the tension. The closest administrator put her hand on Emma's shoulder to reassure her. Emma reached her hand out and picked up the Caregiver Path card. It felt like the right choice. She smiled and turned to the administrator and handed them the card.

"Congratulations Miss Pureheart. You have taken control of your destiny and have many opportunities ahead of you."

The clapping for her commenced, and somewhere in she knew was her dad clapping and hooting so hard that people around would be staring. Before now, she'd never been the subject of so much attention. Her face became hotter than it already was, and she wanted to cover her cheeks to hide the bright red she knew they'd turned. She quickly exited the stage and climbed back to her seat in the colosseum stands.

Though she'd received much praise for choosing, she was now back into anonymity. Many more students came after her, and she clapped for them with a newfound appreciation. When they reached the last student, the administrators concluded the ceremony.

"Congratulations to all of you! Tomorrow, you'll pick up your class schedules and begin your specialized training. But today, we have a celebration planned for you! Enjoy the festivities!"

The horde of students were dismissed and upbeat music began. While the students made their way to the party, the first thing Emma did was find Rina, who was waiting for her and smiling wide. They chatted while they made their way to the festivities.

"So, what did you pick?" Rina asked.

"I got caregiver! You?"

"I grabbed the entertainer card. I'm going to join a guild!"

"That's great! You'll get past the stagehand level in no time!"

"I hope so. I hear it's rough."

There was a buffet-style lunch laid out, and they stood in line to be served. Emma was famished, and so she let the servers load her plate up with a little of everything. Rina let out a scoff.

"Save some for everyone else," she berated, grinning.

"Nope, all mine." Emma clutched her plate tightly.

Emma saw an empty table near the side and pointed it out to Rina, but they were beat to it by another small group. It was big enough for all of them, so Emma sat anyway and introduced them.

"Hi, I'm Emma! This is Rina. What did you all get?"

"I'm Skye. That's Van, and that's Chase," the girl said, gesturing to herself and her friends. "I chose the Builder Path."

"Servicer Path," Van answered.

"Entertainer," Chase said.

This piqued Rina's interest, and she chimed in, "I picked entertainer, too. What guild do you think you're going to go into?"

"Fighter's guild," he answered.

"My dad's a fighter for the UFA," Emma interjected.

"Who's your dad?"

"Phyllip Pureheart. He's been with the UFA for a long time now."

"That guy who got in the ring with The Behemoth, right?"

Emma laughed. "So, I've been told a million times."

"Are you going entertainer, also, then?" Skye asked.

"No, I wanted to do something different. I picked caregiver."

"Oh! That's great! I hear those path cards aren't easy to come by," Van's volume rose with enthusiasm.

She hadn't thought about it before. She just knew she had a desire to help people in meaningful ways, and that path guaranteed it. Each of the paths were designed to contribute to society while providing people with enough money to make a living, but her mother had always pushed having a selfless attitude. Hearing they weren't easy to come by bolstered her confidence in her pick.

The five of them finished eating, and Skye suggested they head out to the open area to dance. While Emma wasn't shy, she hadn't ever danced in public. Rina, however, readily jumped at the chance, and pulled Emma along. Leaving the boys behind, Skye led both of them right into the center, and she and Rina expressed themselves however they felt. Emma eventually gave up her fear of being watched and danced alongside them.

Many others joined in, and the night ended on a high with the three girls worn out. Exiting the colosseum, they headed toward the train and joked with one another.

"I look like an angry chicken when I dance, flapping my arms all around," Emma said, and then clucked a couple times, flapping her arms. The girls laughed.

"I'd be a lumbering tarak with all the stomping I do," Rina said.

"A tarak?" Skye asked.

"A giant lizard myth." Emma bumped Rina with her shoulder. "Rina likes to think they're real."

"They *are*! People have seen them! They might even be in our government!"

"Yeah, right." Emma laughed. "Those people are crazy."

The train pulled up, and the three of them entered. Emma sat on a bench seat facing the window. The train got under way and climbed steeply to reach the tops of the buildings. The sun had set, and Chas was lit up. It never ceased to be an awe-inspiring sight for her.

Before she knew it, Emma's building was announced, and she nearly missed it until Rina poked her.

"Hey, get your head out of the clouds!"

"Oops!" Emma jumped up and headed for the exit. "See you tomorrow!"

Out onto the rooftop, the frigid air bit her skin. The wind was blowing harder than she'd felt it before, and she ran from the platform to the elevator bank. The door opened quickly when she pressed the 'Down' button but, even inside, it was still chilly.

Down to the tenth floor, she exited into her hall and crept quietly to her apartment. Pulling out her key, she entered and found her dad laid out on the couch, ice packs placed all over his body.

"Did you at least win?" she said while jabbing his bare foot.

He pulled an ice pack from his face to respond. "Nah. Anthony got the upper hand in the fight. Knock out in the fifth round."

"Are you okay?"

"Yeah. You hungry? Mom left you dinner in the fridge."

"No, I'm still stuffed from the buffet. I'm going to head to bed. I'll need a lot of energy for the transition tomorrow."

"Okay. Sleep well," he said and returned the ice pack to his face.

Retiring to her room, she readied for bed. It took only a few minutes to change into her sleepwear and pull her braid out. At her vanity, she sat down and retrieved her diary.

The school was huge, and the ceremony long. I met some new people today. Skye, Van, and Chase. Skye seems really fun. The boys didn't come dance with us, but that's okay because I would have been nervous. I got one of the paths I wanted. I'm going to be a caregiver. I just need to figure out what that means for me.

She closed the book and went to bed.

♥

Chapter 2
New Everything

Rina had met Emma at her door as usual, but when they got to school, they separated. They split toward their respective path administrator offices to get their class lists. Emma waited in a short line before entering the Caregiver Path office and sat in the chair. The name on the plaque was 'Mr. Seeker.' He looked up from some papers and smiled at Emma.

"Good morning, Miss Pureheart. How are you feeling about your pick?"

"I'd be lying if I said I wasn't nervous, but this is what I want."

"There are a lot of opportunities out there, and through the next few years you'll get a feel for a lot of different aspects of being a caregiver."

He handed her class list over, with their start and end times, and then a map of the school.

"Do you have any questions for me at the moment?"

"No, not really."

"That's okay. If you do think of any, my office is always open. The rest of the day is yours to collect your materials and locker assignment from the library and locate your classes for tomorrow," he said.

"Thank you!" She nodded and jumped up from her chair.

Racing to the library, she hoped to find Rina done with her appointment so they could stand in line together and maybe get lockers close to one another. Entering the double doors, it was clear finding her was going to be harder than she hoped. The room was packed.

Due to Emma's shorter than average height, she couldn't exactly see over the heads of people to find her, either. She hung back by the doors in case Rina came in while she scanned the crowd.

The doors opened and shut dozens of times before a face she recognized walked through. It wasn't Rina, though. Skye popped in and gravitated to her. Her wild hair and baggy shirt made it look like she'd just rolled out of bed.

"Hey, Emma!" she said, her energy level dwarfing Emma's.

"Hey! How'd you sleep after all that dancing?"

"I was out as soon as my head hit the pillow."

Emma giggled. "You look like you just got up."

"I did!" She laughed. "Waiting for Rina?"

"Yeah. Trying to get a locker near hers."

After waiting a few more minutes, Skye jumped into one of the long lines and waved Emma over. She was reluctant but made her way slowly.

"If she comes in, we'll pull her in with us," Skye reassured.

The line made its way toward the front. Emma kept her eye on the door, and when Rina finally came in, she excitedly waved her over. Rina frowned and approached.

"Sorry, it took a while to get through the administrator's office," she said with an annoyed sigh. "Apparently there was a large wave of people who chose to follow that path."

"Well, we got in line and figured you'd show up eventually," Skye blurted.

Rina squinted at her. Emma knew this was her look of frustration and interjected.

"I was waiting for you, but Skye suggested we get in line and pull you in," she said. "So, what core classes did you get, and what times will you have them?"

They compared their class lists, and Skye joined. Emma was going to share language and general health classes with Rina, and intermediate math and lunch with Skye. She was happy she'd at least get two classes with Rina but sad they didn't share lunch.

"Since we have the same lunch period, we should definitely sit together," Skye offered.

"Uh, sure," Emma replied hesitantly, feeling like she'd somehow betrayed Rina.

After a long wait, they reached the front of their line and got lockers near each other. Their arms were loaded up with heavy books, with Emma's being the tallest stack. She nearly couldn't hold it all, balancing them precariously as she walked.

Rina led them to the elevator, and they went to the third floor. Toward the end of the building, they reached their lockers, and Emma was relieved to be able to set her books down. Inside the locker were bookshelf partitions, which made it easy to organize her books, and she put them in order of her class list. When they were finished, Rina took Emma's arm in hers.

"Ready to go?" she said, anxious to get going.

"Sure!" Emma smiled and closed her locker.

"Wait for me!" Skye called out.

Rina rolled her eyes. Emma wondered why, but she didn't say anything. Skye grabbed Emma's other arm, and as they walked arm-in-arm they took up a large portion of the hallway on their stroll.

They explored the first floor and made their way from one end to the other. Her classrooms were spread out all across the school, and it would be a trial to make it to them all on time if she stopped by her locker between each period.

"I'm not looking forward to my history class," Skye said.

"Which one did you get?" Emma asked.

"Architecture of Salvoa. I don't want to learn about the world's past. It's boring. Tell me about what's going on now, and I'd be much happier."

"History of entertainment should be fun. I want to learn from the greatest examples of people who knew how to draw a crowd and keep them engaged," Rina said, almost as if purposefully being oppositional.

Emma was looking forward to her fundamental clinical skills class. She'd start her hands on training for a possible medical career and helping people. The doctor's office was immediately outside the physical fitness gym on the ground floor.

"I'm going to take a look inside," Emma said. "I'll meet you in the cafeteria for lunch."

"Okay," Rina replied and waved as Emma left. Skye did the same.

The office was a well-lit room, with a reception desk. The room had six beds, three on each side, with draw curtains between each. At the back were supply shelves, where a man in a long white coat organized various things. About halfway in, she cleared her throat to announce her presence. He turned around and pushed his large-rimmed glasses up.

"Yes?"

"Hi, I'm Emma. Are you the instructor of fundamental clinical skills?"

"I am. Do you need medical attention?"

"No. I'm going to be in your class at the twelve-thirty period."

"I have four students each period, times five periods, so you'll have nineteen others you'll be competing with," he said and crossed his arms.

"Competing?"

"That's correct. You'll be competing with your peers at the end of the year, which will also be the final exam. It'll be on what you learn in my class and your ability to treat various injuries. As someone who deals with the caring of others, you and the others are training to be professionals."

This pressure wasn't expected, at least not at first. She already knew those principles were important, and she'd be graded on them, but not that she'd be judged against her classmates.

"I'll have handouts for students tomorrow. The syllabus, standard practices, requirements to pass, and the competition details. If you'll take your leave now, I have preparations to finish."

He wasn't being rude, just curt, but Emma was still taken aback. It was clear he was serious about his job as either a teacher or the school doctor.

"Okay, thank you. I'll see you tomorrow!" Emma kept her cheery tone.

There was still time to kill before heading to the cafeteria, so she wandered the halls. She recognized some kids from her previous school, but none she'd ever talked to. Rina and she were a duo, not really looking to expand their unit until they'd met Skye, Van, and Chase. They'd been friends since she first entered school and been nearly inseparable.

If her father had never been offered a career switch, they'd never have moved from the center of Chas to closer to the UFA building. She'd have never known Rina, and she couldn't imagine her life without her best friend.

Lunchtime came, and she met up with Rina at the doors. It would be the only one she'd get all year with her, so she intended to make the best of it. Rina had an excited buzz about her.

"Guess what?" she said with exuberance.

"What?" Emma replied.

"I was able to get my lunch period changed to yours!"

"That's great!"

With that news, her heart lightened, and she pulled Rina to the lunch line. After making their selections, the two found an empty table to sit at. Skye showed up, with Van and Chase following behind. Rina sighed. It was becoming clear Rina was feeling crowded.

"Hey, look who I found hiding behind the school," Skye said.

The boys waved.

"Did you guys find all your classes?" Emma asked.

"Yeah," Van replied meekly. "Should be easy enough to remember."

Chase only nodded as a response, focused on his food, practically gorging himself. His plate was piled high, and Emma wondered where he packed it all away in his wiry frame.

"That's a lot of food! My clinical skills class falls after lunch, so don't overeat and come in with a stomachache," she told Chase, hoping to illicit a response.

He looked up and gave a half-smile. He wasn't talkative before, either, and Emma wondered if he was also feeling out of place hanging out with new people.

"Rina, you coming to the library tonight?" Emma asked.

"Yeah. I'm in the middle of this steamy romance called *Experience the Rain*. It's about this time traveler who falls in love with someone from his future, and they have this weird unspoken love-angst between them. I need to find out what happens."

"Sounds weird," Skye blurted. "I don't think time travel is possible. Otherwise, some idiot from the future would have come back by now and messed things up."

"That's not the point," Rina fired back. "It's fiction. It's something to read and get my creative mind going. Who knows, maybe it'll inspire me, and I'll be some big author here in Chas."

Skye shrugged and nodded at the same time.

"Yeah, I guess you're right. Do you want to be a writer?"

"I'm not entirely sure yet. Still feeling out my options."

The table became quiet, and they all finished eating.

There were still a few hours left in the school day, and Emma had already seen the classrooms she'd need to remember. The idea of touring the colosseum in daylight seemed fun.

"How about we go explore the colosseum before we head to the library?" Emma asked Rina.

"Sounds good to me," she replied.

Skye didn't miss a beat. "We'll come with you."

They deposited their trays onto the rotating dish rack and headed out. Though she'd already seen it, the colosseum was still awe-inspiring. The sheer size was enough to make people admire it but, once there, they could see the beauty of the detailed columns and arches.

Inside, they walked all around the perimeter. There were many corridors, and Skye wanted to investigate them all. Rina stayed toward the back of their group, and Emma stuck with her.

"I don't know if I want to keep hanging out with Skye," Rina whispered. "It was fine yesterday, but she's too...intrusive?"

Emma wasn't sure what to say. Though Skye was acting a little standoffish with Rina, Emma figured it was probably just her personality.

"She seems to like hanging out with us. We should give her a chance."

Rina grumbled. Emma pushed her playfully and smiled. She pushed back, and they giggled. Skye and Chase were too busy opening random doors to notice Rina's discontent. Van looked back at her, then to Rina, and smiled.

"Besides," Emma pushed her again, "Van's been sneaking glances. I bet he's thinking about how pretty you are!"

"Shut up!"

Rina shoved back so hard Emma almost ran into the wall, which made her laugh. This gained Skye's attention, but she didn't say anything.

They'd circled the whole colosseum and found a few locker rooms, sports equipment, decorations from yesterday, and some poorly lit passageways they didn't dare explore. The afternoon was getting on, and Emma had to make her way to the library.

"Rina, it's about time to head to the train," Emma said.

"See you tomorrow!" Skye said.

Everyone gave a courtesy wave except Chase. He stared off into the distance. She wondered if there was something wrong with him, but she'd have to ask Skye another time.

The duo walked to the train, and Emma looked forward to spending a few hours helping people in their pursuit of knowledge.

♥

Chapter 3
Getting Into Routine

Her night was uneventful. It may have only been helping people find the books they were looking for, but it was satisfying.

When she got home from the library, Phyllip had dinner heating up for her, and they ate together. She could tell he was antsy to get back into the ring because the whole apartment had been thoroughly cleaned.

In the morning, Gwendy prepared a hearty meal.

"You're going to need a lot of energy," she said, referring to it being Emma's first day of classes.

As per normal, breakfast was their family time. She told them all about the school, her tour, and that she'd be put in competition with her fellow classmates in the clinical skills class.

"I'm sure you'll do well, honey, but don't let it consume you," Phyllip said.

"I won't," she replied with a smile.

Rina came over, and they headed to school. The train was packed with students, but there was still sitting room. When they arrived, the campus was more like a zoo than a school. Packs and herds roamed around before the first class. The two of them cut through and headed to their lockers. While Emma was getting out her language book, Skye appeared.

"Hey, Em! How's it going?" Skye said, bouncing like she couldn't hold her energy in.

"It's going okay. A little nervous."

Skye smiled. "Nothing to be nervous about. It's only school."

"I know. I just want to do my best!"

"You will," Skye reassured her, and winked.

Rina approached and practically ignored Skye.

"Ready to go?"

"Yeah!"

Skye waved as they parted ways. "See you second period."

When out of Skye's earshot, Rina sighed loudly. Emma couldn't understand what was causing her friend distress. Did she feel like she was being encroached on? Only Rina could really explain it, and Emma was content to wait for her friend to find the right words.

Emma was average at language studies. She always did her best, but there were always others who outperformed her, including Rina. Rina had a way with words and understood the intricacies, the art of language. During the introductions of the class, Emma thought about her friend's future in entertainment. Though Rina had probably been joking about being a great author, Emma believed it was entirely possible.

Other than introductions around the room, they received the class syllabus. It would help her understand what was coming up, and then she'd get coaching from Rina as needed. The teacher spent most of the time discussing the expectations of the class, and then right before the period was over gave out the first writing assignment: "My Five Year Plan."

"This assignment will not only allow me to see each of your strengths and weaknesses but also serve as a tool for you to get into the mindset of planning for your future," Miss Baker said.

Five years would put Emma past graduation and into her first job. What *would* she be doing? Before she could really dive into thinking about it, the bell rang, and the students left for their next class.

Out in the hall, she and Rina parted ways, and she climbed the nearby stairs to the second floor. At her math class, Skye was looking around, and when she saw Emma, she smiled.

"Hey, you!" she greeted.

"Hi!" Emma waved at her.

"Was your first class as boring as mine?"

"It was okay. Already have my first assignment."

"Ew." Skye crinkled her nose. "Let's sit together so I'm not bored."

Emma nodded, and they entered class. Skye led them to the back of the room and sat in the far left corner. Emma had never sat this far away from the whiteboard, so she wasn't sure how well she'd be able to hear. When the teacher entered and spoke, she could hear him surprisingly well, but only because he projected his voice.

"I'm Mister Yvara, and this is intermediate math. We'll be dealing with real numbers in this class, as they relate to the real world."

"Boring," Skye whispered. Emma giggled quietly.

As he laid out the details of the class, Skye made faces and goofed around. Emma couldn't help but laugh, but she hid it from Mister Yvara. He continued on and jumped into writing math problems on the whiteboard in varying difficulties. He called on students to answer them, and if they got them wrong, he wouldn't move on to the next person. He explained the math until the student could answer a similar problem.

The class was engaging despite Skye's continued distractions. Emma felt confident about this teacher's style. Though she already knew the material, it wasn't as boring as Skye suggested.

Her next class was on her own. History of medicine was exactly what the title advertised. Day one was an introduction to what they would be covering, but it was going to start with current events and work backward. She took a few notes as the teacher tried to make jokes about how awful medicine used to be and hailed their career field as making groundbreaking advancements every day.

It was over before she knew it, and she was excited for her next class. Not because it was interesting but because it was with Rina. They saw each other in the hall and became animated.

"Today has me excited for the rest of the year!" Rina said. "I'm going to learn so much, I don't know if my brain can handle it all!"

"I haven't got to my exciting stuff yet. I'm really looking forward to my clinical skills period."

They continued to chat as they found their way into personal health. Sitting about mid-room, Rina regaled her with a tale of her first taste of entertainment, intro to theater, where they discussed nominations for the school's productions for the year. Rina put up the novel she'd just finished reading to be adapted for the stage.

The teacher entered and began detailing how the class would help them keep their own healthy lifestyles, both with nutrition and physical fitness. Though everyone had to take the class, Emma looked at it as a practical piece of her caregiver training and diligently took notes.

By the end, her stomach was growling to the point she thought it might be heard, even in the noisy hallways. Rina led the way to the cafeteria, chattering away about how she would adapt the book into a play. Emma loved the passion in her friend, and it made her happy to hear her excitement.

In line to get their meal, Emma loaded up with breakfast items while Rina chose more traditional lunch foods. The table they sat at yesterday was empty, so they took seats there.

"So, what do you think so far?" Rina asked. "This is so different than being in one classroom all day."

"It's a little weird, always having to run from one room to the next."

"I'm a little stressed out from it." Rina laughed.

Skye and Chase came from the lunch line and sat with them. Skye sighed loudly.

"I don't know what I was thinking, choosing the Builder Path!" she said while shoveling food in her mouth. "I mean, it was between servicer, builder, or maintenance. I chose builder to follow my dad's path because that's what people do, follow a parent's footsteps. But this is going to be so much work!"

Emma was exasperated at how fast Skye spoke.

"Being a builder gives you lots of options, though, right?" Emma asked.

"Only if I do well in my courses. If I don't, I'll end up with a super menial job like assembly or something."

"There are no menial jobs," Rina said without inflection. "Everyone with a job contributes to society in one way or another. To say otherwise demeans anyone you consider under you, but the fact is, society would crumble without everyone doing their part."

"Well, we'll agree to disagree," Skye retorted and side-eyed Rina. "I want to be at the top of the chain."

Rina exhaled a 'humph' and tried to engage Chase.

"What did you think of the intro to theater class?"

He shrugged. "It's not my thing. I'm just looking forward to getting in a fight ring and showing what I can do. I'm going to be the best."

"Well, we have strength training next," she replied. "We should partner up, keep each other motivated."

"Yeah. Whatever," he said and gave her a quick glance.

At the end of lunch, they parted, and Emma headed to the doctor's office. Every step closer made her more nervous. She was intimidated by the idea of being put on display and judged while under pressure.

Arriving at the office, the three other students in this period filed in, one of which she recognized from history of medicine. The moment they were inside, the doctor began.

"I am Doctor Mansworth," he said and tapped on the nametag on his lab coat. "I am your trainer, and you need to understand this class is more critical to your future in caregiving than any others this year. This is the practical part, and your final grade here will give weight toward what path specialties open up to you.

"As a caregiver, in any position, you will need to know how to provide both general and individualized treatment. In many circumstances, you will be the first responders in a situation and, as such, your responsibility is great."

The speed and accuracy he belted out his speech gave Emma the impression he'd been saying it for as long as he'd been teaching.

"Grab your nametag and put it on. When people see a name, it builds immediate rapport and will help with any interaction you have with someone."

They did as they were told, and Emma raised her hand.

"Yes, Miss Pureheart?" the doctor acknowledged.

"You mentioned yesterday there's a competition?"

"You're jumping ahead, but yes."

He handed them all a syllabus for the class, and she looked over it.

Fundamental Clinical Skills Syllabus 101

1) Basic treatment procedures:

- Vitals assessment

- Therapeutic communication and bedside manners

- Leadership and delegation

- Documentation

- Wound treatment and aftercare

- Pharmacology and pain management

- Slings and splinting

- Cardiopulmonary resuscitation

- Basic tenants of head trauma care

- Minor burn care

2) Bloodborne pathogen and infection control.

3) Demonstrate care related to patients.

4) Application of treatment procedures.

It seemed like a lot to her that they would cover all this and become proficient at it, but she knew not everyone would be cut out for a career in the medical side of the caregiver path. This was just a prerequisite. What path did she want to follow? Did she want to be a doctor? Would she want to be a specialist?

Putting possible life goals aside, she focused on the now. She would put forth her best efforts, no matter what. They all finished reading the pages and turned their attention back to Doctor Mansworth.

"Now you know what to expect, I'll explain the competition. You'll be competing at the end of the year amongst yourselves for the award 'Advanced Beginner Healer,' where all of the skills and knowledge you learn this year will be put to the test. You will be judged, and the person determined as the winner will receive the title and a special commendation to be used toward the career specialty of their choice.

"My class is intense in that, while you will only be learning the most basic of basics, the information you learn will be absolutely critical in your success in any chosen specialty of caregiving. Not everyone is cut out to be a surgeon, or a first responder.

"How well you do here is critical to guiding you to the proper sub-path for caregiving. So, let's not waste time. We'll start now with familiarization of this office. Take a few minutes to learn where things are because you will need to know."

He stepped away from them, and the four students were left to explore the room. Emma began at one side, while the others started opposite of her. One by one, she looked in cabinets and drawers, finding Doctor Mansworth was incredibly organized. In the middle of the two sides of cabinets there was a small freezer with chilled compress packs in it.

When she closed it, she turned and met the others. Though Vera, by her nametag, was in the lead position of the group, AJ and Jakob seemed to be doing things independently. Emma smiled at her but received a cold stare in reply.

"Excuse me," Emma said and moved around her.

She received an upturned nose from Vera, but Emma didn't let it bother her. Her time volunteering at the library put her in contact with people of all temperaments, and it gave her perspective on people difficult to deal with. However, both AJ and Jakob nodded in acknowledgement.

She made her way through the other half of the room, taking note of a tall, clothed, male mannequin in the corner. Upon examination, it had fake wounds on its soft, flesh-like frame.

Emma returned to Doctor Mansworth before the others. He was organizing paperwork and barely noticed her presence. The others returned, and he redirected his attention to them.

"Over the course of the year, we will have no shortage of injuries come through here to gain experience from. In the downtime between my teachings and treating actual patients, you will practice on the mannequin."

The doctor began their first lesson, vitals assessment. Emma pulled out a pad and began taking notes. While Vera didn't show that initiative, AJ and Jakob followed Emma's lead.

They were halfway through the class, and in the middle of practicing on the mannequin, when their first patient came in. It was a sandy blond-haired boy, a bit taller than Emma, being carted in by Rina.

"I told you, I don't need your help." The boy was obstinate.

"Shut up and let me bring you in here."

Rina brought him over to one of the beds, and Doctor Mansworth approached.

"What happened?" he asked.

Rina moved away from the boy and looked down, her cheeks reddening from embarrassment.

"This maniac shoved me into some of the workout equipment. I tripped, and I think my ankle is sprained," the boy said with a sneer.

"You shouldn't have moved my water bottle!" Rina turned and yelled at him. "That was a cheap way to get me off the weight machine!"

"You'd been on it for a while! Your turn was up!"

"That's enough," Doctor Mansworth interjected sternly. "Let me see your ankle."

The boy hung his foot over the side of the bed, and the doctor took a look. He turned to Emma and gave her a directive.

"Retrieve a small icepack and a compression sleeve for his ankle."

Emma nodded and did as she was told. When she came back, she tried to hand the items to the doctor, but he stepped to the side.

"You're going to do it. I'll supervise. First, put the compression sleeve over his foot, then ice and elevate."

Emma did as she was told. She tried to make her movements precise to avoid unnecessary jarring of his injury. The compression sleeve slipped on with only a little difficulty.

She handed the boy the ice pack, and he looked up at her before taking it. It seemed like he wanted to say something by the way he clenched his jaw but didn't. He placed the pack on his foot, sat back against the wall, and Emma retrieved pillows to put under his leg. Emma turned to the doctor, and he nodded.

Doctor Mansworth turned to AJ. "Let's see if you can recall what your parents give you when there's swelling. Get me one tablet of an anti-inflammatory medicine."

While AJ retrieved it, the doctor turned to Rina.

"Dismissed. Head back to class and try not to injure anyone else," he said with a sharp tone.

Rina looked at Emma, and Emma gave her a sympathetic smile. They'd have plenty of time to talk about it later on the train. Rina left, and AJ returned with one tablet of something.

"What did you get him?" Doctor Mansworth asked.

"I got him a Cure-All," AJ answered.

"Good."

As they continued the exchange, Emma noticed the boy looking at her more than the others. It made her a little uncomfortable. Why was he staring?

"What's your name?" Doctor Mansworth asked.

"Denis Lindali."

Lindali. She'd heard that name before. It was her dad's boss's last name. Were they related?

"Okay, Denis. I'll provide you with a note to show your teachers, which will explain the injury and your limitations."

Doctor Mansworth did so and showed it to the students. Emma noted how eloquent he was with his explanation. He handed it off to Denis and proceeded to pull her and the other three away to continue instruction.

♥

Chapter 4
Blossoming Tension

Classes were going okay, and Emma did her best to manage all of the subjects and materials. She had no problem engaging in class, but she was on information overload. Every night, when she wasn't volunteering at the library or going to one of Phyllip's fights, she organized her notes and went over them.

Rina had tried to convince her she was working too hard, but Emma was becoming surer that, if she didn't focus most of her free time on her studies, she wouldn't have a chance at winning the competition.

To add to it, Vera appeared to be doing what Emma was, coming in organized and ready. It was clear Vera wanted to be rivals, as any chance she got she'd attempt to go above and beyond. It backfired when she reorganized the office without permission, and Doctor Mansworth became irritated.

"Everything was where it needed to be for ease of access. After your last class, come back and return things to where they belong," he scolded.

Vera had no recourse. Emma likened it to coming into the library and moving books around so she could find things better but throwing everyone else off.

But the bigger drama in Emma's life built between Rina and Skye. Skye's group was now a daily part of life. Whether it was in class, passing in the halls, or at lunch, Skye constantly sought to hang out with Emma. And Rina by proxy.

Skye's brazenness grated on Rina, and Rina was not short of words to express her frustration to Emma. As they walked from their health class to the cafeteria for lunch, Rina badmouthed Skye.

"She's such a nosy-body, and trouble. We should ditch her. We could sit at another table today." Rina sighed.

"She's not that bad. And Chase and Van haven't done anything." Emma poked her friend playfully.

"Chase is cocky. And she's annoying, and I swear she does stuff to irritate me. Has she said anything about me when I'm not around?"

"No. I would have told you. You're my best friend."

Rina shot her a skeptical side-glance, and Emma smiled sweetly.

They grabbed lunch and sat at the same table they always did. Skye, Chase, and Van were along momentarily. Emma wondered why the boys always followed her.

"Hey!" Skye greeted and plopped down.

"Hey!" Emma waved to the three.

"Want to hang out after school?" Skye asked.

"I can't," Emma replied. "Tonight, I'm volunteering at the library."

"We could come hang out there, then. You could give us a tour."

"It's not a hangout spot, unless you like reading," Rina spoke up.

"It's fine. Do they have picture books? Chase likes the ones with very few words." Skye laughed and elbowed him. He chuckled.

"I need some research materials anyway," Van spoke up. "I'm shooting to be a chef, and that means I'll need about a million cookbooks to learn from."

"There's a pretty good section for that, but I don't know if there's a million," Emma said, laughing.

Skye shrugged and pushed food around her tray.

"I guess we're hanging out at the library tonight, then," she said.

Rina grumbled, and Emma poked her leg under the table. Emma had long finished her food and casually glanced around. On the far side of the room, she saw a familiar face staring at her. Denis looked away the moment their eyes met as if to pretend he wasn't gawking. Embarrassed, Emma got up to put her tray away.

Lunch was nearly over. Instead of sitting back down, she waved to her friends and headed to her clinical skills class. A class was still in session, so she waited outside until it was over. It gave her a moment to reflect.

This hadn't been the first time she'd noticed Denis after treating his sprain. Because she now knew who he was, it was like he stuck out in crowds. She even noticed him more around the UFA building when she went to Phyllip's fights.

The other class ended, and she pushed her thoughts down so she could focus on clinical skills. As the first in, it gave her a few minutes to review notes. The others arrived, and Doctor Mansworth jumped right into proper splinting of various appendages. With no actual patients to work on, they practiced on the mannequin, whom Emma had named Manny.

Her last class, biology, went by quickly. When it was over, she met Rina out in the courtyard. Skye hadn't yet arrived, and Rina was eager to get on their way.

"Can we go, please?" Rina begged.

"We can't ditch them," Emma replied.

"You're too nice." Rina poked her, and Emma laughed.

They goofed around for ten minutes before Skye and crew arrived at the train stop in front of the school. Van stood across from Rina and stuttered his words when he tried to talk to her.

"What are you going to read today?" he asked.

"Not sure yet. Maybe something fantasy."

"Fantasy is a good genre," Van replied. "Maybe after I'm done with my research, you can show me what you found."

Skye sighed loudly and rolled her eyes.

"Shouldn't you focus on getting the career choice you want? Rina can read that stuff because she's becoming an entertainer."

This provoked Rina's anger.

"What are you, his mother?" she responded snidely, and then looked to Van. "I'd be happy to show you."

The train arrived in time to stop the argument. They took up two rows of seats. Rina, Emma, and Skye on one, and Van and Chase on the other. Skye turned sideways, her arm hung over the back of the seat so she could talk to everyone.

"One of these days, my name is going to be on something big like this train. Whether I'm building a train or a skyscraper, I'm going to hide my name in the work somewhere. Like an artist does," Skye stated, making idle conversation.

"Why not become an architect? Then you can have your name on the whole building," Emma said.

"I don't know if I want the kind of responsibility that comes with designing something that large. I think I'll be content to follow someone else's plans."

The city whizzed by below them, and it was a half-hour before the train dropped down to ground level and approached the library. It housed countless books in its four stories and was the biggest in Chas.

There was something about it which gave Emma comfort every time she saw it. Whether it was the inviting nature of the many windows, or the strength of the support pillars surrounding it, it was her third home.

"Now arriving at Chas Master Library," came the conductor's voice through the speaker system.

Before the train was stopped, Emma stood and made her way to the door. The group followed, except for Chase.

"Not coming with us?" she asked.

Chase shook his head. "Naw. Headed to the gym. The UFA is going to have tryouts for a junior league. Need to be prepared so I can secure a spot."

"Oh. Well, have fun!" Emma waved.

The train's doors opened, and Emma was off. Turning around, she beckoned the group and jogged toward the massive archway that was the door.

Inside, she reported to the library supervisor on duty in an administration office to the far right of the first floor. The day's supervisor was Mrs. Grada. She alternated working here and another library down near the center of Chas. Emma loved working for her, and they had something in common. Her husband, Anthony, worked at the UFA, too.

"Good afternoon, Emma," the librarian said with gusto and gave her a hug.

"Good afternoon, Mrs. Grada!" Emma chirped back and returned the hug.

"I have you assigned to floor four today. Please, go to the returned book section and begin sorting."

"Okay!"

As she exited the office she waved and signaled 'fourth floor' to Rina with her hands. Rina nodded, and Emma climbed the first massive staircase.

She *could* take the elevator up, but she rather liked the climb. It was always interesting to watch people from above. From the fourth floor, it was like being disembodied, looking upon a distant world.

Assigned the history section, she looked at the mountain of returned books. While she didn't find the past engaging, someone sure did. Emma hummed a simple tune and organized books onto a cart. As she was setting out to take her first load, Skye appeared and began chatting.

"So, I was thinking, we should hang out more after school. I mean, when you're not volunteering."

"What did you have in mind?"

"Head to the center of the city. There's Asta Park there, and a historic building that might be fun to look around."

"Wanting to see *old* architecture? That doesn't sound like you."

They laughed.

"No, you're right. I actually heard it's haunted, and I figured it would be an adventure."

The word *haunted* sent shivers down Emma's back. Scary stories weren't her thing, let alone a situation which might have an actual apparition. She shook her head while putting books back in their place.

"I don't know about that."

"Are you scared?" Skye smirked. "You are, aren't you?"

Emma felt her cheeks flush. Skye put her arm around her shoulder and pulled her in.

"I'd protect you. We should definitely do it!"

"I think we should find something else." Emma smiled weakly.

Skye sighed and turned away while playing with the books. Emma didn't want to hurt her feelings, but she really didn't want to visit a haunted house.

"So, where do you see yourself going in your career path?" Skye asked.

Emma moved to the next row to continue putting books away.

"I don't know. I haven't really decided on whether I want to be a doctor or some other type of caregiver. To me, it doesn't matter though. So long as I'm helping people."

"That's noble. I guess you live up to your surname," Skye said and smiled at her.

Emma smiled back. It felt like Skye was trying too hard to be liked, which is why, when Rina rebuffed her, she felt sorry for Skye.

After she'd returned at least a hundred books to their homes and helped a dozen people find what they needed, it was time to call it quits. Emma was exhausted and headed downstairs. Skye and Van were nowhere in sight, and she assumed they'd left because there weren't many people left in the library. Rina had passed out, an open book in her lap. Emma shook her gently.

"Hey. It's time to go."

Rina stirred. It took her a minute to come to, and she closed the book.

"Did I snore?" Rina asked.

"Yeah! I heard you all the way up on the fourth floor." Emma giggled. "You going to borrow that one?"

Rina looked at the book and shook her head.

"I'll finish it next time."

They stood and returned the book to the return stacks. On the way out, Emma waived to Mrs. Grada, who was locking up the side office. The librarian waved back.

The air was bitter cold when they exited, and Emma looked forward to her warm bed. The two walked arm-in-arm to the train. They weren't on it five minutes and Rina was asleep again, slumped against her.

There was plenty of time to think about where she was headed, what the future held for her. It wasn't hard to imagine all of the different things she could become. The problem was pinning one specialty down and committing to the years of school.

Nearing her building, she woke Rina. Emma stood and walked to the door. Rina followed. At her rooftop, the doors opened, and she stepped out.

"See you tomorrow," Emma turned and said.

"Mmhmm." Rina waved.

A chilly wind blasted across the rooftops, and Emma ran to the elevator. Inside, she sighed in relief at the warmth. At her floor, she headed to her apartment, hoping her mom would be home.

Emma found her in the kitchen, going over some paperwork. She looked up from her work and smiled.

"Hi, honey. How was the library?"

"It was good. Pretty normal, except I had a couple extra friends come with today."

"Oh? That sounds fun," she replied and stepped back from her work.

"Yeah. Skye hung around most of the afternoon, and then disappeared. I was kind of focused on my work."

"I completely understand." She laughed and pointed to her stack of papers. "Are you hungry? I need a break."

"Sure! Hold on, I'll be right back!"

Emma ran to her room to grab her diary and a pen. She returned and sat on a stool at the counter.

How do I mediate between two friends? Rina's been my friend forever, and Skye's new. Skye is friendly to me but purposely pushes Rina's buttons. I've never had this problem before. I can't exactly keep them separate since we share lunch, and Skye wants to hang out more.

Her mom heated up a pan and began whipping up a batter. Emma knew what she was making: pancakes. She looked at Emma in between movements.

"What's on your mind, Emma? Something bothering you?" she asked.

Emma frowned. "Is it that obvious?"

"I know my daughter well. You get this little dimple in your cheek when you're thinking too much."

Emma rubbed her cheeks and forced a smile.

"It's just that Rina and Skye don't get along. They're my friends, but I don't think they consider each other friends."

"Do they fight?"

"No, it's more like antagonizing each other."

"Want my advice?"

"Definitely!"

"Find a way to give them more common ground than being your friend. You can't force them to be friends, but if you find something they're both interested in, they might be less antagonistic."

Emma thought for a moment and started writing again.

Mom gave me a good idea to find common ground for Rina and Skye. But where to start? They're on different career paths. Rina enjoys reading, Skye doesn't. But if Skye really thinks that place is haunted in Asta Park, maybe Rina will be interested.

Gwendy served up a plate, with a sweet jam and butter spread on the pancakes. Emma dug in.

"Thanks, Mom!"

"Of course!"

♥

Chapter 5
Subtle Suggestions

Every other day someone would find their way into the doctor's office for treatment from the strength training class. Denis was their most frequent visitor, and though his care was rotated through the other students, he always perked up when Emma was his nurse.

Generally, it was something small, like a muscle cramp or an over-extended joint. Emma thought maybe he was faking to get out of class, but even when she wasn't his nurse, she would catch him stealing glances at her. When she noticed, she pretended not to.

Today was different, though. Her group had only just sat down at their normal lunch table when Denis approached and sat. He briefly looked at Emma, and then to Chase.

"Hey, I need a sparring partner next class," he said to Chase.

"What you *need* is to find another table," Rina barked.

Emma slapped her leg, and Rina smacked her back.

"I thought I'd eat with you all today," Denis replied, and then looked to Chase again. "So, what do you say? Spar with me?"

"Sure. Whatever." Chase shrugged and shoveled food in his mouth.

"So, I know what a couple of your career paths are. What about you?" He pointed to Van.

"Servicer. Playing with different ideas for what path I'm going to get serious about."

"That's cool. My pops owns the UFA, so I pretty much know where I'm going."

"Good for you. Want a medal?" Rina snipped.

"My dad works for yours. He's one of the top fighters," Emma said.

"Who's your pops?"

"Phyllip Pureheart, but you probably know him as Lifeshaver." She perked up and her voice raised with pride. "They say he was named that because getting in the ring with him will shave years off your life."

"Yeah, I've seen him around. He's got a match coming up soon doesn't he?"

"Mmhmm."

"What about you?" Denis questioned Skye.

"Builder." She side-eyed him, and then looked to Emma. "Have you changed your mind about our trip to Asta Park?"

"What trip?" Rina asked.

"Just some place I thought would be fun to explore," Skye replied.

"She wants to take me to a house she says is haunted," Emma said.

"You hate being scared." Rina gave her a look of disbelief.

"I haven't agreed to go."

"It's fine. I promise nothing bad will happen. I'll be there," Skye reassured.

"Where's this at?" Denis chimed in.

Rina interjected before Skye could answer him and snipped at her, "I'm sure she'll be fine if *I'm* there with her. We've been friends forever, and she'd feel more comfortable with me."

"I didn't invite *you*. I invited her." Skye's face crinkled in anger.

Everyone became silent, and Emma squirmed in her seat while they ate. It was disturbing to her being in the middle of this tension. It was Denis, the newcomer, who broke the silence.

"You gonna go to your pop's next fight?" he asked.

"Yeah. I usually do unless I'm studying or volunteering."

"Maybe I'll see you there," he said and stood with his empty tray. He flashed her a smile. "I mean, if I don't get hurt again before then."

Emma's cheeks flushed as he walked away to deposit his tray and exit the cafeteria. Rina was furious.

"The nerve!" she grunted. "Who does he think he is, barging into our table like that?"

"Clearly, he's an entitled little boy who thinks he can interject himself wherever he wants," Skye replied.

"Finally, we agree on something," Rina snapped.

Standing, Emma grabbed her tray and walked away from the table without a word. A cluster of feelings were overwhelming her, which she couldn't sift through sitting there. Rina tried to catch up with her, but she was already on her way out the cafeteria doors and headed to clinical skills class.

Did Denis say he wanted to hang out with her? Why were Rina and Skye being so catty? Rina had more interaction with him than she or Skye had, so maybe she had a right to be upset? Things had become more complicated than she was accustomed to dealing with.

All through class, she couldn't focus. She was preoccupied with the dynamic nature of her interpersonal relationships that she nearly missed Doctor Mansworth calling on her to answer a question.

"Can you repeat that, please?" she asked.

Frustrated, he grumbled and did so. "Explain how you would handle this burn on a forearm, which is deep red and has begun to blister."

"I would run the affected area under cool water for fifteen minutes at a minimum. Then, I would want to apply the antibiotic cream, Burn-Heal, and wrap it loosely with gauze. Finally, I would give the patient a Cure-All for pain."

He frowned and walked away from her.

"Wrong."

"What? That's right, though."

"That's partially right, for a *thermal* burn. Where you're wrong is assuming it *was* a thermal burn because, if you'd done that to a chemical burn, you would actually cause more damage with the Burn-Heal. You would also order intravenous fluids and antibiotics."

He was right, and she knew it. The idea that all burns would require the same treatment was definitely incorrect, and her first action should have been to ask questions about the burn.

"If you want a chance at winning the year-end competition, you're going to have to study harder. I have a top pick for the projected winner already: Marcus Bones.

"If you're thinking about seriously competing, you should know he has completed half of the school year's required assignments."

Emma wasn't caught off guard. She knew his name from other classes because he was also the top student there. But for him to have done that much already, he had to be spending every waking hour on his schoolwork. She wondered what his home life was like for that to even be possible.

"Vera, demonstrate on the mannequin how to properly sling a shoulder."

"Yes, Doctor," she said with cheer, and then gave Emma the stink-eye.

While Vera did as instructed, Emma's thoughts drifted to how she could get ahead, like Marcus. She hadn't really thought of having a rival, no matter how much Vera tried to push her into it. Now, though, since Marcus had progressed so far so early, she needed to come up with a stronger study strategy.

She jotted down different ideas on her notepad, while still paying attention to Doctor Mansworth's critiques of Vera's sling. He tested AJ and Jakob's skills as well, and she wondered if they'd want to form a study group.

A team effort would help them all excel, but she reasoned they would eventually become her direct competitors. Would they be able to work together without constantly trying to compete when they didn't need to?

Her thoughts persisted into her biology class after clinical skills, and Marcus was now on her radar. Though distracted, she was diligent in note taking. She hadn't chosen a career but felt her best chance at opening up opportunities was to win the competition.

Marcus was cool and collected. Any answer he gave, and he gave many, were concise. Not only was she taking notes on what the teacher said, but what Marcus's answers were. To her, it was rational to record his answers, to maybe understand how he was so good at being a student.

She'd filled four full pages, front and back, by the end of the class. When the bell rang to end the school day, she watched Marcus. He stood and picked up a rather large backpack. He shoveled his books in and slung it up over his shoulder. Rather than returning to her locker to put her book away for tomorrow, she followed him and thought about starting a conversation.

He spoke to no one. He didn't visit his locker. He headed straight out from the school and got into a motorized vehicle waiting for him. While formerly common as transportation, motorized vehicles had become widely unused in favor of the citywide train system. The ground vehicles, which were in abundance were first response vehicles, whether it was medical, fire, or law enforcement.

It was clear; he took all of his school's materials home. He was dedicated. Whether it was to win the competition, or to be the best in general, he had a drive she had yet to find for herself.

Emma returned to her locker, and Rina was there.

"You're late," Rina scolded. "But it's okay because you missed Skye."

"I had to check on something."

Instead of putting her books away, Emma copied Marcus, and loaded her bag with as many books as she could. It wasn't large enough to store them all, so she chose the ones most pertinent to helping her win the competition.

"Are you taking those home?" Rina asked.

"Yeah. I need to do some heavy studying."

"Okay. Well, let's get out of here before we miss the second train."

Outside again, they approached the train station. When it pulled up, they got on, and sat in their normal seating. Rina leaned on Emma, and they watched their ascent to the top of the skyscrapers.

"What do you hope to be doing in five years?" Emma asked.

"Star as the leading role in a production. You?"

"I don't know. I'm still deciding. There's a boy, Marcus, who is really good at everything, who is probably going to win the Advanced Beginner Healer award. He seems like he's probably had his answer since he could talk."

"What about being one of those first responder doctors? You'd get to ride around the city. Probably even learn to drive."

It was a great idea. Becoming a doctor for that would provide her with the greatest opportunity to do what she craved. She'd help people and give them a fighting chance to live. She knew it would be a long road and would require her to focus on becoming the best caregiver she could be.

"Thanks! I think I'll look into that." She smiled and hugged her.

"What are friends for?" Rina hugged back.

Upon arriving home, she said bye to Rina and skipped off the train. More and more, the thought of being a first responder became appealing.

Chas was so large, in her entire life she'd only seen a fraction of it. To be a first responder doctor, riding on a mobile hospital, would give her the opportunity to reach beyond her local neighborhood and do good for a greater number of people.

By the time the elevator hit her floor, she was practically bubbling. At her apartment, she burst through the door and proclaimed the epiphany.

"Mom? Dad? I think I might try to become a first responder."

"That's great!" Phyllip stepped out of his bedroom. "What made you think of that?"

"Rina suggested it. Honestly, I don't know why *I* didn't."

"Well, she is your best friend. It makes sense she'd know you well enough to make that suggestion," Gwendy said, coming from the kitchen.

"I need to study hard so I can have a chance at something important like that position. I'm going to head to my room."

"Okay, dear. I'm getting dinner ready before I have to go to work. I'll let you know when it's done!" Gwendy said.

"You're still going to make time for your old man's fights, right?" He chuckled.

"You mean watching you get thrown around? After having to rest up after that last one, they ought to change your name from Lifeshaver to Nap-taker," Emma jested.

"You wound me! Know any good first responders?"

This made Gwendy laugh, and it egged Emma on.

"You know I wouldn't miss one of your fights. Unless I have something more important going on," she jabbed again.

"My feelings!" Phyllip threw himself at the wall and fake sobbed.

"Don't worry. Rina will come along to cheer you on. I'll be rooting for the other guy." She giggled. "Okay. I'm going to study now!"

In her room, she sloughed off her backpack next to her desk. It wasn't large enough to hold all of her books, so she stacked the ones not currently in use on the floor next to her chair.

She pulled out the textbook for Doctor Mansworth's class, the one he never referred to, and opened it to the first page.

♥

Chapter 6
Infatuations

Home, school, home, repeat. The only deviation she allowed herself was volunteering and for her dad's return fight.

Rina had begun to complain about not seeing Emma as much. They didn't have many hang out days after school, but Emma knew she understood her studies were important.

Her mind felt like it was on overload while she juggled what she'd studied at home and what she learned in school. Things started coming together, and what her teachers said made sense, but with every right answer she provided, Marcus supplied two. He continued to stay a step ahead of her without even knowing she viewed him as her rival.

She watched him, and his demeanor. He was stiff. Calculated. It was clear he was dedicated. Outside of the classroom, he didn't interact with anyone, and sat alone at lunch. Emma wondered what caused him to be so closed off.

In their history of medicine class, they received an assignment to pick an era of medicine to study and elaborate on what it meant for the time, how it advanced medicine to today, and what more innovations could mean for the future.

Marcus began writing the moment the teacher had finished giving the assignment, as if he already knew what he was going to write about. Was this in the syllabus, and she just hadn't noticed? She checked. The item wasn't *that* detailed.

In an effort to keep up, she also began writing, but it was only brainstorming ideas for what she could write about. Thinking of the future, she wasn't sure where medical advancements would go. Ideas of what future medicine might be were already out in the world, but their technology hadn't advanced far enough for machines to do the healing.

While she jotted down ideas, she watched Marcus out of the corner of her eye. He continued writing with purpose, barely pausing for more than a few seconds. It was overwhelming to think of what he must put himself through.

The bell rang, and the class exited. They had the next class together, too, personal health. Today was an alternate day, which meant they were working on fitness. There were many options in the class, divided between guided and self-guided activities.

Most kids opted only to follow the teacher in instruction, but Marcus chose to do solo laps around the colosseum. He didn't seem to care about excelling at athleticism. Emma didn't either but, to her, it was an interesting insight to his character.

"What do you want to do today?" Rina asked.

"I'm not sure. What have you been doing in strength training?"

Emma's eyes weren't on her friend. They were on Marcus.

"Everything. Weightlifting, core strengthening, eating pastries," Rina said.

Emma caught the oddity. "What?"

"Oh, good, you were paying attention. What are you looking at?"

"Nothing."

"You can't lie to me. You're distracted."

"Just checking out the competition for the Advanced Beginner Healer award."

Rina looked to where Emma had been looking, and she spotted Marcus.

"Checking out the *competition*, or *checking out* the competition?" Rina poked her and laughed.

Emma hadn't thought of him that way, and so her face flushed now Rina had planted the thought.

"Definitely not checking him out. Just wondering what makes him tick."

"That sounds like a crush to me."

"It's not!" Emma bumps her shoulder into Rina's.

"Okay, okay! How about we do the class directed workout...so you can do some more reconnaissance." Rina smirked.

Emma squinted at her, which only prompted her grin to grow. They jogged to where the class gathered for their routine and followed the stretching poses.

It was there now. She couldn't get the weird romantic idea out of her head, and she silently cursed Rina. She acknowledged it was an infatuation with him but kept having to rationalize that it was over his academic performance, rather than attraction.

In her clinical skills class, she did everything she could to push ahead and impress Doctor Mansworth, but due to his demeanor, he was impossible to read. All she could do was perform to the best of her ability and hope it was enough. She even performed a splint, lift, and transport perfectly with Jakob, but all they received was a nod.

As the class ended, Vera, AJ, and Jakob gathered at the door, and Emma approached.

"Hey, so I've been thinking. I know at the end we'll all be in competition for the title, but since Doctor Mansworth mentioned another student was currently his prediction for the winner, I thought we could team up and do some study sessions together."

Vera sneered at her and stuck her nose up in the air. Emma knew what that meant.

"I'm fine, thank you very much," she said, throwing her shoulders and head back.

"I wouldn't mind doing some group study," AJ said, ignoring Vera's attitude.

"Great!" Emma replied. "How about you, Jakob?"

"I could use some extra help."

Vera sighed and left. The boys stayed a moment to complete the plan.

"Okay! I think the Chas Master Library would be a great place. I volunteer there, and could book us a side room to study in."

"When do you want to meet?" Jakob asked.

"I'll set up a day, and let you know!"

Emma opened the door and led the way out. Minus Vera, they were all going to their final class of the day together, and it was an opportunity for comradeship.

"So, what are your strengths and weaknesses?" she asked.

"Strength: biology. Weakness: history of medicine," AJ replied.

"Mine are clinical skills and biology. Same order," Jakob said.

"I'm decent at clinical skills, and I'd say my weakness is wanting to beat Marcus in the competition," Emma joked. This elicited a laugh, and she felt good about starting this study group.

Between biology and planning their first study session, she also thought about her dad's fight coming up that evening. It wasn't an effective use of her time but, right now, she couldn't help it.

Anything she didn't fully understand in class, she made note of to read up on later while waiting for the fight. The class flew by quickly, and when the bell rang, she bolted from the room toward her locker.

As she was loading her bag, Skye approached and leaned on the locker next to hers.

"Hey, so when are we going to hang out after school again? The library was pretty boring since you had to work."

"Not sure." Emma smiled at her. "I have a pretty full schedule right now with studies, volunteering, and my dad's fight tonight."

"Well, we need to do *something*. How about you figure out a good day and let me know. I'll plan something for that day."

Rina appeared in the hallway from the crowd of kids.

"What are we planning?" she asked.

"Nothing," Skye responded.

"Just another day to hang out," Emma said.

"Hmm. Are you going to have time for that?"

"I'm sure I can find some extra time somewhere. I'm making time for the fight tonight."

"Are we heading straight there, or we stopping by your apartment for food first?" Rina asked and put her books in her locker.

"Food first."

"Watching a fight sounds like fun," Skye jumped in. "Think I could come?"

"Sorry." Emma frowned. "My family gets front row seats, but they only give us three spots. Rina's been going with us for so long, I believe they think she's my actual sister."

"Oh." Skye looked down, dejected.

Emma felt bad because she hadn't seen Skye hang out with any other girls besides her and Rina. It made her want to set that date of when they could hang out. Empathy. That was her true strength. She hugged Skye, and it seemed to perk her up.

Rina tugged at her arm, and she nodded.

"If we're going to stop by your place first, we should get going so we can catch the train before the one that's always packed," Rina said.

"Yeah."

They walked away, but Emma turned back to wave at Skye one more time. Skye watched and waved back.

"She's so needy," Rina commented once they were outside.

"She wants to be friends," Emma replied.

"She wants to be *your* friend. She couldn't care less about me."

"You're being overdramatic," Emma said with a smile.

It wasn't a true jab at her friend. She understood where Rina was coming from, and also that it did seem like Skye was trying hard to become closer with only her. It was a little weird as Emma and Rina had been inseparable growing up.

On the train, Emma pulled out her Biology book. She studied while Rina rested quietly against her. When they arrived at her building, they disembarked and headed down. Neither Gwendy nor Phyllip would be there. He would already be at the UFA building, and she would meet them there after work.

Inside the apartment, Emma tossed her bag on the floor next to their kitchen island, and Rina took a seat on one of the stools.

"So, what can I get for you, miss?" Emma played like she was a servicer.

"Hmm. I'll have a giant helping of whatever's leftover in your fridge."

Emma looked in the fridge. Her mother was meticulous in keeping leftovers neatly packaged in single portion dishes for easy reheating. Pulling a few out, she set them on the counter and turned the oven on.

"Looks like we have a casserole, beef stew, and a lasagna," Emma said.

"I'll have all of them. What's left in the fridge for you?" Rina joked and laughed.

"Har har."

"The casserole."

"Yes, ma'am!"

Emma spun, put the dishes into the oven, and returned the unchosen to the fridge.

While the food heated, Emma tried to study more. Rina became restless and walked to the window. Though she tried to focus, Emma's mind wandered, and she joined her friend. The streets below bustled with people walking, going into and out of buildings. She wondered what their lives were like.

"One of these days, I might try to leave Chas," Rina said out of nowhere.

"Where would you go?"

"So many different places to see in the world. I could join a traveling show and go see them. I hear Gowar is nice all year long, right by the beach."

"That would be an interesting place to see."

"Any place would be. Our whole lives have been here!"

After ten minutes, Emma returned to the oven and retrieved their food. They sat at the island and ate. Emma savored her bites while the light dimmed outside. It signaled that it was about time to head out.

They finished, washed the dishes, and grabbed light jackets. Their train took them to a transfer station several buildings over to get on the one to the UFA tower. As predicted, it wasn't crowded yet with people who would also be going to the fights.

It was a thirty minute ride and didn't go all the way to the tower as there was an open space all the way around the monstrous building. They exited the train to the platform and made their way to the elevator.

On the ground looking up, the tower's top couldn't be seen. It was the tallest building in Chas, dwarfing even the highest skyscraper. The entryway matched the grandeur, with a large, patterned arch over the frame and several well-lit revolving doors.

The two never used them, though. Those were for ticket holders. Around the side, she and Rina approached the employee entrance, where Samuel and Samson guarded.

"Good evening..." Samuel said.

"...Miss Emma, and Miss Rina," Samson finished.

"Hi, Samuel! Hi, Samson!" Emma gave them both a hug.

Rina waved.

"Your father is waiting..." they continued to speak in turn.

"...inside for you. Floor five..."

"...room five-oh-five."

Rina moved to Samuel's side and turned him so Samson couldn't see, then held up seven fingers.

"Samson, how many?"

"Seven."

Samuel smiled, and Emma and Rina moved to enter. Rina gave both their large bellies a pat as they passed.

"One of these days, I'm going to trip you up, and you'll get it wrong," Rina joked with them.

"We always know..."

"...what the other knows."

"But how? What's your secret? Are you telepathically linked or something?"

They chuckled and gave no answer, and the door closed behind Emma and Rina. The corridor they entered went in a square around the outside of the building, with dozens of entrances into the main floor's different areas. Most of them were off limits to non-employees, so Emma never knew exactly what was beyond most of them. They made their way over to a bank of employee-only elevators and called one. Inside, Emma pressed the button for the fifth floor.

As it rose, she couldn't recall ever being higher than the fifteenth, though it definitely went higher. Each floor was a stadium, with a fight ring, and a large number of seats, so on the fifteenth floor, they towered over the city. Her father had started on that floor, and when she first saw Chas lit up at night, from above, she was in awe of what could be accomplished.

The elevator dinged, and they were deposited into a fighter's staging area. Emma led the way, following the room numbers. When she reached her dad's room, she knocked. He answered, already dressed to fight in his white and red boots, shorts, and gloves.

Some fighters chose to keep their costumes simple, while others went all out with body suits and capes. The idea was not only to fight and win, but to entertain, and so each fighter was encouraged to create a persona to give the crowds a character to cheer for.

"Dad, when are you going to grow up and put on real fighter clothes?" Emma said with a laugh. "You need a cape."

"Never." He laughed and pulled her in for a hug.

The three stepped into his changing room. Emma and Rina sat while he warmed up on a punching bag.

"You ready for your return?" Rina asked with a smile.

"I couldn't stand all that time off. It's one thing to go on vacation but entirely another when you're stuck at home recovering from wounds."

"Well, you know we'll be rooting for you out there," Emma said to encourage him.

"You better!" He laughed. "Your mom should be here soon. You'll be in row one, seats fifty-five through fifty-seven. You should grab some snacks before the fight begins."

He handed over a credits card, retrieved from his personal clothes.

"Thanks, Dad!"

"Get something for your mom, too."

"Will do!"

She and Rina exited and headed through the staging area to the arena. The air was already abuzz, with people taking their seats. The line for concessions would be long, but they made it with plenty of time to spare.

At the back of the line, they waited patiently. Looking around, she happened to catch a glimpse of Denis. He was hanging around with a few of the security guards and seemed to be giving orders. Rina also saw him and grumbled.

"Little twerp…"

"Don't be rude, Rina," she said and swatted her friend's thigh.

He turned and roamed the hallway.

"That's right, walk the other way," Rina said only loud enough for Emma to hear.

When they reached the front, she ordered a burger meal for her mom. Rina ordered a sausage link meal, despite having just eaten. Emma was content with a package of soft candies. The cashier took the credits card and swiped it through the PayPad.

He handed the card back, and they stepped to the side while their order was assembled. The servicers were efficient, and Emma and Rina were headed to their seats in no time.

They arrived as Gwendy was taking her jacket off and preparing to sit down. She reached over and hugged Emma and Rina.

"Hey, honey," Gwendy greeted.

"Hi, Mom. How was work?"

"It was good. Nothing out of the ordinary."

Emma handed her mom her meal, and they sat.

"How was school for you two?"

"It was good," Rina chimed in first. "We're preparing our first play. I'm going to be in the rafters, working some control cables."

"Well, make sure you let us know when it is, and we'll come see it."

"Front row seats!" Rina said and winked.

"My day was good. I'm forming a study group with other kids following the Caregiver Path, so we can help each other in our areas of weakness."

"That's great! You're going to do well in the competition."

"Thanks, Mom."

A few minutes passed before the overhead lights turned on and beamed into the fighting ring. Emma studied the ring and predicted what her dad would use as leverage to get the advantage. This particular ring was a closed cage, with various-sized obstacles the fighters could use as cover, or possibly as a launching point for an attack.

After she'd looked it over, she pulled out her clinical skills book, and reviewed things she'd learned in the first weeks, to keep it fresh. To her, it would be worse in the competition to remember complex procedures, but not be able to carry out the basics.

Despite the fact the increasing number of people taking their seats also raised the volume, Emma was able to focus on the book and block some of it out. Her mind was deep into the text when shadows came to hover over her. A throat cleared, and she was startled, causing her to jump a little.

"Sorry. Did I scare you?" Denis asked from in between two tall security guards.

"Yeah. I wasn't expecting someone to sneak up on me while I was studying." She smiled.

Rina huffed. He glanced at her and kept it cordial.

"Hey, Rina."

"Who's your friend?" Gwendy asked.

"This is Denis. His dad is Mr. Lindali," she replied. "We met in school, when he got hurt and had to come into the doctor's office."

"You must be Mrs. Pureheart." Denis held his hand out to Gwendy. "It's nice to meet you."

They shook hands, and he occupied the seat right next to Emma. He waved off security, and when they were gone, he relaxed in the chair. Rina sighed loudly, but Emma couldn't smack her leg this time without Denis noticing.

"Your pops is in the second matchup tonight," Denis stated.

Emma put away her book, understanding she wouldn't get any more studying done.

"Yeah. He's going up against Firefeet."

"Pretty solid contender. He'll use mostly lower body attacks to try to wear your pops down."

"In his downtime, Dad's been working on some new techniques. He once showed me a full body swing after someone tried to kick him. Lifted the guy right up and spun him in the air."

"Nice. I don't know what kind of fighter I'm going to be yet. I've been studying various different techniques, but I haven't really found my strength."

"Since your dad owns the UFA, why are you going into entertainment as a fighter instead of servicer for business?"

"Eventually, I'll cross train and become a dual-career. But if I don't know the business from the bottom up, I can't be a good boss later."

"That makes sense. I suppose with the popularity of the UFA, he has enough money to send you back to school for the second career."

"Yeah."

They went quiet, and Rina nudged her shoulder into Emma.

"So, for the first play—"

The lights dimmed, and an announcer came on over the speaker system, interrupting Rina before she could finish her statement.

"Ladies and gentlemen, tonight, we have a lineup of four matches, and the return of one of your favorite fighters: Lifeshaverrrrrrrrrr!"

The crowds cheered.

Denis leaned to Emma and whispered, "Is it all right if I sit here to watch the fight?"

"Sure," she whispered back.

He sat back, and Emma looked around. Not another seat in the stadium was empty. Had he specifically reserved this seat, or was someone else supposed to be sitting there?

"For our first matchup, in one corner, we have Visceral Vik! And in the other, Mighty Maz!"

She wasn't interested in these fighters, and while they began, her mind wandered to her writing assignment. She wondered how many people would pick Cure-All as their topic. It was an easy target, and that wasn't her style. She had to think of something different.

Denis leaned forward, clearly doing his own studying. He watched the fighters move about the ring, and she wondered what kind of fighter he'd be. He held an air about him which made her think he might be pretty aggressive in the ring.

"Watch right here," Denis said, pointing to the fighters. "He's setting up for a throw."

Emma leaned forward, and he was right. Mighty Maz waited for Visceral Vik to come in for a one-two, as he'd been doing. On the second jab, Maz grabbed his arm, swung him around, and slammed him into the cage. Maz stepped in for an assault and pummeled Vik.

"Visceral Vik's moves aren't hard to read," Denis said.

Rina sighed loud enough to hear, a feat amidst all the noise from the fighting and the crowd cheering. Emma looked, and Rina glowered, staring past her at Denis. Her friend wasn't having fun, and she couldn't understand why Rina's attitude had changed lately. It was clear it wasn't only Skye but toward anyone intruding.

Emma grabbed Rina's hand and, before the fight was over, stood up and pulled her along. In the public area outside the arena, away from anyone, she looked to her friend with compassion.

"What's wrong, Rina?"

"Nothing…"

"Don't lie to me, please. You've been agitated lately, and you haven't shared what's really going on."

"I don't like Skye, and I don't like Denis. I'm allowed to not like people."

"But why, though? Did I do something wrong?"

"It's not—"

"Hey, what's up?" Denis approached and asked, interrupting Rina.

Rina scoffed.

"It's nothing, we just need a little girl time." Emma replied.

"Okay. Well, I wanted to let you know your pops is up next. Vik made a comeback and knocked Maz out."

"Thank you. We'll see you back in there." Emma smiled and waved him off.

Rina waited for Denis to walk away. Her eyes watered. Emma pulled her into a hug, and Rina let it out. It wasn't a long cry, just enough for her to release what had been pent-up. When she was done, Emma smiled softly.

"It was always just you and me," Rina said. "And now everything's changing. I feel like school and people are getting in between us."

Emma leaned against her and spoke reassuringly, "I understand how you feel, but they're not. We're best friends forever, okay?"

Rina nodded and sniffled.

"You ready to go back in?" Emma asked.

She nodded again, and they walked arm-in-arm back into the arena. They settled back in their seats, and Denis looked over. He didn't say anything but seemed concerned.

"Next up, we have the return of Lifeshaver! And his opponent tonight is Firefeet! Betting is still open, so head to the booths and see what the odds are!"

Phyllip strutted out and put on a show for the audience. They cheered. He was goofy at home, but here, he took it to a completely different level. Climbing on top of an obstacle, he raised his arms up in the air, and then beat his chest. It was a persona he'd developed. The audience encouraged him by getting louder.

Firefeet came out in shorts and gloves similar to her dad. He didn't entertain the crowd as much, and the look on his face was that of displeasure. He sneered at Phyllip.

"All right! Let's have a good match!" the announcer said, and then the bell rang.

Phyllip stayed on his perch, waiting for Firefeet to approach. When he came near, Phyllip dropped to the mat. Jab. Block. Kick. Counter. They were into their dance. Firefeet worked in as many kicks as he could, low, mid, and high. Phyllip picked and chose which ones he countered and which he allowed through.

He went on the offensive, making several hard blows toward Firefeet's torso. They were blocked, but with the amount of force he was putting into it, Firefeet would have bruises in a day or two. They moved about the ring, and Phyllip used the obstacles effectively to avoid blows.

Firefeet became infuriated when Phyllip reached across a waist-high block and popped him in the mouth with a solid jab. Firefeet climbed up on the obstacle and began hitting Phyllip with a flurry of downward kicks. He could only block for the moment, or risk getting kicked in the head.

"C'mon, Dad! Don't let him get you like that!" Emma jumped up and yelled out.

He backed away, and Firefeet leapt from one obstacle to the next to keep up. The barrage of kicks continued.

"Don't get pinned at the cage," Rina yelled.

The kicks slowed for a fraction of a second, and that's when it happened. Phyllip took the opportunity while one of Firefeet's feet was in the air, and he made a palm-strike on the grounded ankle. Firefeet lost his balance and toppled back down to the stage.

Rather than take advantage of him being on the ground, Phyllip waited for him to get back up to make it fair, and then launched his counterattack. He charged in with his shoulder, and Firefeet's block couldn't withstand it. He was back on the ground.

"Yeah!" Emma and Rina screamed.

Struggling to get up before another attack, he stumbled a bit, and Phyllip was there to deliver more blows. Punch, punch, punch, shoulder-ram. Repeat. Firefeet couldn't recover and became pinned on an obstacle, where Phyllip proceeded to pummel his ribs.

Ding. The sound of the bell signaled the end of the first round. Phyllip retreated to his starting corner, and Denis stood and walked over there. She and Rina looked at each other questioningly, as approaching fighters during any part of their fights was unheard of. It was a brief encounter, and Denis came back.

"What did you say to him?" Emma questioned.

"Just mentioned that Firefeet's favoring his left side."

"Can you do that?" Rina scowled.

"Since I'm the son of the owner, it'll be all right. For all anyone knows, I told him you said 'hi.'"

"Seems like cheating to me," Rina remarked.

Denis shrugged.

The fight resumed, and they went at it again. Firefeet had a renewed energy, but so did Phyllip. It was intense, but Emma noticed he didn't focus on Firefeet's left side. Instead, his attacks were balanced. He wasn't using the information he was given, and it made her proud.

Firefeet made a mistake in his steps. He kicked too high and was a hair too far away to connect. Phyllip grabbed his ankle and went in for the takedown. Firefeet landed hard on his back and was quickly locked into a choke. It took him all of a second to realize if he didn't concede, he would lose consciousness. Firefeet tapped his arm on the mat, and the bell rang. The fight was over.

"Ladies and gentlemen, the winner: Lifeshaver!" the announcer called out.

Phyllip and Firefeet stood and shook hands. Emma, Gwendy, and Rina cheered. Denis clapped. She was excited her dad's first day back in the ring was a success. Unable to wait for them to exit, Emma led Rina and her mom out, to head to his changing room.

When she looked back, she noticed Denis followed and wondered what he was doing. They beat Phyllip to his room and waited inside. He entered, and Gwendy was right there to congratulate him with a kiss. He hugged her tightly. Emma stepped up to hug him, too.

"Congratulations, honey," Gwendy said.

"Yeah, congratulations!" Emma echoed.

"Thanks. It was good to be back in the ring."

Emma took his arms and began examining them for injuries. The tissue on his forearms was soft, and he winced.

"There doesn't appear to be any major damage from Firefeet's kicks. Just going to be a little bruised," Emma told him. "You'll want to ice the tender areas for the next two days."

"Thanks, Doc," he said and smiled at her. "I know I'll be in good hands with you caring for me."

"Of course!"

Denis stepped over, extended his hand to Phyllip, and they shook hands.

"Mr. Lindali." He nodded at Denis.

"Denis is fine. I don't run the business yet, and I'll be a fighter alongside you for a while before my pops is ready to retire. That was a good fight."

"Thank you. You have a good eye for openings," he complimented. "I appreciate your advice out there, but I had already sized Firefeet up and had my own plan ready."

"You did, and it was a good one. Congratulations."

"Are you here on behalf of your father?"

"Nah. Just hanging out with Emma and Rina."

"Well, thanks for stopping by." He nodded at Denis, and then looked to Gwendy. "I'll be ready to head out in a few minutes."

"Okay, dear."

Phyllip headed for the changing area in the room.

"It was fun hanging out. See you at school tomorrow," Denis said and waved on his way out.

It wasn't more than ten seconds before Rina sighed in relief.

"Finally! What a nuisance."

"Rina, that's not very nice," Gwendy scolded.

"Sorry, Mrs. Pureheart," Rina looked down. "It's just that since the first day, when he took my water bottle to get me off workout equipment, everything he does irks me."

"He seems like he just wants some friends," she replied.

Emma's dad came out in his regular clothes, with his bag in hand.

"It's hard being on a pedestal. Mr. Lindali is an important man in Chas, second only to the governor. And because the UFA is a popular place, people come from all over Salvoa. It must be hard for Denis to live up to that kind of reputation," Phyllip said.

That made Emma think. Was it the coincidence her father worked for the UFA which drew Denis to want to hang out with them? Or was it the odd first meeting in the doctor's office?

♥

Chapter 7
Introspection

Since the first time he'd done so, it had become a regular thing for Denis to sit with them at lunch, and Rina had remarked more than once about it being too crowded. Emma wasn't sure who Rina wanted to leave more, Skye or Denis. Either way, Emma tried to make it less awkward, and kept their conversations light.

This day, though, he encroached a little more into Emma's personal boundary. After lunch, Denis walked with her to the doctor's office before heading off to his class.

"You wanna hang out after school?"

"I can't. I have study group. The Advanced Beginner Healer competition is at the end of the year, and I have to work hard to compete."

"It's that important?"

"Yeah. I'll get a credit, which I can use toward specialized training. I think it'll really help me get on the path to becoming a first responder doctor."

"Nice. If you need any help, I can get you into the medical office at the UFA for some hands on training."

"I might take you up on that," she said and smiled.

The bell rang for the lunch period to end, and she waved to him. He waved back, and she entered the office. Doctor Mansworth was restocking supplies, and though class hadn't started yet, Emma helped.

"Miss Pureheart, what are your ambitions in life," he asked casually.

"To help people," she replied without thinking.

"There are many ways to do that. Elaborate."

It made her stop what she was doing and wonder what he meant.

"I want to save lives."

"Don't stop," he said and pointed to the supplies. "More detail."

She was unsure of what he was going for. What kind of answer did he want? He was fishing, but she didn't know why. Returning her attention to the supplies, she thought about the best way to answer, and Doctor Mansworth interjected.

"Marcus wants to become a surgeon, but not just any. He intends on being a top surgeon of muscular and skeletal systems."

"I think I want to be a first responder doctor and provide life-saving care to those in immediate need. I want to give people a fighting chance to get better and live," she said with confidence, knowing now what he was going for.

He sized her up and let out a 'hmm.' He moved onto the others. Vera, AJ, and Jakob had come in, and he asked them the same, starting with Vera. Not realizing she'd be put on the spot, she stammered her answer out.

"I-I want to be an early childhood doctor. Provide care for newborns."

Doctor Mansworth pointed to AJ.

"A mental health specialist, so I can help people who are struggling."

And last, Jakob.

"I guess I want to help wherever I can. Maybe a nurse who's able to help a variety of people."

"You all need to work on your initiative. You are training to be caregivers, and you need to be assertive in the role, and life, if you want to succeed. People will be counting on you," he chastised.

Doctor Mansworth briskly walked to the mannequin and knocked it over. Emma jumped as it clattered to the floor. With a scalpel, he cut the shirt Manny the Mannequin was wearing, and he scribbled on him with a red marker to simulate wounds. He stepped away, after leaving him *bloodied*, and practically yelled.

"Emma, Jakob, you're first responders. This man has just been in an industrial accident. He's unconscious. His face and chest are lacerated with deep cuts. He's going to bleed out. Triage!"

Emma and Jakob understood and began treating the patient. She grabbed rolls of gauze while Jakob retrieved scissors to cut the clothes off.

"Wrong!" Doctor Mansworth barked. "You should be applying pressure to wounds and checking if he's even breathing! With an injury on and around the head, neck, and torso, it's possible his throat was also impacted!"

Flustered, Jakob applied pressure to the largest red area, and Emma tilted Manny's head back to open his airways. She put her ear to the nose.

"Is-is he breathing?" Jakob asked Emma but looked at the doctor.

Doctor Mansworth nodded to her.

"Yes, he's breathing. Keep pressure on the wounds, I'll get bandages."

"You two…" Doctor Mansworth turned to Vera and AJ, "get the gurney. You're transporting!"

They did as he said while Emma cut bandage strips to apply to the wounds. As Vera and AJ brought it over, the four of them started to lift Manny onto it.

"Wrong!" the doctor yelled again. "You're moving an injured person without first securing his neck. He could have spinal damage and you'd be making it worse!"

Emma was close to tears. She wanted to do well, but with this much pressure, she began doubting herself. Doctor Mansworth hovered over them all with condemnation for their actions.

"Get the neck brace!" Emma yelled at Jakob, not meaning to.

He pulled the classroom's neck brace from its cabinet, and she secured the patient's neck. They moved Manny onto the gurney and continued to treat.

"Is there any debris in the wounds?" Jakob asked.

Emma peeled back the gauze one by one to look, and then looked to Doctor Mansworth for the answer. He shook his head.

"Are there signs of any other types of wounds besides lacerations?" Emma asked with a choked voice.

The doctor shook his head once more.

"Everyone, lift all at once," she commanded.

The four of them moved Manny carefully to the gurney, and they stood it up on its wheels. She elevated the head of the gurney, to keep his head wounds above his heart, and they wheeled to the other side of the class. Turning back to Doctor Mansworth, they waited for his criticism.

"If you want to save lives, you need to be the best in your fields. If you can't dedicate yourself to that ideal, you might think about a more realistic goal within this path."

It was difficult to choke down, and she could tell from the unease of her classmates they felt the pressure, too. No one spoke for a minute, but despite the fear she felt, she wasn't going to let Doctor Mansworth bully her.

"I'm going to be a doctor. I'm going to be a first responder, Doctor, and if I fail this class, and the competition, it will be a failure on your teaching methods!" Her voice was rushed, and it quivered, but it was out there now.

He said nothing. She wanted this to be some sort of test he'd concocted to weed out those who might not have the strength and drive to keep at it, despite overwhelming odds. But there were no congratulations. Jakob stepped up next to her, to show he was with her. AJ did, too. Vera was the last, but she wasn't going to let Doctor Mansworth get her down either.

"Fine," the doctor said and returned to zero inflection. "Get your books out and let's study."

When the day was through, she met up with Rina at her locker. It wasn't hard for her to tell Emma was a bit down, as she asked, "What's wrong?" the moment they met.

As Emma explained, she bagged up her books to take to the library, and they headed out from the school. Rina fumed over Doctor Mansworth's rudeness.

"Want me to make some trouble for him?" Rina joked. "I could go in and mix up all of his supplies and leave him a nasty note."

Emma laughed. "No, then he'd suspect one of the four of us in my period, and he'd make us clean it all up."

The train arrived, and they boarded. Rather than rest her head like normal, Rina wrapped her arm over Emma's shoulder. It comforted her. They rode to the Master Library and disembarked. AJ and Jakob would arrive within an hour, which gave her ample time to secure their study room and set it up.

Rina headed off to find another book to dive into while Emma entered the office. Mrs. Grada was ready for her and handed her the keys she would need both to access the room and to get into the kitchen for glasses and a pitcher of water.

By the time Emma had laid out all of their study books, the two boys walked in and set their bags down.

"Hey!" she greeted. "It's a big table, so I laid out everything, and we can work through the subjects one by one."

"Sounds good," AJ replied.

"Mansworth was such a beast today," Jakob spouted.

"I think he's only trying to prepare us for the real world." Emma didn't like defending his methods.

"You were amazing, though, standing up to him like you did," AJ told her.

Emma blushed and shook her head. "I don't know what I was thinking."

"Well, I agree with AJ. Someone had to put Mansworth in his place, and despite all the venom Vera has for him outside the classroom, she was the last to step up."

This made her even more leery of how she was perceived by Vera. Vera was already snippy with her, and she didn't want to make things worse. Rather, she kind of hoped Vera would join their study group so they could all work at getting better together.

"I know he was rude today, but let's not focus on Doctor Mansworth and put our energy toward our studies!" Emma said exuberantly.

Both the boys nodded, and they began. Their time was spent going over the most difficult materials for each of them.

AJ was adept at explaining the anatomy portion of their biology studies, and Jakob took notes as they discussed the musculoskeletal system.

Because no one was strong in the history of medicine, they spent the most time on that subject, and discussed the project they'd been given.

"What if we teamed up for the project?" Emma suggested.

"Would Mrs. Uni accept that?" AJ asked.

"Wouldn't hurt to ask," Jakob replied.

"I'll ask on our next school day," Emma said.

After hours of studying, Emma was spent. She was getting tired, and she saw it in the others' faces, too. It was time to call it. To give them the signal, she closed up all of the books and began putting them away. Jakob sighed in relief, and AJ put his head down on the table.

"We need to rest up. We have a few days off to recuperate and let it all sink in," she said.

"How often do we want to meet?"

"Every few days? We should bring all of our notes to compare," she replied.

Jakob nodded. "That sounds like a good plan."

"Then, I'll see you in a couple days," she said cheerfully and slung her bag on her back.

They cleaned up their mess and broke from the room. When she found Rina, she was passed out with a book folded open on her chest. Emma picked it up and rummaged through Rina's stuff for a bookmark. When she found one, she dropped the book right back onto Rina's chest and startled her.

"Wake up, sleepyhead." Emma giggled.

"How long were you in there?"

"Too long." Emma shrugged. "But we made some good progress."

"We leaving now?"

Emma held out her arm as an answer and helped her friend to her feet. Rina checked her book out, and they exited the library. The last train would be leaving soon, and if they weren't on it, they'd have to walk a long way to get home.

She hurried Rina along, and they arrived as the train was pulling up. The heated car was a welcome change from the cold of the night, and the moment they sat, Rina snuggled up to her. After such a long study session, her eyes burned. It was hard to keep them open.

She couldn't do it. Even though the train ride wouldn't be long, the seat was comfortable, and her friend made for a nice pillow. Her eyes closed, and then she startled awake, afraid she missed her stop. She recognized the next stop as several before they needed to disembark.

As the train sailed along the rooftops, she watched the city below, now mostly dark. Rina proved difficult to wake, and even when she stirred it was only to sit upright and lean on Emma's shoulder again.

Arriving at her building, she pulled Rina up and guided her off onto the platform. Because of the wind, she rushed them to the elevator.

"Why am I getting off here?" Rina asked through a yawn.

"You're too sleepy. You'll miss your stop. I'll call your mom on the holo and let her know you're staying over tonight."

"All right. Your bed is comfy anyway."

Rina woke up enough to not need Emma's support to make it to the apartment. Gwendy was there, and she was busy about the kitchen.

"Hi, Mom," Emma greeted.

"You're getting home late."

"The study group went long. Rina's staying over tonight."

"Okay. Want me to call her mother?"

"I'll take care of it."

Emma turned to find Rina had disappeared. There was no question she'd already found the bed. She approached the holo's base stand, and a list of people is projected upward in a column. She used the down arrow to select 'Mr. & Mrs. Gladia.'

A few moments passed, and their call connected. Mrs. Gladia's image appeared from waist up on the holo.

"Hi, Emma," she said groggily.

"Hi, Mrs. Gladia. Rina stayed late at the library with me, and she's going to stay here for the night."

"Okay. You two sleep well."

Mrs. Gladia's image disappeared, and Emma turned back to the kitchen island. Her mom had prepared a sandwich in that short amount of time, and Emma was glad to have it. The ham and cheese were simple, delicious, and gone in a matter of a couple minutes. Gwendy took the plate, washed it, and returned it to the cupboard.

"Thanks, Mom."

"Of course, sweetie. Now, you should go get some sleep."

She nodded and headed to her room. Rina had already passed out and hadn't even bothered to get under the covers. Emma snickered and went through her nighttime routine. Because of her tiredness, she had to stop and think about what she was doing a few times, which made the satisfaction of finally getting in bed even greater.

It took some wrestling, but she was able to get Rina covered up. How long had it been since they'd had a sleepover? Soon after, Rina snuggled her, her cool body sucked heat away from Emma.

It didn't bother her. The blankets soon warmed up, and she became comfortable. It took some time for her mind to decompress after the intense study session. Her eyes became heavy, and she fell into a deep sleep.

In the morning, she sprang out of bed while Rina snored loudly. Wanting to do something nice for everyone, she got out all the necessary ingredients to make omelets. The pan hadn't even fully heated when her dad appeared and began helping her.

"Morning, Em," he said.

"Morning. How's training?"

"Good. Got a fight next week. Denis has been asking a lot of questions about you. Like if you ever come to my trainings."

"H-he has?" She blushed.

"Pretty sure he likes you," he stated.

She couldn't see her face, but she was sure it was as red as a tomato. He wasn't joking, and he didn't make anything of it. This caught her even more off guard, and she left him to cover the pan while she prepped dishes.

Rina appeared from the hallway, rubbing her eyes. Emma wasn't sure if she'd heard anything, and she turned her face from her friend to hide the embarrassment.

"Morning," Rina said through a yawn.

"Hey, sleepyhead," Emma replied, hoping her redness had gone down enough.

Rina didn't seem to notice her discomfort when she sat at the island, and Emma breathed a silent sigh of relief. She plated an omelet, cut an apple in half, and set it all in front of Rina. The fork was barely out of the drawer when Rina snatched it and began digging in.

"Thank you!" she said with her mouth full.

Phyllip was already working on the next one, but she shoved him out of the kitchen area.

"Go. Sit." Emma waggled her finger at the other side of the island.

Phyllip went to wake Gwendy, and they both returned. Three more omelets done and plated, and she sat to eat with them. Conversations varied from school, to work, to extracurricular, but never back to the subject of Denis possibly liking her.

While they talked, she wasn't sure what she thought of him. It was clear he was trying to hang out with her more, but romantic thoughts had been far from her. Now, though, she wasn't sure how to proceed. Just knowing he might like her was going to make her awkward around him.

What would she do if he said something? Would she pretend to not have noticed? Her head swam with thoughts about him now, to the point that she spaced Rina was talking to her. Rina poked her with her fork.

"Hey, I'm going to head home. Mom and I were going shopping later today."

"Okay. Want me to walk you up to the train?"

"Nah, I think I can manage now that I'm awake." She smiled. "Thanks for letting me stay over."

"Any time," Gwendy said.

They hugged at the door, and Rina was off. Emma shut it behind her and returned to the kitchen. Phyllip had started washing the dishes, while Gwendy had moved to the living room to work on a painting.

Emma kept her voice low while talking with her dad, not sure if she wanted to bring her mom in on the conversation yet.

"What do I do?" she asked quietly.

He caught onto her hushed voice and kept his down, too. "Well, it depends on how you feel. Do you like him?"

"I don't know how I feel. Until you said something, I hadn't even thought about it."

"If he does like you, he'll eventually tell you. Until then, I'd say go with the flow."

"Thanks, Dad."

"Of course."

Emma retreated to her room to gather fresh clothes for after a shower. There was no rush because it was the weekend, but she did want to get back to her studies.

The day drifted by, and she felt more confident in what she was studying. Phyllip had brought her lunch, and dinner, giving her the freedom to focus.

It was as the sun was setting that the doorbell rang, and she wondered who it was. Being nosy, she crept to her door and poked her head into the hall while her mom answered it.

"Hi, are you Emma's mom?"

She recognized the voice. It was Skye. How did Skye know where she lived? Emma exited her room and began heading for the living room.

"Yes, I am. Are you one of Emma's friends?"

"Yes! I'm Skye."

"It's nice to meet you."

Emma poked her head around the corner and saw Skye dressed warmly. There were other voices in the hallway, muffled by the walls. She appeared, and Skye waved fervently.

"It's nice to meet you, too, Mrs. Pureheart."

"Would you like to come in?" Gwendy asked.

"Actually, I was wondering if Emma wanted to come hang out with us," Skye replied. "We're going to take a train ride around the city and get dessert from my mom's shop."

Gwendy looked to Emma and smiled. She was leaving it up to her. Skye had been bugging her about hanging out, and up to this point she hadn't committed to anything. Now that it was sprung on her, she felt it would be rude to decline. She needed a break from studying anyway.

"Is it okay, Mom?"

"Sure, honey. Don't stay out too late."

"I won't!"

She grabbed her denim jacket and put her shoes on. In the hallway, she stopped dead in her tracks. Chase was expected but, instead of Van, Denis was there. He waved, and she felt her face get hot again.

♥

Chapter 8
Intention

It was too late to back out. The door was closed behind her, and Skye had taken her arm. The boys took places at their sides, Chase with Skye, and Denis with her. Pulled along, she felt the most awkward she ever had.

"So, I thought we'd head around the city, see the different sights at night. I hear City Hall is pretty all lit up," Skye said.

"It is," Denis replied. "My pops has taken me there a few times on business."

They ascended to the train station, and boarded one which would loop around the outer edge of the city. They took up two benches facing each other. Emma was thankful Skye sat next to her, rather than Denis. She could see he was trying to appear aloof, however their eyes met every once in a while.

The train hurtled along, and Emma stared outside, imagining what the other people in the city were doing right now.

"How's your studies going?" Denis asked her.

"They're tough, but I think I'm doing okay."

"She's going to win that competition," Skye boasted and nudged Emma. "Then, she'll go on to become the best doctor there is."

Emma smiled. "It's a little more complicated than that."

"Don't forget my offer. If you need more hands-on, let me know and I can get you in with the UFA's medical team."

"Would they accommodate a group? I have classmates who might be interested."

"Let me see what I can do. I'll let you know."

He smiled at her, and she smiled back. Averting her gaze, she returned to looking out the window and hoped she hadn't blushed too hard.

The train turned to follow the buildings, giving them an unobstructed view of City Hall. In the dead center of a wide open space sat the second largest building in Chas, both in girth and height. Emma marveled at the glass pyramid, all lit up like a beacon. They were too far away to tell if anyone was still in there, but she imagined the bustling masses at peak hours.

After stops around City Hall, they pulled away, and the building shrank in their view.

"How's your training going?" Emma broke the silence.

"It's good. Me and Chase have been sparring and working with the UFA trainers to build techniques."

"That's great!"

"Chase is fast. Sometimes it's like he's a blur. Always keeps me on my toes."

"Someone's gotta," Chase said, his first words of the night.

"You're a quiet person," Emma remarked.

"I say what needs said, when it needs it." Chase shrugged. "Skye gets it."

"Well, how are we supposed to get to know you better?" she said playfully.

He shrugged again. Skye laughed and nudged her.

"It's all right. When he does actually have something to say, it's like a runaway train."

They stopped, and Skye stood up. She motioned for them to follow off onto a platform. While they waited in the cold for a different line to arrive, Skye wrapped her arm around Emma, and side hugged her.

"It's a bit chilly. I'm going to steal your warmth," Skye joked.

A new train arrived, its sign lit up with the words "City Center." After changing to the new train, Emma spaced out until they arrived. Skye pulled her off, and they walked arm-in-arm to the elevator.

"Wait until you try my mom's ice cream. It's the best. She loves to try new things to enhance flavors. Once, she ground up some hot pepper seeds, baked them, and then sprinkled them into her chocolate-chocolate recipe. It was amazing!"

Skye's enthusiasm for sweets rubbed off on Emma, and her mouth watered. On the ground, Skye sped them up to a brisk walk.

The boys chattered behind them about seeing an upcoming fight, and she heard a familiar name: The Behemoth. He was currently the top fighter in the UFA.

"It's going to be a private match for governors from all over Salvoa. Pops is preparing it special for the hundred year anniversary of the regions coming together."

"Who is Driesen up against?" Chase asked.

"Mich the Bonecrusher."

"That'll be a really good fight."

"Yeah. I'll get us seats in pop's office; best seats in the house."

"I'm going to put my bet on Bonecrusher," Chase said. "Wouldn't have anything on me though. I'm going to be undefeated."

Emma turned to look back. "I'll take that bet. What do you have to offer?"

"If Driesen wins, I'll be nice to Rina," he said and cracked a smile.

Seeing he had opened up a little bit, she wanted to nurture that. She stopped right in his path, so he walked into her, and then she elbowed him gently in the ribs.

"You'll be nice to her anyway!"

They all laughed.

"Fine. Fine. I'll keep Denis out of her way for a week."

This provoked Denis to playfully push Chase.

"And if Bonecrusher wins, I'll bring you homemade lunches for a week," Emma offered.

Chase stuck his hand out to make a deal, and she shook on it.

They laughed and chatted more, Chase coming out of his shell a little. Emma wondered why the universe had deemed this year as the year she would make more friends.

A bright neon sign with the words "Destiny Desserts" greeted them, and Skye pulled the door open.

"We're closing in ten minutes," a voice came from the back.

"It's me, Mom," Skye announced.

A tall woman appeared. If Skye hadn't mentioned it was her mom, they could easily be mistaken for sisters.

"Oh, hi! What have you been up to?"

"Nothing, just spending time with some friends. I brought them by to try some of your newest concoctions."

"Great! I'm working on a new strawberry ice cream combination, and my taste buds are burnt out. I can't tell if I'm making it better or worse."

She ushered them over and dished some ice cream into little test cups, with tiny wood spoons. The ice cream was pink, as Emma expected, but it had dark red bits in it. Taking a small spoonful, she put it in her mouth. The bits were impossible to avoid, and she bit into one. It was beetroot, but there was also a hint of some other spice she couldn't identify.

It was unique, to say the least. She hadn't ever thought of whatever this combination was, and it wasn't something she'd go out of her way to try. But because it was Skye's mom, she wanted to be objective.

"The flavor is interesting. It's mostly sweet, and the little bits of beetroot add a good texture, but I'm not sure about the other flavor in there," Emma commented.

"Jaderoot, imported from Ralt. I bought some to test it out, but no matter what I mix it with, it doesn't seem right," Skye's mom said. "The only upside is that the taste grows on you the more you eat."

"I'm sure you'll find the right place for it, Mom."

"So, what can I do for you all? Desserts on me."

"Do you have any of that puff-pastry with the chocolate filling left?" Skye's eyes lit up.

"Sorry, they were gone early this morning. Had a big client come through, and they took the whole lot."

Skye pouted and looked in the ice cream case.

"Can I get some berry-cream with candies?" she asked.

Her mom set out to get her a small bowl of it, with tiny multicolored candies on top. She handed it to Skye, and then looked expectantly at Emma.

"I'll have some of what she's having, please." Emma smiled.

She was handed a bowl and picked up a spoon from the container on the counter.

"Thank you!"

"You're welcome!"

Skye had already gone to sit at a table, and Emma joined her while the boys picked out what they wanted. Still very unsure of how to feel about Denis liking her, she tried to sit by Skye. Except Skye put her feet up and grinned in a suspicious manner.

"Sorry, reserved for Chase," Skye said with a giggle.

Emma's eyes went wide, and she knew what Skye was doing. This made Skye giggle louder. She sat across from her, and when Denis sat next to her, she kept her head down. Skye kicked her foot, causing her to startle.

"You all right?" Denis asked.

"I'm fine." She smiled at him, and then gave Skye a look.

Skye grinned mischievously. The boys went back to talking about fighting while they ate, and Emma just sat and listened while they discussed technique. Every once in a while, Denis would look over and smile at her.

When the four of them finished, Skye grabbed their dishes and ran them behind the counter and through a door into what Emma presumed was the kitchen. She came back out, followed by her mother. Emma stood and approached.

"Thank you for the ice cream!" Emma said.

"You're welcome. Come by any time. I'm always trying to make new desserts."

"Thanks, Mrs. Torrie," Chase said.

"Yeah, thanks for the dessert. I'll tell my pops about this place, about how good it is."

"I appreciate that. You kids heading back out?"

"Yeah. Just for a bit," Skye said. "And then I think I'll take Emma back home."

"Okay. Don't stay out too late. They say *Walkers* come out about the middle of the night," Mrs. Torrie said, with a grin.

"Come on, Mom. There haven't been gangs in Chas in a hundred years." Skye laughed.

They headed to the door. Skye and Emma turned back to Mrs. Torrie and waved. Mrs. Torrie waved back. Out into the night, Skye grabbed Emma by the arm again, and they walked together. As the boys hung back, Skye whispered.

"So, do you like Denis? He definitely likes you."

Emma was flustered. "I don't know. I hardly know him."

"Well, this is a good time to change that. I'll pull Chase up here, and you and Denis can walk together." Skye was excited, and this made Emma more nervous.

"No, don't. It's—"

"Come on, it will be fine."

Skye didn't wait for a rebuttal and dropped back to grab Chase. She pulled him by his arm and began running toward an opening in the city. Denis stepped up to Emma and gave her a questioning look. She shrugged and looked down.

The other two were getting far ahead of them. Due to her short stature, she had a hard time keeping up and had to jog. Denis kept pace with her, never passing.

Past where the buildings ended, they found themselves at a tree line, and Emma knew where Skye had taken them. They were at Asta Park, and thoughts of the possible haunted building at the center caused her to become instantly clammy.

Emma stopped dead in her tracks, causing Denis to overtake her. Skye and Chase stopped ahead, across the street.

"Come on!" Skye urged.

"I was thinking Rina would want to come, too."

"You don't always need to have her around. We're your friends, too," Skye said and sounded hurt.

"It's not like that." Emma flushed with embarrassment.

"If you're scared because of what I told you before, don't be. It's a legend people tell in good fun. Nothing's going to happen."

The three of them looked at her and she felt pressured to go along. It made her uneasy, but she didn't want to ruin the night. She stepped up to Denis and offered her hand to him.

"Would you hold my hand, please?"

He was taken by surprise but didn't recoil.

"Of course."

He reached out and took her hand in his. It felt massive compared to hers, but that made her feel safe in his charge. Emma caught Skye's smirk right before she turned around and hooked her arm through Chase's. Led into the park, on a well-lit paved path through the trees, Skye seemed to know exactly where she was going.

It was only a few minutes of quick striding when the building came into view. It was in a clearing of its own. A two story house lay in the center, with neatly kept grass, and an apple tree near the border. The lights were off but, even in the dark, she could see it was well kept, not at all what she would expect from a place which might be haunted.

As they approached, Emma hoped the door was locked. Chase reached for the knob, and it opened with ease. There was a faint whine from the hinges, and Emma's heart thumped hard. Anxiety crept up and she clutched to Denis.

"Okay, so we'll start with the *creepiest* area first. The basement. Legend is that the ghost is a twenty-something-year-old man, said to have died of a broken heart," Skye said.

She led the other three into the home, and the first room was a kitchen. The interior was dated. She couldn't tell when the appliances were from, but her best guess was at least a hundred years old.

In the back corner, next to a fridge, was a door. Skye pulled it open, and a loud creak echoed in the room. A cold breeze rushed by, and Emma shivered. Terror gripped her. Her heart pounded. Denis brought her in close as they descended into the black.

Skye pulled out a flashlight and turned it on. This had been her plan the whole time. Shining it around, the light hit the shelves and created eerie shadows against the far wall. She looked back at them with a mischievous grin and shined the light on her face.

"Some say they've seen him roaming, looking for his lost love, moaning her name in despair."

At the bottom of the steps Skye pointed the light at yet another door. Edging toward it, Skye rattled the doorknob. Denis led the way and beyond it was more storage, with archaic, rusted yard tools. Skye popped up in her face.

"Emmaaaa," Skye moaned. "Emmaaaa!"

She screamed and buried her face in Denis's chest. He wrapped his arms around her.

"Knock it off," Denis chided.

"Calm down," Chase interjected. "It's all just good fun. There's nothing here."

After a few moments, Emma pulled away from Denis, feeling foolish. Around a wall centered in the middle of the room, there was no sign of a ghost. They explored the items of the near past, and like the appliances upstairs, they weren't too far removed from modern day tools. It reminded her of her assignment to evaluate how far medicine had come and where it could go.

The slight reprieve from terror was interrupted when Skye led them back toward the stairs.

In a spooky voice, Skye continued her narration, "It seems the specter does not reside here, but there are still many rooms to explore in the house."

Back into the kitchen, and past the fridge and island counter, they pushed through a swinging door. Skye shone her light around to reveal a living room, with a musty couch on the left, and some bookshelves in a recessed nook on the far right side of the room.

To their immediate right was a hallway, and in it was a set of stairs leading to the second floor. The light lit the hallway, and though it illuminated all the way to the end, it left pockets of shadows along the way.

"Up or down?" Skye asked.

"Up," Chase responded.

"Up," Denis also chimed in.

"Up it is, then."

They climbed the creaky, wooden stairs, and at the top lay another hallway. There were plenty of doors to choose from on either side. Skye moved to the first on the right and opened it. The hinges whined, and they entered.

"This was said to be *his* room, and he liked to collect artifacts. It may not look as if there's anything out of the ordinary here, but let's look around anyway."

Skye set her flashlight so it pointed straight up and illuminated some of the room. Skye and Chase broke away to sit on the bed, while Emma and Denis moved to the closet.

There were some clothes in there, sealed in clear garment bags. They were all custom pieces, and embroidered on the right shoulder of each shirt was an orange chrysanthemum. Emma knew someone had gone to great lengths to craft them.

"Do you like clothes?" Denis asked.

"Only a little. I don't really put much thought into what to wear, so long as they're my overalls. I like to feel comfortable."

"They look good on you."

Emma looked away and blushed.

They moved to the dresser in the room and inside were more sealed clothes. At the bottom of the top drawer was a paper lining and something that made it bulge up slightly in a rectangle. Emma looked back for the flashlight and found Skye and Chase kissing on the bed.

Emma grabbed the flashlight and shone it into the drawer. The lining's corner stuck up, and it begged to be pulled. She did, and underneath was a neatly laid out, well-preserved letter. The handwriting was exquisite, neat and uniform, but her heart beat hard in her chest when she read the greeting.

Dearest Emma,

Only two words into the letter, the image of a beautiful, young woman flashed in her head. Brown hair, with a blue ribbon tying it up in a ponytail; a white blouse and white denim pants. A stranger, and yet there was a weird feeling of familiarity. She let out a yelp and startled everyone.

"What's wrong?" Denis asked, a little panicked.

"Is this a joke?" Emma uncharacteristically turned and yelled at Skye, tears in her eyes.

Skye jumped up and came to see what was wrong.

"What are you talking about?"

"This!" Emma shoved the letter at Skye.

Skye looked at it, and her face paled.

"I-I don't know what this is! I swear!"

She took a few moments to read it, with Chase looking over her shoulder. It left Skye speechless, and she tried to hand it back to Emma. Not wanting it, Emma tried to push it away, but Skye was insistent.

Her throat constricted, making it hard to swallow. It felt like someone had turned a heater on. Denis put his hands on her shoulders, and she could feel herself shaking under them.

"It's okay," he whispered in her ear. "Look how old it is. It's probably for someone named Emma who died a long time ago."

She knew they'd look at her as crazy if she tried to describe the vision of the woman. What *was* that? Skye held the light on the page, and Emma read.

Dearest Emma,

By the time you read this, much time will have passed since my writing it. I can't tell you how I knew you'd be here, or how I knew you'd read this. You have a long road ahead, and we believe in you. You're going to do great!

We miss you dearly. Life feels weird without our family together but, right now, it's better this way. For now, live in the moment, cherish your friends, become everything you want to be. You're strong, and nothing can stand in your way.

One day, we will come and see you, and I'll bring you a gift. A pure, heart-shaped Vradix crystal.

Until we meet again.

Love,

Ami

Whoever Ami was, she'd practically called Emma by her full name. A *pure*, *heart-shaped* crystal? That couldn't be coincidence. Were it not for the strange vision of this woman in her head, Emma would be completely convinced this was a prank. The paper, however, was old enough that it felt like if it was mishandled in any way it might crack and fall apart.

Did Skye know about it and was pretending to not know? Or was she clueless? It didn't matter. Emma didn't want to be there any longer. She threw the paper back in the drawer and ran out. Skye and Denis called after her, but it wasn't until she was halfway out of the park they caught up. Emma couldn't help but tear up, partly from the terror, and partly from the cold air stinging her eyes.

"Emma, I swear, I don't know anything about that," Skye pleaded.

She tried to touch Emma's shoulder, but Emma wrenched away. Denis approached.

"Please, take me home, Denis," Emma managed to choke out.

Denis gave Skye a sympathetic look and offered his arm to Emma. She took it and pulled into him. He led her back to the nearest building with a train stop.

She shook the whole way. It wasn't until they were on the warm train, and she'd curled into him, that the shakes stopped. Could she trust Skye when she said she didn't know? What would be the point of scaring her like that?

Denis held her tight, sharing his body heat. His arm around her was a small comfort, and she felt safe. They switched trains to one which would go to her apartment and, after arriving, he walked her to her door.

"Hey, I'm sorry about all that. I had no idea what was going on," he apologized.

Emma shook her head.

"I don't think Skye planted the letter. That paper was old. There's no way she put it there," Denis rationalized.

She looked up at him. He was being sweet, trying to console her, and salvage what Emma thought of Skye.

After a few moments of silence, he spoke. "Do you want to come out to the UFA tomorrow?"

She shook her head.

"I have to start working on a paper."

"All right. Another time?"

She nodded.

"I'll see you at school, then."

She headed inside, and Denis waved as she closed the door. After the latch clicked, she looked out the peep hole and watched him walk away.

Her parents were relaxed on the couch, talking. She bypassed them and started heading to her room, but Gwendy called out.

"How was it?"

"It was okay, but I'm really tired," she dodged.

Emma didn't want them prying, and so she immediately headed to her room. With her door closed, she got ready for bed, and pulled out her diary.

I'm a little freaked out right now, so I'm writing until my mind calms down. I went out with Skye, Chase, and Denis tonight, and something happened. I found this really old letter I'm positive was meant for me. I can't explain it. It was like it was possessed or something. I saw this flash of a young woman in my head when I touched it. I didn't recognize her, but I kinda felt like I should have.

Maybe my imagination was running wild because we were sneaking around an old house at night, with no lights on. Did I scare myself because Skye said the house was haunted? Maybe I'm overtired. At least hanging out with Denis was okay.

In bed, she covered herself up past her head, to hide from non-existent ghosts. Finally exhausted enough, her mind drifted.

♥

Chapter 9
Explosive Behavior

They stood on the platform, waiting for the train to take them to school. Emma recounted the terror of the other night, and Rina's face grew red with anger.

"She did what?!" Rina yelled.

"It's okay—"

"No, it's not! She doesn't get to torment you and get away with it."

"I don't want you to get in a fight with her. She made a mistake, that's all."

"Emma, we've been best friends forever. Have I ever done anything like that? No. Friends don't terrorize their friends."

The train arrived, and Emma waited until they were inside to continue the conversation. At least in here, Rina would keep her voice at a reasonable level, Emma thought.

"I'm not okay with her, Em. I don't want to hang out with her, and I really don't think you should either."

Emma was torn. Skye hadn't meant to be mean, she was sure of it. If anything, it was her attempt to be better friends. Skye had introduced her mother, they'd ate ice cream together, and she used the outing to push Emma closer to Denis. Skye wasn't bad, but Emma knew Rina's frustration was reaching a boiling point.

"She thought we were having a fun time. The letter was some creepy coincidence." She said *coincidence*, trying to convince herself the letter didn't call her out by name.

"I don't care. I can't stand her."

Emma feared Rina was headed for an ultimatum of *me* or *her*. She hadn't said it yet, but the way Rina turned her head and avoided looking at her, it was likely coming.

Once they arrived, they headed to their lockers. Rina was there only long enough to pick up the Language class book.

"I'll see you in class," she said hastily and rushed off.

Emma was dropping off her unneeded books and assignment materials when Skye showed up. Her downturned lips told Emma all she needed to know; she was sad and sorry.

"Emma, I don't know how to apologize. I feel like saying sorry isn't enough."

Emma didn't want to make her feel worse about it.

"It's okay. I think I overreacted because I was scared. I mean, it's just some really weird coincidence I found that letter."

Again, trying hard to believe her own words.

"Definitely. Can we forget about what happened?"

Emma nodded. "I have to head to Language class. We'll talk in math."

She waved solemnly, and Emma packed up and headed for her classroom. As she entered the room, Rina briefly looked over, and then returned to staring out the window. Emma took her seat next to her.

"I want it to go back to you and me at lunch," Rina said abruptly.

"What about Van, Chase, and Denis?" Emma asked.

"Van and Chase come with Skye, and Denis is just a menace. I don't want any of them there. I want it to be you and me."

"I don't think I can do that." Emma looked down to her desk.

Rina crossed her arms in anger, and Emma couldn't think of a time when she'd seen her so upset. With the situation as it was, and being faced with an impossible decision, Emma could hardly focus on the class.

Her distraction followed her into the next class with Skye. She mustered enough of her attention span to take notes on how to solve certain equations. Skye tried gaining her attention a couple times, but Emma did what she could to stay focused on the material.

The day went terribly. It wasn't a spontaneous catastrophe, rather a slow burn to confrontation. Skye would want to sit at the table, Rina would refuse. Emma tried hard to think of a way to calm the storm.

Lunch came, and all she could come up with was to not go. At the end of their personal health class, she and Rina exited, but Emma excused herself to the restroom.

"Want me to wait for you?" Rina asked.

"No. That's ok. Thank you."

Emma entered the bathroom, hid in a stall, and waited a few minutes until she was sure Rina had gone. Poking her head out, she looked both ways. The hallway was clear. Emma briskly headed to the front door of the school and out to the colosseum.

Inside, she entered one of the passages she'd been down with the group and found a room to hide in. Alone, she was able to let out the sadness and anxiety in the form of sobbing. Tears rolled down her cheeks in a steady stream.

What could she do? How could she fix this? She didn't want to lose friends over a misunderstanding. She needed to be strong enough to be the bond between them all, but leadership wasn't a strong suit of hers.

After spending the lunch period in hiding, she made her way to her clinical skills class. It wasn't hard to go the rest of the day without seeing any of them. She knew the basic patterns of their daily movements, and the only common place they might meet was the lockers. She could skip going to hers, and then catch an earlier train home. If anyone came over, she'd have her dad tell them she wasn't feeling well.

It worked perfectly. But she couldn't do it again tomorrow, or the next day. It was up to her to come up with a plan to settle things down.

All night she stewed about it, and all she could come up with was basic psychology. Sit them down. Talk it out. Rina had to get her feelings out. Skye had to explain it was a mistake. If she could get them to talk, Emma could mediate, and it would be okay.

The night came and went. She'd never before felt this much pressure to get something right. It was worse than trying to please Doctor Mansworth.

Rina came to the door the next morning. The look of worry in her eyes, instead of anger, put Emma's mind a little at ease.

"Hey. What happened to you yesterday?"

"I wasn't feeling well. I'm still not."

"Oh. You should have said something. I was worried when you didn't show up at lunch. I went looking for you."

"Sorry." Emma looked down.

"We have a few minutes. Don't forget to eat something."

Her stomach was in knots, and she wasn't in the mood to eat anything. If she didn't, though, she wouldn't have enough energy to make it to lunch. She made peanut butter toast.

They headed out while she was eating her second slice. All the way to school, Rina kept looking at her. It was clear she wanted to talk, but she didn't. Emma was okay with not answering the unasked, still working on a plan.

She was able to focus better in classes, but lunch came around, and she didn't feel ready. If anything happened, Emma would have to deal with it in the heat of the moment. In math class, Skye had a million questions about where she was yesterday. Emma avoided them by redirecting her to the teacher.

It came. The dreaded moment. Her stomach knotted up as she entered through the double doors to the cafeteria, with Rina at her side. They went to the line to get their food and made their way to their usual table.

Skye and the others were only a couple minutes behind. Denis sat next to Emma and smiled at her.

"Hey, we missed you yesterday. What happened?" he asked.

"I wasn't feeling well," she replied and took a bite of her sandwich.

"What happened? You seemed okay in math yesterday," Skye replied.

"Like you'd know how she feels," Rina quipped under her breath.

"What?" Skye snapped.

"You can't really read a person, can you?" Rina said louder.

"Stop," Emma said but was talked over.

"I don't know what your problem is—"

"My problem is you disregarding *my* friend's feelings."

"You have no idea what you're talking about. I apologized—"

"Half-heartedly?" Rina sneered.

"STOP!"

They ignored Emma's outcry, and Skye stood up and slammed her palms on the table.

"What's your problem, *Rina*?"

"My problem is you, *Skye*!"

Rina reciprocated the gesture and practically flipped her food tray at Skye. Emma grabbed Rina's hand and pulled on her. She wrenched it away and continued to go at Skye.

"You invade our space, you push yourself on Emma, making her do things that cause her to feel uncomfortable."

Tears began streaming down Emma's cheeks. She couldn't help it, and it felt like her chest was caving in.

"Uncomfortable? You mean like how you're making her feel right now?" Skye blurted. "You think it's healthy to live your life with minimal interaction, having only one friend your entire life? If anyone's pushing themselves on Emma, it's you and your insecurity."

"All right, that's enough," Denis spoke up loud enough to break through their yelling.

Emma put her face into his shoulder and cried. The whole scene was embarrassing, and she was sure the entire cafeteria was watching.

"You two need to walk away," Denis raised his voice. "There's no need for this."

"No. Skye's right," Chase said and stood up. "Rina's being petty and jealous that her *only friend* has made new friends."

This silenced the table for a brief moment.

"You need to step it back there," Denis warned Chase.

"Nah. See, Skye shouldn't have to take this. All she did was try to have fun. And we've all noticed how Rina has been acting, even toward you."

"I don't have to put up with this!" Rina barked.

Denis broke away from Emma and stood.

"If you actually value your friendship with Emma, leave, now," he addressed Rina, Skye, and Chase.

"I'm not going anywhere! I'm sitting with Emma and having lunch with her like I have for our whole lives," Rina protested.

"Emma's *my* friend, too, and I'm going to have lunch with her whether Rina likes it or not." Skye got louder.

Three standing turned to four as Chase puffed up his chest and glanced at Denis.

"I'm with Skye. Rina's the one with the problem. Let *her* leave."

Emma couldn't bear it anymore. The weak cohesion binding the group had disintegrated, and now it was a squabble over who had *rights* to her.

"That's enough! I want all of you as my friends, but it's clear that isn't going to happen. You're too interested in having a power struggle instead. Maybe *I* should leave!" is what she wanted to say.

Rather than confronting them, she bolted out of the cafeteria, with the lot of them calling after her. They tried to follow, but she turned and yelled at them in the hallway.

"Don't follow me!"

She ran and exited the school. Out into the courtyard, she made a beeline to the colosseum again, and retreated to her hiding spot. On the floor, she put her face into her knees and cried.

It had all gone wrong. She wasn't strong enough, outspoken enough, to stop their fight. All she could do was run away. Was that how it was going to be when it came to the competition? Was she going to back down under the pressure and let Marcus have the win?

She wasn't alone more than five minutes before the door to the storage room opened. Hiding behind some stacks of boxes, she didn't want anyone to see her.

"Emma?" Denis called out. "It's only me. Not the others."

How did he find her? she wondered. Rather than make herself known, she sucked in a breath and stayed quiet, hoping he would go away. He didn't.

"Hey," he said, standing over her.

She didn't acknowledge him and felt his presence as he sat next to her. It took her a few minutes of sitting there for her to say anything.

"All I wanted was for them to get along."

"I know what you mean."

"You do?"

"Yeah. Pops has had to quash a few rivalries at the UFA, and I've seen it firsthand. But, sometimes, no matter what he did, those fighters would never get along. Then, there's people like you and your dad, who get along with everyone.

"I think Skye and Rina only put up with each other because you're their friend, but I don't think they'll ever be friends with each other. It'd probably be best if you hung out with them separately."

"Rina has been my best friend since we were little. We're practically sisters. I can't ditch her to hang out with Skye more."

"You're loyal. I get it. And she's loyal to you."

Emma rested her chin on her knees and stared at the boxes in front of her. Confrontation: she was going to have to get better at handling it and other stressful situations. She wouldn't always be able to run.

"What about Chase? I don't know what's going on with him."

"I don't either. He might just be defending Skye, but he's taking it too far. I'll try and talk to him."

"Thanks, Denis."

"Don't worry about it," he replied.

He pulled a tray from his side and handed it to her. It was her lunch. Smiling weakly at him, she nodded in thanks.

Denis was quiet while she ate, and when she was done, he reached out for the tray. Hesitant, she handed it over slowly.

"I'll take it back for you so you can go to your next class."

He helped her to her feet and walked her back to the school.

♥

Chapter 10
Betrayal of Feelings

Emma had become weary of the constant voices in her ears. Skye on one side, Rina on the other. Both reasoned that they weren't the ones at fault and bashed the other. It was stressful.

She tried persuading both of them to drop it and leave it all be, but it only worked for a short amount of time before they started up again. Skye worked overtime trying to get Emma to come with her on excursions after school. She politely declined with the valid excuse of making sure her studies came first.

The time she really looked forward to was at the library. It was now a sacred haven from the drama. Both Rina and Skye had tried to interject during studying or volunteering, and Emma informed them both she needed to focus. Both took it hard, but they gave Emma her space.

Denis, on the other hand, was the one person she was okay with stopping by when she volunteered. He didn't need anything and would show up just to hang out while she put books away.

"Don't let Rina or Skye see you," she'd told him.

"Why?"

"I told them when I'm here, I'm busy. The truth is I needed a break from them both."

This went on for a few weeks, their clandestine meetings, and she never knew when he was going to appear, if at all. Her heart fluttered as she thought about him.

On the third floor, she returned engineering books to their proper shelves when he snuck up on her. He tapped her shoulder, and she yelped. She didn't even have time to cover her mouth to stifle it. Her face turned beet red.

She was thankful this section was devoid of people, but she still looked around to see if anyone caught her embarrassing moment. Playfully, she smacked his chest, and he grinned.

"Hey, I don't have much time today. I've gotta practice," he said. "Pops says he'll allow me to try out for the Junior League."

"That's exciting!"

"You'll come watch me, yeah?"

"Of course. Rina and I will be there. That actually brings me to something I needed to talk to you about."

Emma looked down and became bashful. Her words were hushed.

"After that blow up with Skye, Rina wants it to go back to me and her. I've already told her I don't want that though…"

He looked at her and tilted his head inquisitively. There was more she wanted to say. She wanted to tell him she liked being around him. It wasn't easy, and she chose the path of least resistance.

"So, I need you to be her friend, too."

"I was a jerk at the beginning, but I view her as a friend now."

Emma shook her head. "She doesn't view you that way. You haven't earned her trust or respect yet, and she won't give those up easily."

"It's important to you, so it's important to me. Just give me some pointers, and I'll do whatever I need to."

She didn't even realize she'd done it until she was in the moment. Her arms up around his neck, she hugged him tight.

"Thanks!"

He reciprocated. They parted ways, and the rest of her night was quiet and uneventful. There were even a few moments to study.

What started off as time for her to decompress from Rina and Skye turned into *their* time together. It became their space. Sometimes, they talked about a lot, and other times, nothing at all. It was a nice reprieve, and she felt giddy now simply entering the Master Library's doors.

Today, though, Rina came with, intent on checking out new books. The discussion on their way over, thankfully, had not included anything about Skye. It was instead about learning the fate of a fictional character in a newly released novel.

"I don't know how the writer can possibly continue the series with *her* dead. I mean, she was the main character. I was so mad when the book ended and there was no resolution."

"Mmm," Emma replied.

"What do you mean 'mmm'? Do you have no empathy for me?" Rina made a face, her mouth downturned.

"You know me. I've never really been into fiction. I can't imagine myself in those worlds like you can."

"You just haven't found the right book. Maybe you need some steamy romance novel. No fantasy or science fiction. Just a good ol' love story."

That turned her thoughts to Denis, and she blushed. Rina was sure to notice, so Emma turned away.

"I don't think that would interest me either."

Rina elbowed her.

"Don't tell me that kind of thing embarrasses you."

Emma shook her head, and then buried her face in her sweater.

"I'll pick a good one out for you. I promise!"

When they arrived, Rina left to pick up her reserved book, and Emma started working. The return stacks were enormous today, which would make the time go by fast but also gave her no opportunity to study later in the evening.

It was a few hours into her shift when *he* showed up. She saw him before he saw her and couldn't take her eyes off him. The way he looked at her, and how the right side of his lips upturned into a smile, made her heart flutter.

"Quick, hide over here! Rina's here getting books today," Emma whispered playfully and pulled him in between bookcases when he approached.

It was a rush to be sneaking to see each other, and she looked around to see if Rina was anywhere to be found. She wasn't.

"Sorry, I wasn't really thinking about it. Just wanted to get in here and see you."

"Well, if you don't want me to kick you out, you better help me put books away!" She picked up a book and planted it in his arms.

He laughed, and they teamed up to tackle the huge workload. Emma made note of how much easier talking to him was now they were familiar with one another. He certainly wasn't someone she'd have picked out of a crowd to have a conversation with, but she was glad fate crossed their paths.

"So, you're going to be a fighter but eventually get a dual certificate and take over your dad's business?"

"Yeah. Pops told me the only way he'll pass the UFA on is if I first understand the fighters, to learn everything at its core, and then he'll pay for me to go to school again."

"What do you think it was like before this school and career path system?"

"If you can believe I have smart friends besides you, I've got a history fanatic friend who loves to throw tidbits out. It was bad. Crime was rampant because a substantial part of Chas was unemployed. There was this gang called Walkers, and they'd kill and steal to survive. Finally, another group rose up to bring the idea of a better society. The class system was developed and implemented within a decade."

Emma was baffled. No one had ever told her this, though if she'd have chosen the social engineer card at Celebration Day, she was sure it would have been part of her curriculum.

"Wow. I never knew."

"It wasn't that long ago either. That house we visited with Skye? Turns out it was the place where the people who came up with the class system lived. It's why the place is preserved as a historical site."

A chill ran down Emma's spine as she thought of the letter again but was quick to push it from her mind.

"I wonder why they don't teach this to everyone," Emma pondered.

"I guess it depends on what knowledge we need for our careers. Entertainers wouldn't really have use for that, but I'm sure I'll learn it in my second bout of schooling."

The pile of books on her carts dwindled to a few, and her shift was ending. The two of them were hid out on the second floor, near the back shelves. She reached down to grab the next book just as Denis did, and their hands brushed.

Instead of pulling back immediately, she let her hand rest there next to his. Their eyes met, and she smiled and pushed loose hair back behind her ear. It was becoming clearer every moment they spent together that she was falling for him.

He smiled back and took the book from her to put it away. She snatched it from him and tried to put it up on the shelf. He reached his long arms across her to get at the book, but she put her shoulder into his sternum and held it away. They playfully fought, and she clutched the book to her chest. He put his hands on her hips and drew her in close.

Being so close together, looking up at him was like craning her neck at a skyscraper. He looked down, and she felt him draw her in. Her heart raced at the thought of her first kiss. What did lips pressing together feel like? Was she ready to date? Would it interfere with her schooling?

She was unbelievably warm. It felt like her whole body was flushed. Her breathing was shallow, and she closed her eyes. He pulled her in and wrapped his arms around her back, but the attempted kiss was interrupted.

"Denis? What are you doing?" Rina screamed at the top of her lungs. "Get away from her!"

The moment was shattered. Emma had completely forgotten her friend was here.

Rina charged like a wild animal and simultaneously ripped Emma away and shoved Denis into the shelves. Caught off guard, he listed, and took a dozen books with him as he flailed his arms in an attempt to not fall over.

"Rina! What are you doing?" Emma exclaimed.

She broke away from Rina and helped Denis regain his composure. He didn't react, or fight back, but his fists were clenched. She put herself between the two of them, so Rina wouldn't attack again.

"What do you mean, *what am I doing*? What are *you* doing? I thought you were supposed to be putting books away!"

"I-I was. We were just… Denis stopped by to say hi, and then was helping me."

Rina's face was red with anger, unlike Emma had ever seen before.

"Don't lie to me!" she yelled.

"I'm gonna go," Denis said quietly in Emma's ear. "I'll see you later, okay?"

He moved away from her and tried to pass Rina.

"Stay away from her! You and Skye," Rina stepped in his path and warned.

Ignoring it, he pressed on and left the two of them standing there. Emma had never seen her friend in such a fit. She could be moody, sure, but she'd never seen her aggressive.

Emma picked up the books and put them back on the shelf, but Rina wasn't done.

"Look! He didn't even pick up the books he knocked over!"

Emma was reaching a breaking point. She loved her friend dearly, but this petty jealousy was becoming too much.

"It was your fault," Emma quipped back.

"My fault? Did you forget what he did to me at the beginning of the year? He's a jerk! The only reason he didn't do anything back is because he's trying to impress you!"

"Yeah? Well, what if he *was*?" Emma was finally speaking up.

"What? Do you like him or something? Are you kidding me? First, Skye tries to break our friendship up, now Denis is butting in! It was better when it was only the two of us!"

"I am okay with making new friends! You are the one who can't accept it! If you don't like it, then maybe you should take a step back!"

It wasn't out more than a fraction of a second before Emma regretted saying it. She wasn't trying to push her friend away, but she had to say something, or she feared Rina would get worse.

The look of hurt on Rina's face was gut-wrenching. Before she could apologize, Rina turned and stormed off toward the stairs.

"Rina, wait!"

Emma chased after her.

"No, you go ahead and do whatever you want. I'm going home!"

"Rina, I'm sorry!"

They bounded down the stairs, making a scene throughout the library. People looked, adding to the pain Emma felt.

"Stop following me!" Rina yelled at the top of her lungs.

This halted Emma in her tracks. Rina kept going, and slammed the front doors open as she left. The urge to cry was building rapidly.

When Mrs. Grada approached to see what was going on, Emma couldn't hold it in any longer. Throwing herself into Mrs. Grada's bosom, she sobbed and heaved. Mrs. Grada wrapped her arms around her.

A few minutes passed, and there was no sign Emma's tears were going to let up. Mrs. Grada led her into the administration office, away from the prying eyes, and sat her down. She waited patiently for Emma to calm down before inquiring.

"What happened?"

It was hard for Emma to form words in between the self-induced hiccups.

"I made new…hicc…friends at…hicc…the beginning of the year, but…hicc…Rina doesn't get along with them. And I…hicc…I think I just told my best friend I didn't want to be friends anymore!"

This set Emma off again into renewed anguish, and she sobbed again. After a few minutes, she calmed down, and Mrs. Grada was able to speak. She handed Emma tissues to wipe her face and smiled.

"Emma, dear, you are not the first to go through a fight with your best friend, and you won't be the last. I don't know the specifics, but I do know you and Rina have been friends for a very long time. I'm sure she just needs some time to cool down."

"I don't want her to hate me."

"She doesn't. Whatever it is you're fighting about, just sit down and talk with her. Tell her how you really feel, because the most important thing in any relationship is communication."

Emma nodded. Deep down, she knew this. Her parents always talked things out, which is why, in the moment, she didn't know how to respond to the way Rina reacted. For all of her parents' successes in raising her, this was something they failed to prepare her for.

"When you've made up with Rina, come back and I'll tell you about the time Anthony and Driesen had their worst fight and how they resolved it."

Because both of them were UFA fighters, Emma's imagination put them in a fighting ring in her mind's eye. The two were completely mismatched, not even close to the same weight division.

Emma frowned and stood.

"I should be getting home," she said.

"Of course. Good work with putting the books away tonight." Mrs. Grada winked at her.

Emma grabbed her stuff and headed out to the train. It had begun raining at some point in the night, and she had no umbrella to shield her. Sprinting did no good, as she got as wet as if she'd walked, and she had to wait at the platform for ten minutes for the next train.

Could the night get any worse?

♥

Chapter 11
Missing

Morning came too soon. When she got in the previous night, every last part of her was soaked. The cold had permeated deep. She had grabbed warm sleepwear for after a hot shower, and then put a second blanket on her bed. It felt like hours before she was warm again.

Startled awake, she checked the time, and it was before her alarm was set to go off. Try as she might, she couldn't get back to sleep. Anxious, she threw the covers off and picked up her diary and flipped through to the next blank page.

I've never had a fight before, let alone with my best friend. She caught me and Denis right as I think he was leaning in to kiss me. At the moment, I'd never felt so excited. It would have been my first. But Rina saw and freaked out. I don't understand why she's been so hostile lately. She's never been like this.

I don't want things to go back to the way they were before Celebration Day because then I wouldn't have my new friends, but I want the old Rina back. I have to talk to her, away from everyone.

My heart is so heavy, I don't want to go to school today. I want to crawl back in bed and sleep. That would be irresponsible, though. First trimester testing will be coming up in a month, which will give me a view of how close I am to Marcus Bones's level.

She closed the book and returned it to the desk. Everything seemed duller today, and she was unmotivated to get dressed. After a half hour she was changed into her overalls, with a pullover sweater on top of it.

In the kitchen, Phyllip was cooking waffles and eggs. He saw the pained look on her face and served her breakfast before saying anything.

"Is something bothering you?" he asked.

The lump in her throat returned, and her emotions threatened a takeover. She regulated her breathing, and it helped.

Recounting everything, he faithfully listened. When she was done, he came around the kitchen island and hugged her. She felt safe in his strong arms, and it allowed her to let his love wash over her pain.

"I take it she hasn't told you yet, and it would explain why she's having a rough go of it," Phyllip said.

Emma looked up at him, confused.

"Rina's parents are divorcing. You were her constant, and because you're growing in a different way than she is, I'm sure now she feels like she's lost everything," he told her.

The revelation hit her like a train. Why hadn't Rina said anything? It made her sadder, but also angry. Who doesn't share that kind of thing with their best friend?

"When?"

"At the start of the school year. Her dad came to me and asked my advice."

Everything became clear; that first day she lashed out at Denis and put him in the doctor's office wasn't because he was rude to her. It was her unleashing anger. Rina had subtly changed, and now her attitude toward everyone who wasn't Emma made sense.

Phyllip let go and returned to the other side of the island to begin cleanup. While eating, she thought hard about how she could reassure her friend. Rina hadn't come to her with her problems, and Emma figured it meant if she brought it up, Rina would get defensive.

She needed to help Rina without letting her know that she knew. But what about her relationships with Skye and Denis? Skye was her friend, too. And Denis. She wasn't sure what he was to her yet, but she didn't want to push him away while being there for Rina.

After she finished, she prepared for school and hoped Rina would show. When she didn't, Emma rode the train alone and looked for her when she got to school. There was no sign of her anywhere, even at her locker. Emma began to worry.

Skye approached with a confused look and opened her locker.

"Where's *she* at?" she asked while motioning to Rina's locker.

"I don't know. She didn't stop by my apartment this morning."

"Maybe she stayed home sick?"

If that were the excuse for not being here, Emma knew it was a lie. She felt guilty because she was so absorbed in her own life she couldn't see her best friend was hurting.

"We'll keep you company at lunch." Skye smiled, retrieved her first period book, and nudged Emma playfully.

Maybe she was running late? She held out hope that in their first class, she'd show up. But she didn't, and Emma was becoming more worried. Even more so than the other day when she couldn't concentrate, there was no way she'd be able to focus today.

Without Rina at lunch, a hole existed, and she wasn't sure how to deal with it. Denis sat down and looked at her with a raised eyebrow. Emma shrugged and shook her head.

"Probably still mad," he said.

Her eyes became wide, and it was only right then she didn't want Skye knowing what happened. The almost kiss. The blow up. Even though he saw her reaction, it was too late for him to take back the words. She slyly shook her head at him.

"Mad about what?" Skye asked.

He hesitated and diverted.

"Oh. It's nothing," he replied.

Her squinted eyes said Skye didn't buy it, but she didn't pressure him either. Lunch was far from quiet, though.

"So, I know you're both trying out for the Junior League," Skye started, referring to Denis and Chase. "I was thinking about getting my mom to bake you a cake to commemorate."

"That sounds like a good idea. I haven't been to the UFA building. Maybe we could have a small party afterward," Van said.

"I'll see if my pops would be up for that. Maybe he'll let us use his Skybox Elevator."

"What's that?" Skye asked.

"He has an office besides his penthouse at the top, and it can go to any of the floors so he can watch matches."

Van's mouth dropped. "Whoa. That sounds amazing."

Emma already knew about it. She'd seen Mr. Lindali using it many times while at her dad's matches. But she'd never been inside. Would

Rina want to go, knowing Skye and Denis would be there? She'd have to find her first, in order to ask.

The group carried on, and Emma listened. She was preoccupied with thinking of a way to make amends with Rina.

Throughout her clinical skills class, she did everything in her power to do exactly as Doctor Mansworth instructed. It wasn't enough and, soon, she found herself singled out due to the improper compression of a hematoma on Manny. She'd bound the bandage too tight, and before she could fix it, she was scolded.

"Miss Pureheart, if you bandage *any* patient that tight, you're likely to cut off circulation completely."

"I'm sorry, Doctor. I realized my mistake before you said anything and was going to redo the bandage."

"Your attention has been lacking today. While you've been getting higher marks lately, and are closing the gap to Marcus's skill level, you need to make sure your attention is firmly planted on the treatment of your patient at the time."

"Yes, Doctor."

"Good. Jakob, you're next. The mannequin has suffered a laceration on their heel tendon. Triage."

Emma stepped back and watched him work. Their study sessions really had been helping them excel in all of their studies.

With the end of the day closing, she planned to go to Rina's and find out if she was okay. In such a tough time she was going to make sure she was the friend Rina needed, whether she liked the intrusion or not.

At the end of the day, she grabbed study materials for an upcoming test and ran to the train. She stared out the window and purposely skipped her stop. Onward, she headed to Rina's apartment four stops over. Before the train came to a halt, she leapt up and stood by the doors.

They opened, and she darted to the elevator. Down to the second floor, she entered the hallway, and ran to the Gladia's apartment. Emma rang the doorbell. Mrs. Gladia answered.

"Emma?" she said, poking her head out and looking around.

"Hello, Mrs. Gladia. I came to see if Rina was feeling okay."

"What do you mean? Isn't she with you?"

Her heart thumped hard.

"No. She didn't come to school today. I thought maybe she wasn't feeling good."

Mrs. Gladia's face paled.

"She left this morning," her voice hastened. "You didn't see her at all today?"

Emma shook her head and panicked. Where could she be?

"Come in, have a seat on the couch. I need to call her father."

Inside, she removed her shoes, and placed them with the others on the shoe rack. Instead of sitting on the couch, she headed down the dark hallway to Rina's room.

The room was upheaved, something completely abnormal. Papers and schoolbooks were strewn about on Rina's unmade bed. Examining them, it was schoolwork she'd neglected to finish. Emma mentally beat herself up again for not knowing she'd been struggling.

Mrs. Gladia's voice emanated from the other room, and she was frantic. A brief look through everything didn't reveal any clues to Rina's whereabouts, so she returned to the living room.

"...not with you?"

There wasn't much to do, other than listen to their conversation.

"I haven't seen her. She didn't come by my work," Mr. Gladia said over the holo.

"Okay. Can you leave early?"

"I'm in the middle of an important experiment. Leaving now would compromise the results. Have you checked anywhere yet?"

"No, *Horatio*, I only just found out she didn't go to school. Emma came looking for her."

"Okay, so she hasn't been home since this morning. I'll finish what I'm doing here as soon as I can. You need to call public services and have someone assigned to help us find her."

Mrs. Gladia huffed and ended the holo call. She promptly dialed up the Public Services, and a pleasant man answered.

"This is Detective Brack, how can I assist you?"

"My daughter has been missing since this morning. She usually goes over to her friend's house, and then to school, but her friend says she hasn't seen her today. I need someone assigned to help me find my daughter."

"Yes, ma'am. If you'll provide your address, we'll have a nearby investigator assigned to help."

After providing him with her details, the holo call ended, and it was only a couple minutes before the doorbell rang. Mrs. Gladia answered, and a well-dressed woman in a long, brown coat entered.

"Mrs. Gladia, my name is Cris Prentis. I'm the investigator assigned to help you find your daughter. Please, tell me everything."

Mrs. Gladia briefed the investigator on everything she knew and didn't spare the detail she and Mr. Gladia were currently estranged. Investigator Prentis diligently wrote everything down in a notebook.

"Has she ever run away before?"

"No, never."

"Children who are going through parental separation tend to do things to lash out or get attention. Do you believe she's in imminent danger, either by putting herself in harm's way or intentionally harming herself?"

Emma stood and approached.

"I don't think she would do that," she said.

"Are you the friend whom she was supposed to meet?"

"Yes, ma'am. My name is Emma Pureheart."

"Have you checked your home, to see if she's there?"

It hadn't really occurred to her since she hadn't come over this morning. She shook her head.

"I'll call my dad. He should be home."

Rushing over to the holo, she scrolled through the contacts list and found her home listing. It hummed while it attempted to connect. As expected, Phyllip answered.

"Dad, is Rina there?"

"I haven't seen her."

"She didn't come to school and isn't at home. If she comes by, can you please call Mrs. Gladia?"

"Of course, hon. Do you need me to come help look?"

"There's an investigator here. They're going to help us, I think."

"Okay. If you need me, call."

"I will."

The call ended, and she didn't have to relay any of it. The two women were standing right behind her.

"Do you two have any place you frequent or hang out?"

"The library. I haven't checked there because I came directly here after school. But I don't know if she would go there right now."

Emma explained what happened the night before, and again the investigator wrote everything down.

"Despite that, it's our best starting place besides here and your home. Shall we go check?" Investigator Prentis asked.

"Wait, shouldn't someone stay here, in case she comes home?" Emma asked.

"Horatio will hopefully be here soon," Mrs. Gladia said. "He can wait here."

They made their way out and up to the station. The train was arriving, giving them plenty of time to get on. It sped off, and they were headed toward the Master Library.

The ride was all but silent, as Mrs. Gladia and Investigator Prentis discussed the details of the night before. Rina had come home, ate, and gone to bed, all without a word. Emma had nothing to add, so she watched the cityscape out the window.

When they dipped down from the building tops to the Master Library train stop, the three of them stood and headed for the doors. As soon as they opened, Emma bolted toward the building.

"Wait up!" Investigator Prentis called out.

She didn't, though. Emma ran so fast when she got to the doors she practically collided with them. The ground level lounge area was populated with people reading, but Rina wasn't there. Her next thought was to check in with Mrs. Grada and rushed to the administration office.

"Mrs. Grada?" Emma said while bursting through the door.

She wasn't there, but Emma did manage to startle the librarian who was.

"Oh! I'm sorry!"

"Mrs. Grada's not here today. It's her day off," he replied.

"Can you check the system, see if my friend checked out any books today?"

He looked at her with a quirked brow.

"She's missing, and I need to know if she was here today!"

"Do you have her ID number?"

Of course, she did. It was impossible not to know it after years of coming here. She gave it to him.

He accessed their electronic database and input the number on his touch screen. He tapped a few more times and wrote down the time and the name of the book she checked out. He pushed it to her, and she looked. Rina had been there when she should have been in school.

"Thank you!"

Emma leapt up and left the administration office. Out into the foyer, she ran into Mrs. Gladia and Investigator Prentis. Thrusting the paper at them, she was proud she found something to help.

"So, she was here earlier. But that was hours ago. Might she still be here?" the investigator asked.

"It's not uncommon for her to spend her time here while Emma is volunteering," Mrs. Gladia replied.

"That's right. She could be here, but the library is huge. How should we look for her?" Emma asked.

"I want you to stay here, Emma, to watch the door for her," the investigator instructed.

Emma was displeased at the idea of staying put, but if that's what it took to find Rina, she would do it. While the two women searched high and low, Emma kept her eyes open and alert. It took some time for them to return, but Rina was not with them.

"Are there any other places she might go?" the investigator asked.

"The school would be locked because it's after hours, but I suppose she might find a way to get into the colosseum," Emma suggested.

"Which school?"

"Chas Elite Academy."

Increasingly her heart ached for Rina. Fear like she'd never known before crept in. Intrusive thoughts and urban legends mixed together. What if a bad person found her? What if the Walkers gang still exists? She'd never known the city to be unsafe, but it didn't mean it couldn't happen. Emma tried to push the thought down while Mrs. Gladia headed to the public holo booths. She was only in there for a few moments before she returned.

"Horatio is there at the apartment. She hasn't come home yet."

"Do you want to head to the school, then?" Investigator Prentis inquired.

The sky was now dark and clouded over. They'd have no help from the stars or moon. Their only hope would be to contact someone from the school and have the floodlights turned on.

"Is there any way you can pull any more investigators in on this?" Mrs. Gladia asked. "That colosseum is large."

"There are also a lot of hiding spots there," Emma chimed in.

"Emma, I want you to head home. No sense in having you out later than you need to be. You can contact me if Rina shows up."

Investigator Prentis handed Emma a business card.

"Mrs. Gladia, we can walk to the local precinct in this section of Chas and call ahead to the one closest to the school."

Leaving the Master Library, she walked to the train station while watching the women head off toward the block of buildings to her right. The ride home was lonely, and she was scared for her friend. Fear became anger, because even though they'd had a fight, she was going to give Rina a piece of her mind about everything.

The train reached her building, and she hurriedly made her way from it to the elevators to avoid the chill. As she rushed to exit at her floor, she tripped over someone sitting outside the elevator doors. When she hit the carpet, she cried out in pain and startled them. It was Rina. Jumping up, the roles reversed. Emma towered over her friend, who was still just sitting there.

"Rina! What are you doing?" Emma let her fury out. "Where have you been? Do you know how worried we all are? Your mom called Public Services, and an investigator came out, and now they're headed to the school thinking you might be there!"

Rina didn't immediately respond to any of the inquiries, and so Emma became even more furious.

"Get up! We're going to call the investigator right now!"

♥

Chapter 12
Being the Solace

"Marina Gladia, you are in an incredible amount of trouble!" Mrs. Gladia scolded over the holo.

"I'm sorry, Mom." Rina looked down, ashamed.

"When you get home, we're going to have a long conversation about today, and why what you did is not appropriate," Mr. Gladia said.

"Hello, I'm Investigator Prentis. Miss Gladia, are you okay?"

"Yes."

"I'm going to have to take a statement from you about the incident. When would be a convenient time?" the investigator asked.

"I don't know. After school, I guess…" Rina kept her head down, and her voice low.

Phyllip approached from behind the two girls.

"Hi, Mandi, Horatio. It's a bit late, and I wouldn't feel comfortable putting Rina on the train by herself. What would you say to letting Rina stay here for the night? We'll look after her, and Emma can make sure she gets home after school tomorrow."

Rina's parents looked between one another and seemed to silently agree. Horatio nodded.

"Rina, I expect you to be here after school lets out tomorrow," Mr. Gladia said.

"I will be."

They finished their short conversation, and the holo image shut off. Phyllip returned to the kitchen where Gwendy was cooking. He patted the stools as he passed them and moved around to the other side of the island. Emma and Rina sat on them, and it was clear from the rare face he was making that Rina was about to get a lecture.

"Rina, I didn't send you home tonight because it's likely what's happened is going to cause a fight," he started. "It's better if your parents can work through that just themselves."

As Emma watched Rina's eyes tear up, her anger wavered.

"I know you're having a hard time with everything right now. Emma has told us about your confrontations with Skye and Denis. I won't pretend to fully understand, but part of becoming an adult is learning to deal with difficult emotions in healthy ways."

"I don't want them to divorce!" Rina cried out.

The urge to hug her built in Emma. She wanted everything to be better for her.

"It's like they didn't even think about me when they decided! How am I supposed to feel?!"

Gwendy lowered the heat on the stove and came to the island as well.

"Rina, dear, I don't think it was that. Sometimes, people grow apart. When I talked to your mom, they'd already tried seeing a marriage counselor and couldn't reconcile their differences. It's not your fault. It couldn't be."

"Then, what am I supposed to do?" Rina's tears streamed.

Emma brought her stool closer and hugged her friend. She couldn't be mad at her, not now.

"I wanted things to go back to how they were, but everything keeps changing. It's not just them! It's everyone!"

"Hon, change is part of life. But something that won't ever change is that we'll always be here for you," Gwendy said.

Rina sobbed and said, "I'm sorry," about a hundred times. Emma held her friend and stroked her hair. After a few minutes, Rina calmed down, and it gave an opening.

"How about we go get ready for bed. You need some sleep," Emma suggested.

The two of them headed to the back of the apartment. Rina opted to shower while Emma wrote in her diary.

Rina scared me today. When she didn't come to school, when she wasn't at home. I don't know what I would do if something had happened to her. Just because Chas is a safe place to live doesn't mean she couldn't have had an accident.

I'm glad I found her safe, though I was mad at her for making us worry. I can't do anything about her parents, and I don't want to give up my new friends just so we can stay the same. I don't know how to help her, except to be there for her. Is that enough? It's going to have to be, I guess.

Changed, lights off, and the two in bed, they rested after a long day. Rina intertwined her fingers with Emma's, and Emma squeezed lightly to let her know it was okay.

In the morning, Emma found herself alone. The spot where Rina had slept was already cold. Fearing her friend might have left to run away again, she threw the covers off and ran out into the living room. Rina sat at their dining table, looking out the window at the city.

Emma sighed in relief. Rina looked over and gave a weak smile. She smiled back and returned to the room to get ready. They ate breakfast and headed out. On the train, Rina turned to Emma with a serious look.

"Skye's going to be nosy and ask, but I don't want her knowing, or anyone else."

"It's between us. Just tell them you were sick, and I'll back you up."

At school, things were almost as if Rina hadn't been absent except for gathering the work from the day before. Now that Emma knew what was really going on, they would handle it together.

The day was typical, and the classes flew by. Lunch came, and the group converged on their table. Ignoring the fight Rina and Skye had, and the almost-kiss Emma and Denis had, things had returned to being stiff but cordial.

"So, the Junior League tryouts are next week. Chase and I will be competing, and Pops has agreed to let us use the Skybox Elevator for an after party," Denis beamed. "We're gonna invite the participants and their families."

"Great! How many should we bake for? Me and my mom will make sure there's enough cake for everyone," Skye replied excitedly.

"Thirty seems like a good number."

"What about second helpings?" she asked, and then didn't wait for an answer. "You know what? I'll tell my mom to do a whole cake sheet."

"Will we have tickets?" Van asked.

"Not really. Because this isn't an actual fight, tickets won't be sold. We'll make sure Samuel and Samson have a list of names."

"Who's that?" Skye asked.

"Basically, the building's ground floor security." Emma let out a small laugh. "They're so big, only someone truly insane would try and cross them."

"They were the heaviest class in the duo competition, and the reigning champions before retirement. The Trouble Twins," Chase chimed in.

Rina was silent during the conversation. When she was finished eating, she got up and put her tray away. Emma quickly followed, leaving the group behind.

"Hey, wait up!" Emma called out.

Rina stopped only for a moment and looked over her shoulder.

"We didn't get any time to talk about things last night...I mean, things here between everyone," Emma said.

Rina led them out of the cafeteria, and they went upstairs toward their lockers.

"I don't like them, but you want to be friends with them, so there's really nothing to talk about," Rina replied, not angry, but more matter of fact.

"There's also Denis. And what happened the other night," Emma's voice lowered.

"You mean that he was trying to kiss you?" she replied with disdain.

Emma played with her braid and looked down. She wanted Rina's approval, because this was a first for her. Neither of them had really considered dating before because they were content with it being just the two of them. But life was different now. Their lives were expanding in front of them, and Emma wanted to experience new things.

"I like Denis."

"He's a jerk, and he's only nice to you because he likes you. How long have we been going to the UFA? Forever? And only now does he notice you?"

"We probably passed each other before, but maybe he's like us. Maybe he's now seeing things beyond a limited view of the world."

Rina shrugged, and they continued their walk in silence. At their lockers, Emma gathered materials for her clinical skills class, and they waited there until the bell rang. Before she could walk away, Rina unexpectedly clasped Emma's hand and pulled her in for a hug.

"I don't want to lose you as a friend," Rina said.

"You won't. Ever. I promise."

They split to head to their next classes. Emma approached the doctor's office. The door flung open, and she was bowled over. She dropped to her butt, and it sent a zing up her spine.

"Watch where you're going." Marcus sneered while passing by.

As others exited the office and tried to help her, she brushed them off, leapt up and turned to him.

"*You* bumped into *me*! How about you watch where *you're* going!"

He paid her no attention though, which infuriated her. She wondered if his intelligence was related to his attitude. In the office, Doctor Mansworth was at his desk writing in a spiral notebook. Looking up, he handed her a form.

"Give this to your parents tonight. We're going on a field trip next week where you'll spend the day shadowing a healthcare professional. You've already been pre-excused from all of your classes that day, so make sure you pick up that day's materials the day before."

She nodded and put the paper in her bag. On one of the beds, was a student with a face mask on. She coughed loudly, and Emma heard the mucus built up. Not waiting for class to start, or direction from the doctor, she came to the student's side.

"Hello, I'm Emma. Is there anything I can get you at the moment? Some water?"

The girl nodded, and Emma put on disposable gloves and retrieved some for her. While the other students came in and were greeted by the doctor, Emma aided the patient in sitting up so she could take the water. Her eyes were red and puffy, and her nose whistled when she breathed.

"Shouldn't you be going home?" she asked the girl. "If you're ill, it's better if you're at home where you can get proper rest."

She nodded.

"Miss Setam's mother is coming to pick her up," Doctor Mansworth replied.

Emma smiled at her and helped her lay back down.

"That's good. If you need anything, let us know," she said.

In an attempt to gain favor with the doctor, she wanted to display her knowledge. Her hard work studying could only get her so far, and this was a good opportunity for practical application.

"How is our patient's vitals? Does she have a fever?"

"Blood pressure is slightly elevated, but nothing serious. She is running warm, but was given fever reducer an hour and a half ago. Her mother will be here before it's time for another dose," he replied. "Let's get on with our studies."

"Doctor Mansworth, we've been studying and practicing on Manny…I mean, the mannequin since the start of school with only a handful of patients to give us actual hands on. If it's okay with our patient, can we use her as our subject of studies today?"

He mulled it over and gave Emma a curious look. It felt like her attempt to get on his good side worked. He gave a slight nod.

Throughout the class, the doctor asked each of the four aides questions related to immunology and virology. The class went by quickly, and Emma felt much better about all the information she'd been doing her best to absorb.

The following class, Biology, she gave Marcus dirty looks every chance she got, even to the back of his head. She took notes, asked and answered questions, and did everything to make sure he knew she was a contender. Whether he'd acknowledge it or not until she beat him in the competition, she couldn't say, but it was still satisfying to keep up with him.

At the end of the day, she felt proud and had a renewed sense of drive. The feeling of having to catch up was waning, and a new desire to push ahead was taking its place.

When she was loading her bag after school, Skye came over and smiled.

"Me, Van, and Chase are heading to the markets near the center of the city to pick out decorations for our after tryouts party. You should come with us."

"I can't. Rina and I are heading to her place."

"You can go to her place anytime." Skye tugged lightly on Emma's arm.

"Sorry, Skye. I can't today. Maybe we can do something another day?"

Skye pouted and crossed her arms, but when Emma didn't budge, she relaxed and nodded.

"I'll find some place really fun for us to go. Just the two of us."

Rina approached and retrieved her study materials from her locker. Skye waved goodbye and left. Rina gave Emma a sideways look but caught herself and stuffed books in her bag.

The train ride was silent again between them, and it was getting to Emma. It wouldn't be the right place to say anything, but the urge was there to break privacy etiquette. The ride was long to Rina's apartment, and the time to talk was dwindling. Emma was sure once they got there, Rina's parents were going to want to have a talk with her, alone.

"What are you going to say to your mom and dad?" Emma asked.

"I don't know yet. They're going to scold me, and then they're going to fight."

"Would it help if I came in?"

"Probably, but only until you go home. It's going to be bad no matter what."

"At least I can be there for you."

Rina turned her head, and it looked like she wanted to cry. She didn't, though. Emma held Rina's hand, and they watched the city whiz by.

At Rina's apartment block, they disembarked and headed down. She hesitated at her own door, but when Emma squeezed her hand it broke the spell, and they entered.

Around the corner, and into the living room, Rina's parents were talking in low voices. One was on the couch, and the other in a chair across the dark, wood table. They became quiet when they noticed the girls, and Mrs. Gladia patted the couch for Rina to come sit.

The two girls sat down, and it was clear neither of the parents knew how to begin. Emma half-expected they might ask her to leave, and so she preempted them.

"Would it be okay if I stayed, for Rina?" she asked.

"Of course, Emma. We're family, and this affects you, too," Mrs. Gladia said.

Rina's hand tightened, and tears fell.

♥

Chapter 13
Fight Night

The UFA Junior League tryouts were upon them. Phyllip and Gwendy knew Emma would be gone most of the night, and it wasn't going to be a problem since there was no school the next day. It would be a few hours after school ended before the first tryout match began, which gave enough time to drop stuff off at home and get ready.

The doorbell rang as she changed into a heavy, pullover sweater. It was Skye. Emma had agreed to help pick up and carry the baked goods Mrs. Torrie made for the party.

"Hey!" Skye said and launched a hug-attack at her.

Emma stabilized herself and held Skye up long enough for her to break away.

"Hi!"

"You ready?"

"Yep!"

They headed out and took the long trip over to the bakery. Mrs. Torrie had everything ready on the counter. Two pastry boxes and a cake box. Emma peeked at the cake to see Mrs. Torrie had hand drawn the UFA logo by piping it, and the quality was perfect.

"Thank you, Mrs. Torrie!" Emma smiled big. "They're going to love it!"

"You're quite welcome, Emma. I'm glad I could help make this night special for you all."

"You're the best, Mom. I'm not sure when the party will be over, so I'll call you when I'm on my way."

"Okay. Have a wonderful time!"

Skye took the cake, leaving Emma the two pastry boxes. They weren't heavy, just a little cumbersome. Back to the nearest train station, they boarded one which would take them around to the UFA tower. The two made light conversation on the way.

"So, have you ever been outside Chas?" Skye asked and scooted closer.

"No. I've seen pictures, though."

"Yeah, but that's not the same thing. My mom saved enough that we're going to take a trip and go to the ocean."

Emma wondered what that was like, or how far it was. Chas was surrounded by farmland, and hills in the distance.

"Maybe someday. I don't know if my parents have left Chas either, actually," Emma said.

Skye came even closer and brushed her hand against Emma's. Emma suddenly felt nervous.

"I wonder if my mom would let you come with us," she said, turning more toward Emma. "Would you want to?"

What was Skye doing? Was she trying to be her best-friend? More? Why would she have pushed Denis and her closer together? She'd only begun to acknowledge the idea of being romantically involved with Denis, so this gesture by Skye confused her.

"I wouldn't impose myself on someone else's vacation. It would be really awkward for me." A truth.

Their stop was coming, and it gave Emma an excuse to stand. Carefully, she cradled the boxes and readied to disembark.

The walk to the UFA tower was chilly, and she couldn't wait to get inside. Samuel and Samson guarded the back entrance, as per usual.

"Hello, Miss Emma…"

"…Denis is waiting."

"Please, go inside…"

"…and go to floor thirty."

"Okay! Thank you! Have a good night!"

"You…"

"…too!"

They found their way through the employee area and up to their floor. All of the arena doors were open, but the hallways were nearly empty. There was a lot of commotion coming from inside though.

Down near the stage had been decorated and enormous banners had been hung with the words 'Junior League Tryouts' printed on them. Many families were gathered in groups around the arena, and there was a buzz of excitement in the air. On the far side was the Skybox Elevator, with several people inside. Denis was there.

"Miss Emma," a deep voice called.

She looked, and it was a man so large she felt like just standing in his presence could crush her. It was Driesen, The Behemoth. He was smartly dressed and wore a round, brimmed hat.

"Mr. Lindali is waiting for yous," he said and held out his arm in the direction.

He led them around the upper ring to the Skybox and held the door for them. It was almost comical, as he had to duck and squeeze through the already oversized doorframe.

The Skybox was quite large. It was going to easily accommodate the party, and still have room. They placed the boxes on a table, and Driesen waved for them to follow. But he didn't lead the girls to Denis. He kept going to the far back, where there was a man doing paperwork behind a desk. It was the owner, Mr. Lindali. His slicked back, deep brown hair, and strong jawline gave him a certain handsomeness. Denis definitely got his looks from his dad, minus the hair color.

As they approached, nervousness built. She was in the presence of an incredibly influential person in Chas. Someone who made their family what it was. He took notice, and she expected he would be cold, and disconnected. He wasn't. He smiled widely and stood to greet them, hand outstretched for a handshake.

"Emma, welcome. I'm so glad you could make it."

"Thank you, Mr. Lindali. I'm glad to have been invited."

"Please, call me Trevor. You're practically family. I keep up with all my employees families, and Phyllip tells me you're going to be a great doctor someday."

"Dad loves to embellish! I don't know exactly what I'm going to do. But I hope I help a lot of people. This is my friend Skye. Her mother is the one who baked sweets for the contenders and guests."

"It's a parent's right to boast about their kid's accomplishment," he said, and then put his hand out for Skye.

"I'm Skye. It's a pleasure," she said and shook his hand.

"The pleasure is mine, young lady. I've heard good things about your mother's baking from Denis. He was quite impressed."

"I'll make sure she knows her reputation preceded her!"

"Of course. Now, if you'll excuse me, I've got some boring business stuff to look after. I'll see you two around."

Emma was stricken by him. Because she had growing feelings for Denis, it was hard not to project them onto his father as well. A man of stature.

Denis was still young, but he was on the path to growing up to be like Trevor in more ways than one. One day he would be a powerful man. A feeling of inadequacy formed in her head. Why did he like her? Did he find her cute? What was it she liked about him?

Forcing herself not to dwell on it, she led Skye to where Denis was. The group he was with talked and laughed. They were having a good time. Emma hadn't met most of the people there, including the other Junior League tryout participants, so she stuck with Skye. Denis noticed her hanging back and broke away from the group.

"Hey."

"Hi," she said, smiling.

"Rina coming?"

"She should be here soon. She had some stuff to do at home."

"Sounds good." He turned to Skye. "Chase is down in the locker room getting ready. You want me to let him know you're here?"

"Nah. He can come say hi after. Have you seen Van?"

"He came with me and Chase. He's probably getting a tour from one of the fighters right now, because we have time before starting." He turned to Emma. "Speaking of which, do you want a tour of the medical facility?"

It was as good a time as any. She would be going on her career shadowing field trip soon, and this would give her an excellent opportunity to close the gap to Marcus's level.

"Yeah! Let's do it!"

Her exuberance made his face light up. He offered his arm, and she took it. They left Skye, and he took her to the elevators. Inside, he hit the twentieth floor button, and they descended.

"We actually have multiple healthcare stations across various levels, but we're going to a floor dedicated to the healing of our fighters. Pops wanted to make sure his employees got immediate healthcare instead of having to call emergency services."

"I bet he's thought of everything. He seems very savvy."

"Smartest man I know."

The door opened, and the layout of this floor was completely different than any other. They entered into a sterile white area, and on either side of the room were separate recovery rooms. Against the back wall were a few sets of double doors spaced out.

A large staff of healthcare professionals bustled about, and she noticed that despite how much was going on, the place was immaculate.

Denis walked over to a receptionist for the area, and an older, balding man addressed him.

"Please, state the nature of your medical emergency."

Denis laughed. "Nothing, yet. My match isn't for a few hours. I wanted to know if Doctor Elanda was in."

"Doctor Elanda is in her office. Would you like me to page her?"

"No, that's okay. I'm going to show Miss Pureheart around, and then introduce them."

"Please, do not enter any of the occupied rooms and keep your voices at a lower level to promote a soothing atmosphere."

"Yes, sir."

For the next twenty minutes, he showed her around the different accessible triage stations while pointing out the doors which led to surgery areas.

"They can treat almost anything here. Very rarely is someone in such a critical condition they'd need to be taken to a bigger hospital."

"That's amazing. I bet the caregivers love it here, having whatever they need."

"I've never asked, but you can ask the head doctor yourself."

He led them into a side hallway and down a way to an office with Doctor Elanda's name on the door. Denis knocked politely before opening it. The doctor was faced away from them at one of several data entry terminals against the wall. Each had biometric data displayed for different individuals.

"Good evening, Doctor Elanda."

She turned and lifted her glasses off her nose and planted them in her dark, curly hair.

"Did your father send you for injury reports?"

"No. Actually, I wanted my friend to meet you and get a tour of our facilities. She's on the Caregiver Path."

"What specialty are you going to follow, Miss...?"

Doctor Elanda motioned to the chairs in front of her desk, and they sat.

"Pureheart. I'm shooting for first responder doctor."

"That's ambitious. You're aware that job is quite stressful?"

"I like to think that I rise to challenges, and I can work under pressure."

"Absolutely crucial traits required of anyone in this path, but good you recognize that in yourself now, rather than later. So, what do you think of our facilities?"

"They're quite nice. Very comprehensive."

"We have things pretty well figured out here. Our fighters get the best care possible, and thanks to Mr. Lindali, innovative technologies are acquired not only for the UFA, but the hospitals across Chas."

"Doc, I was wondering, would it be possible for Emma to volunteer here?" Denis asked.

"We don't have a system setup for that as our staff are hired on here after completing their degrees due to the specific needs within the Fighter's Guild members."

"That's okay," Emma said, not bothered. "It was still nice to get a tour of your facility. I have a career shadowing field trip coming up, and I'm sure that will be enough for me for now."

"Make sure you take extra notes from whomever you're shadowing. They will be able to give some important pointers," the doctor replied.

"Can I ask you something though?" Emma half-smiled.

"Sure."

"How did you know this was the right field for you?"

"Got path-jitters?"

"A little."

"Honestly, it wasn't until my second year into the young child caregiver specialty that I was sure I wanted to be a doctor. It took me another two years to move into the nursing specialty, which was more time to think. The truth is, even today I what-if myself. But really, so long as you love helping people, I think that's what matters most. You'll find your place in our field."

"Thank you."

"You're quite welcome."

"We should head back. The matches are going to start soon," Denis told her.

After quick goodbyes, the two of them headed back to the Junior Tryouts. Emma was directed back to the Skybox. In front of the glass, seats had been set up. There was an open seat for her just past Rina, with Skye and Van on the other side.

"Hey!" Emma greeted them.

"Hey, Emma!" Van replied first. "Isn't this amazing? I've never been in such a place!"

"It is incredible. I've only ever seen the Skybox from the outside."

"I can't wait to see Denis and Chase in their matches," he said.

Emma sat and received a questioning glance from Rina.

"Where have you been?" she asked.

"With Denis. He was showing me the UFA medical facilities. They have a really nice setup!"

"Oh, really? Is that all you two were doing?" Skye joked.

"I... What do you mean?" Emma blushed. "It wasn't anything like what you're probably thinking!"

Skye only smiled cheekily in response.

The matches soon began. Emma and Rina guessed who would win, as they had done so many times in the past. Skye and Van got in on the action. Soon, they were making up stage names for the tryout participants, and betting with food items.

"Two cookies on Short-Stack there," Skye wagered. "He's clearly the underdog of the match."

"I'll take that bet. Handsy-Reach will win by second round," Emma offered.

Rina smirked. "I'm in. Two on Short-Stack."

"Refrain," Van said.

"What do you mean, 'refrain'? Pick someone and ante up!" Skye challenged.

"I just don't know enough."

"It doesn't matter," she said and elbowed him. "You're not playing with credits."

"Okay. Two on Handsy-Reach."

The match began, and immediately Handsy-Reach dominated. Wild swings, kicks, and finally a tackle ended the fight. It was more of a brawl than what UFA fights were supposed to be. It was still exciting, though.

The next few matches, Van accumulated a whole pile of cookies as his luck in picks was good. He laughed as the three girls piled them on the plate in his lap.

After a while, Emma wondered when either Denis or Chase were going to enter the ring. It dawned on her they were probably going to get matched against each other. She didn't have to wait long for the confirmation.

When their turn came, they entered the ring, and the betting began. This time though, it wasn't met with nearly as much enthusiasm because they were now betting for or against a friend.

"Chase is going to win," Skye said confidently.

Van was hesitant. "I think I'm obligated to go with Chase since I've known him longer.

"I'm not betting this round," Rina replied.

Skye looked over to Emma with a mischievous grin.

"Well? Are you going to put a bet on your *boyfriend*?"

"What? He's not!" she practically yelled, and then looked around and covered her face.

"He might as well be," Skye prodded.

"Just shut up, Skye," Rina snapped. "Don't tease her."

"Shut up yourself. I'm playing around."

"Stop!" Emma glared at both of them. "We're here to have a good time, and I won't let you ruin it over a silly argument!"

The peace returned, and Emma sat mortified. Looking around, she saw others had noticed their little outburst, and it made her embarrassment worse. She was glad Denis or Mr. Lindali weren't in there to have witnessed it.

He wasn't her boyfriend. They had only hung out. A kiss was interrupted. She wasn't sure what her true feelings were about him other than liking his company.

Denis and Chase entered the ring, and they tapped fists to signal the start of the match. Denis was the first to take a swing, and the second. Chase dodged, and Denis resumed a defensive stance. Chase came in with a few blows right at Denis's forearms, and then turned his shoulder inward and rammed him.

Denis shoved back, but it didn't push Chase far, and he kept on top of him. A few low kicks caused Chase to back away. They danced around the ring, both looking as though they were trying to wear the other out. Jab. Block. Kick. Counter.

Emma rooted silently for Denis, but her excitement was hard to contain. On the edge of her seat, she felt the urge to mimic Denis's moves.

He cornered Chase but was pushed back hard when Chase used the ring post as leverage and put both feet into Denis. He stumbled backward, and Chase took advantage. Emma thought her vision blurred for a moment. Chase seemed to speed up beyond human capabilities. He tackled Denis, and they wrestled for domination.

Emma leapt out of her seat.

"Come on! Get up!" she yelled despite that Denis couldn't hear her. It was foolish, but she couldn't help herself.

Chase came out on top, flipped Denis onto his stomach, and twisted his arm behind his back. Denis slapped the mat twice, and the match was over.

They stood up and the referee declared Chase the winner. They bowed to the clapping audience in the stands, and then took their leave toward the locker rooms.

Because she was still standing at the glass, the embarrassment of having stood up set in. Trying to play it off, she headed over to the snack table and poured a cup of juice. Rina came to stand beside her, and thankfully she didn't make it awkward.

"That was a surprisingly good fight. I was rooting for Denis at the end."

"It was fun to watch. I hope Chase winning it doesn't disqualify Denis," Emma frowned.

"I doubt it. He *is* the boss's son," she whispered and looked over her shoulder.

"I don't think being the boss's son would matter. Mr. Lindali seems like a fair man."

While waiting for Denis to return, she explored the office with Rina. When they made their way to the back of the office, she noticed a photo of Trevor and a couple, a man and woman. She recognized them from one of her own family's photos. They were the couple who took her parents to the UFA the night her dad fought Driesen. Who were they? Did they know Trevor before, or did they meet him at the match her parents went to?

"Hey," Denis said from behind, and startled her.

She spun and smiled.

"You did great out there!"

"I did all right. It wasn't a real fight, so we didn't go all out."

"Looks like you'll have to work on getting out of pins, though," Rina commented.

"That's true. I'll have to spar some more."

An announcement came over an intercom and interrupted them.

"This is your Junior Tryouts results announcement. Those whose names are called have passed into the Junior League and are to report one week from today. The names are Rip Garlan, Anika Axcie, Freddy Marchuk, Zander Builder, Jake Feller, and Denis Lindali."

There was an exclamation of anger from Skye and Chase. Emma was shocked, and when she looked to Denis his expression told her he didn't see this coming.

"That's not fair!" Skye yelled.

Chase strode over to Denis to confront him, amidst all the other guests in the Skybox.

"What is this?" Chase pointed and shoved his index finger into Denis's sternum. "I beat you. I should be on that list!"

Denis raised his hands up in the air in surrender. "I had nothing to do with this, I swear!"

"Don't lie," Skye followed. "You're the son of the owner, *of course* you'd get in, even though *Chase* won."

"Stop!" Emma interjected. "He said he didn't do it."

"It doesn't matter if he didn't. Someone did on his behalf. Maybe it was even his father!" Skye kept on. "This whole thing is rigged!"

"Hey, don't put this on me or pops! I didn't do this, but I'll get it fixed," Denis said, raising his hands to fend them off.

"This is idiotic. I don't want to be a part of this trash organization anyway," Chase yelled and shoved Denis. Emma caught him the best she could, but they nearly toppled over.

"That's uncalled for!" Denis recovered and shoved Chase back. "Get out and don't come back!"

All eyes were on them. Emma saw Chase thinking about retaliating, but he stormed out and slammed the door. Skye scowled and glared. After a moment, she followed Chase.

"Van, let's go," Skye ordered.

Awkward silence.

"Let's go. I need to go talk to my pops about this."

♥

Chapter 14
Unexpected Engagements

Denis tried to repair their friendship and explained he talked directly to his *pops*. He expressed that he believed the judges made an error to his father. The answer he received was that there were extenuating circumstances and that Mr. Lindali wanted to speak directly to Chase. Chase refused.

Chase couldn't be soothed. The damage was done. Hostile feelings grew between the now fractured group, with the timider people like Van and Emma caught in the middle.

Days passed and the void grew. Van became reclusive. Skye no longer talked to Emma during class. The two groups now sat at opposite ends of the cafeteria during lunch.

There wasn't anything special about the day that Emma knew of. She and Rina entered the cafeteria and got in line to get their food. Skye and Chase unabashedly cut directly in front of Rina, who was about to grab a tray.

No sideways glance. No acknowledgement of her presence. Only complete disrespect. Skye took the top tray and collected her lunch. Chase followed. Rina was visibly angered, and Emma tried to calm her before the outburst by placing her hand on Rina's shoulder. A futile attempt. Rina pulled away.

"What is your problem?" Rina yelled.

Skye ignored her, and Rina reacted. She pushed past Chase, grabbed Skye by the shoulder and spun her around. Skye shoved her into Chase. Rina rebounded and slapped Skye's tray from her hand. The clatter made Emma wince.

"Keep your hands off me!" Skye barked.

Emma got in between Rina and Chase but couldn't restrain her friend if she wanted. Rina lunged and tackled Skye to the ground, and the two girls caused a commotion large enough to draw the attention of everyone.

Chase shoved Emma out of the way to pull Rina off Skye. She hit the floor hard and, out of nowhere, Denis came to her aid.

"Are you okay?"

Emma was close to tears, but she nodded. He helped her up and moved to intervene in the now two-on-one that Rina was in. Just as Chase was lifting Rina up roughly, Denis moved in and chopped down with his arm in Chase's elbow crease to break his grip.

"Let go of her," Denis ordered.

"How about you go jump off the top of the UFA building," Chase shot back and shoved Denis.

The four were now in full on brawl mode, with trays, food, and fists being flung around. Emma retreated, and it took several administrators to come in and break up the whole debacle. The four were separated and filed out of the cafeteria. Emma followed.

Away from the prying eyes, they were sat down on benches outside the headmaster's office. Emma sat in-between Rina and Denis on one, while across the hall, Skye and Chase glared. One by one, they were called in, with Emma being last.

"Tell me what happened," Headmaster Greene instructed as she sat in a cushioned chair in front of his desk.

"We had entered the cafeteria and were about to get our food when Skye and Chase cut in front of us…"

As she explained, she felt it necessary to volunteer the information about the Junior League tryouts being the catalyst to the outburst.

"It was a mistake on the judge's part, and Denis tried to fix it, but Chase and Skye won't accept his apology, and so they're acting out because of it."

"Miss Pureheart, while I understand you didn't have direct involvement in the altercation, we need to make it known to everyone this behavior will not be tolerated, as it's certainly not out in the real world.

"The school has resources for conflict resolution, and I am putting in that the five of you will attend a sixty-minute session after school each day for a week, starting next week. It's important to learn these skills now rather than later."

"Yes, sir."

She would have to work out a revised schedule with her volunteer work, as well as figure out how to make up any lost study time. It didn't seem fair that she was also required to go, but she wanted to remain optimistic it might be beneficial in some way.

When the meeting was done, lunch was over. There was no time for them to get any food. A couple minutes late for clinical skills, she entered and caught flak from Doctor Mansworth.

"Miss Pureheart, if you can't be on time for my class, then you might as well apply for a career path change now. Consider this your only warning. I won't tolerate tardiness and will speak with the headmaster about a change if it happens again."

Frustrated and sad, she figured it would be pointless to try and explain what happened. All she could manage was a nod. The rest of the day, she was sullen and withdrawn. Everything happening all at once was overwhelming, and it felt like the world was weighing her down.

Even the ride home after school was quiet. Neither she nor Rina said anything about what happened. Mr. and Mrs. Gladia already wanted Rina home right away because of her disappearance. Now, there would be a reason for them to impose more restrictions on her.

At her stop, Emma said goodbye to Rina and disembarked. Rina simply waved and stared out the window.

In the apartment, Gwendy was there. It was one of her days off, and Emma felt like it might be better to talk with her woman-to-woman. It wasn't that she didn't have faith her father could guide her adequately, but her mother *was* the better negotiator in the household.

"Hey, honey. How was school?"

"It was awful," she said and tossed her bag on the floor near the island counter.

"What happened?"

She told her mom about all of the fighting, and her mom listened closely.

"That sounds like a lot going on."

Emma was frustrated.

"There's nothing I can do to fix it." She fought the urge to raise her voice. "I don't know what I'm going to get out of the conflict resolution class. I guess I'll just have to find out."

"Growing up is hard for everyone and, sometimes, these kinds of things can't be fixed. I am sure, though, the conflict resolution training will be helpful for this and future situations."

Emma sighed and got some juice from the refrigerator.

"Why would Skye and Chase act like this, though? I understand why Rina's been abrasive lately, but Skye doesn't seem to have any problems except the ones she makes."

"Just like not knowing Rina's parents were separating, Skye and Chase's struggles may be invisible. Some struggles are physical, some are emotional. But there's no way for you to know why without knowing every detail about her life."

"What should I do, Mom?"

"Just keep being you. Your empathy is one of your greatest virtues, and I have no doubt you will overcome this obstacle."

Emma offered a half-hearted smile. She didn't feel any better, but her mom was wise, and it gave her a little perspective. Grabbing her backpack, she trudged to her room to get ahead on her schoolwork. Gwendy brought her dinner so she didn't have to stop.

The doorbell rang, but it barely registered as the numerous details from her biology book clouded her mind. It was only when her mom knocked on the door and opened it was her concentration broken.

"Em, Denis is at the door. He said he wanted to tell you some exciting news."

Exhausted, she stood and followed her mom back out to the living room. When he saw her, his eyes lit up. He smiled and waved.

"Hey!" he said.

"Hey."

"So, I talked to my pops and told him how you're studying really hard to be able to win the Advanced Beginner Healer award. I told him Doctor Elanda said there wasn't really a way to have you volunteer, but I thought it would be great for you. So, he talked to her, and they're going to make a volunteer spot just for you!"

She was at a loss for words. Doctor Elanda was clear that there wasn't any sort of program set up, so for Denis to get his father to make one felt wrong. Emma wanted to be thankful for the opportunity, but it felt like she'd cheated a system.

"I..."

If he could convince his dad to make a volunteer position where there was none before, was it possible he actually did rig the Junior League tryouts? With this seed of doubt sown, what would her conscience do to her if she accepted?

"I can't accept, Denis. Thank you."

"What?" The look of shock on his face was that of hurt. "I don't understand."

"Doctor Elanda and the staff are busy people. My presence there, where they'd have to watch over me, babysit me, would be a burden. I can't do that to them, if it means they'd have to sacrifice the care of others."

"But it won't be any problem," he said. "I want you to win your competition."

"It's not only about the competition, Denis. If I'm to be a caregiver, I have to respect boundaries of all kinds, personal and policy. I *do* appreciate it, but I won't put the doctor out like that."

His hurt turned to frustration.

"I don't get it. I practically begged to get you this opportunity, and you won't even give it a shot?"

Not willing to compromise her morals, she rebuked him.

"I didn't ask for you to do that. It wasn't your place to go over Doctor Elanda's head and have your dad force the situation. I was happy I even got to see the facility and meet some professionals."

"Then, think of how happy you'd be working side by side, learning from those same professionals!"

"No, Denis," she said, getting frustrated. "It was nice of you to think of me but, in the process, you disregarded the other people who this will affect."

Having reached an impasse and both upset, he sighed.

"All right, I guess that's it, then. I'm going to head out," he said and walked down the hall.

After everything that happened today, she didn't want him to be angry, but it couldn't be helped right now. Emma figured after some time to cool down, they might get closer to seeing eye-to-eye on the matter.

Closing the door, she turned to find Gwendy was there to console her. Emma shrugged and sighed.

"I'm proud of you, honey. You stuck to your principles, and I'm sure it was difficult considering what he was offering."

They walked to the kitchen, and she watched her mom wash dishes.

"It would really help having an opportunity like that. But it didn't feel right. He used his dad's position of power to manipulate a situation."

"That is the world sometimes. We live in a time where inequality is minimal, but there are still people with more wealth and power than others."

What did that mean to her? Was Denis a bad person for using the power? Or simply misguided? Under either circumstance, she knew if they were going to continue to be friends, she'd have to make it perfectly clear to him he can't do that anymore.

"Thanks, Mom. I'm going to get back to my studies."

♥

Chapter 15
A Life Worth Living

The drama that had entered Emma's life caused her head to spin and, when it came time to do job shadowing, it was a nice break from everything.

Doctor Mansworth had scheduled the day off school for all of his clinical skills students for the field trip. Even with all of the extra students, Emma felt most comfortable sticking with AJ, Jakob...and Vera. The two girls sat on either end of the bench seat, with the boys in the middle, while they rode the train to Asta Memorial Hospital.

The simultaneous conversations made the interior of the train car incredibly loud. Even AJ and Jakob contributed, with their enthusiasm about getting to see the things they'd been learning used in a real world setting.

"I wonder what kind of people we'll get to shadow," AJ said.

"I'm sure we'll just be put with nurses across the different departments," Vera answered. "They won't stick us in any high-profile setting, that's for sure."

"I hope Doctor Mansworth was able to get a couple emergency room opportunities," Emma said.

"I know we've seen injuries at school, but even the smallest sight of blood nauseates me. I hope I don't see anything gruesome. I prefer the doctor's red ink all over Manny," Jakob said and laughed.

Asta Memorial wasn't too far from the school, as they'd only been riding for twenty minutes before reaching it. They stopped on the roof of one of many buildings. Despite already being incredibly high up, the other buildings surrounding were even taller. Nothing that could touch the height of the UFA building, or the governor's office, but still quite awesome.

Doctor Mansworth led them out onto the roof and met with an administrator waiting for them. They spoke quietly for a moment, and then he abruptly turned to the students and bellowed.

"Students, you will follow Doctor Lark down into the administration area, where you will wait to meet up with your assigned professional. Ask questions, take notes, learn. The shadowing will take all day so, when we are done, you don't need to return to school."

With that, Doctor Lark waved them on, and before Emma could move, Marcus pushed between her and Vera.

"Jerk," Vera snapped.

At the elevators, Doctor Lark informed them to descend to the first floor. The students split into groups, and there were many administration booths when they reached ground level. Doctor Lark directed them to form two lines to keep the other booths free for incoming patients.

While in line, she looked around, and the hospital seemed busy. She people watched until it was her turn to check in.

"Name?"

"Emma Pureheart."

She was handed a plastic nametag with her name engraved on it, the letters painted in white. Pinning it on made her feel special, like she already had a permanent caregiver position.

"Please, step to the side and wait for Nurse Hawker."

It was only a few moments before a young man approached her wearing a simple, standard blue nurse uniform. His nametag said 'Nurse Marv Hawker.'

"Miss Pureheart, welcome to our facility. You'll be shadowing me today, and I'm hoping you walk away with a better understanding of the path you've chosen. Are you ready?" His voice was smooth, as was the smile he flashed.

"I am!"

He led her back into the halls of the hospital. Everything was immaculate. The walls were lined with artwork, images which evoked feelings of calmness and serenity. A picture of the ocean drew her attention, but she didn't look long as Nurse Hawker kept going.

"Which specialty do you work in?" she asked, trying to keep up with his long strides.

"I work in maternity, floating between antepartum, labor and delivery, and postpartum. My favorite is assisting mothers in caring for their newborns."

"That sounds rewarding."

"It is. What specialty are you hoping to get into?"

"First responder. I want to be the first on scene to help save lives."

"That's a really good goal. I have a friend who does that. He says it's stressful, but he has the same passion. I could put you in contact with him, and maybe you could go on a ride-along."

"Wow! Really?! I would love that!"

He chuckled at how animated she became.

Through a set of secured doors, they entered the maternity ward, and he had her sign in on a visitor log. A couple other students were there also, including Marcus. She wondered if he would be smug here, too, but he signed in and passed her without even a glance in her direction.

She spun on her heels to face Nurse Hawker, and he led her to his assigned station. They began by familiarizing themselves with the shadowing protocol.

"There are several things you need to know for today. First, anything you see and hear about patients is confidential, and I need you to sign this form stating you won't talk about it outside here," he said and passed her a clipboard with a page on it.

She read it over, and it seemed like the penalties were harsh for sharing detailed personal patient information. Though she had no intention of breaking the rules and laws, she still became instantly nervous. The penalties ranged from reparations to jail time. Signing it, she handed it back to him, and he filed it away in a cabinet.

"The second thing is going to be that you are here as an observer. Your primary goal is to learn how the medical field operates. You're welcome to ask questions and take general notes. I won't be relying on you for any actual care or treatments of the patients today."

"Understood!"

"If a patient does happen to ask you a question, redirect them to me, and I'll take care of it."

She nodded, and he continued with the minutiae of what to do in emergency situations. He wasn't like Doctor Mansworth, or anyone else she'd met, really. There was a professional calmness about him, and it was pleasing to hear him talk.

Writing down the notes of the things he'd just discussed, he waited for her to finish. She looked up at him and nodded.

"Ready?"

"Yes, sir!"

"Just Hawker is fine."

"Okay, Hawker."

Accessing an electronic health system, on a screen similar to the PayPad system down at the markets, he was able to obtain a list of current rooms he was assigned to. He seemed to memorize the list in a short amount of time, and then turned the screen off.

Waving her on, she followed and watched the other interactions. Nurses talking to doctors, students going through the same spiel as she did, people checking in.

At the first room on the stop, he cleaned his hands at a sink outside and knocked on the door before entering. Emma followed his lead and washed hers, too.

"Good morning, Mrs. Jaster," he said and began prepping fresh linen.

"Good morning," she replied with a yawn.

"Will today be the day?"

"I certainly hope so!"

"So do we. The doctor will be in a bit later to discuss options for birth but, for now, I'm going to give you a clean bed spread. Can you stand?"

With Hawker's help, she slowly stood, and he was incredibly fast at changing the bed. He replaced her pillow and all the dirty linen was placed in a portable hamper in the room. When he was done, he helped her back onto the bed, and she smiled in appreciation.

"Is there anything you need at the moment?"

"Ice chips!"

He chuckled at her enthusiastic request. "No problem. I'll be right back with those."

Out into the reception area, he retrieved a tall blue plastic cup filled with ice.

"That's it?" Emma asked. "That seems...easy."

"That's because it was an easy one," he replied with a cheeky smile and led her back to the room.

He passed off the cup of ice.

"Would you like to put in your lunch order now?" he asked.

"Grilled cheese, tomato soup, crackers," she blurted.

"Got it. I'll make sure it's sent up in a few hours. Let us know if there's anything else you need."

"Thank you!"

They exited, and he closed the door.

"I chose an easy one to start you out. I've found it works better that way. It's how the person I shadowed did it, too."

"How long ago was that?" she asked because she was curious about their age gap.

"About ten years."

It didn't stop her from thinking he was handsome, but it was too great for her to consider crushing on him.

A gentle chime came across the announcement speakers, and she didn't need any explanation for what it meant. A mother had given birth. A couple nurses emerged from one of the stations, with fresh cut flowers and a balloon that said 'Congratulations!' on it and headed down the hall.

"Who sent the flowers?" she asked.

"No one. We do it for every mother after they've given birth."

"That's sweet."

They visited half a dozen patients, and Emma took diligent notes on processes and interactions, but not details on the people. Though she passed her peers every once in a while, there weren't any interactions with them until it was Hawker's scheduled lunch break.

He led them down to the cafeteria, where they had their choice of various food and drinks. After choosing, they sat down at a table with Marcus and the nurse he was shadowing.

"Hey, Quinn," Hawker greeted.

"Hey, Hawker. How's the day going so far?"

"Good. Just walking Miss Pureheart through the daily routine. And you?"

"Good. Mister Bones has been telling me about following in his father's footsteps."

"Oh, yeah? Any relation to Doctor Bones here?" Hawker asked.

"Indeed. My father's the department head of the head, neck, and spinal clinic two buildings over. He's the leading expert on paralysis reversal," Marcus said with a tone of importance.

"I've read some of his papers on the matter, but I'm afraid because that's not my area of expertise, most of his reconstruction methods went over my head," Hawker said.

"I'm not surprised. He pioneered the technique, and doctors from all around Salvoa seek to be taught. He ensures the most talented amongst the doctors are taught the methods."

It felt to Emma like he was proud of his father but also that he was using his father's clout as his own. As if he was better than the others simply because of his parentage.

"Sounds like you have a big pair of shoes to fill," Hawker said with a hint of contempt for Marcus's tone.

Marcus gave a quick glare and took a bite of his food.

"What about you?" Quinn asked Emma.

"I hope to become a first responder. I've always wanted to help people, and it seems like it might be the greatest opportunity to do that. I could save lives."

"That's great! I thought about that, too." Quinn got excited. "I was going to take the specialized on-the-job training course for it, but life kind of got in the way."

"It's never too late for a new specialization, is it?" Emma asked.

"No, not really. I just need to do some brushing up since it's been a few years since I graduated with my nursing degree."

"You should come by the Chas Master Library. I volunteer there, and I can familiarize you with the medical section!" Emma offered.

"I might do that. Thanks."

"First responders don't really save the lives. They're not equipped to. They simply keep the people from dying until the doctors in the emergency rooms can save them," Marcus stated.

"Of course, they save lives," Emma snapped. "What you said doesn't make any sense because if the first responder wasn't there to stabilize them, they'd end up dying before they ever reached the emergency room."

"I'm just saying, if you want to save lives, study hard and become a regular doctor."

The gall. Emma couldn't tell if he was saying these things because he truly believed them or if he was trying to antagonize her. She was torn between ripping into him or keeping quiet and letting him look stupid.

The latter thought prevailed, and she simply ate her sandwich. Neither Hawker nor Quinn said anything either, and she assumed they also had the internal struggle to let the matter drop. Marcus sat there, looking smug as if he'd won the argument.

Returning to the maternity ward, they resumed the shadowing experience, and Emma was glad she was away from Marcus. His snobbish attitude irritated her but, with distance, her mood returned to normal.

As they were coming out from another expectant mother's room, a few nurses and a doctor rushed by. There was a sense of urgency in the air, and Hawker joined them when they waved for him. Not knowing what to do, Emma instinctively followed, and she heard a woman grunting and crying when they grew close to where they were headed. At the door, Hawker turned to her.

"Stay here."

She and a few other students congregated outside the room. From the loud wailing coming from inside, and the doctor's elevated and commanding voice, there was no doubt they were having an emergency.

"We need to get her to surgery, now."

"Clear the hall!"

"What's going on? Is she going to be okay?" a man frantically asked.

"Let's go! Move!"

Hawker emerged and ushered all the students along.

"Come on, out of the way!" he ordered and led them to the nearest nursing station.

He accessed a holo, and the call was immediately answered.

"State the emergency," the operator on the other line said with haste.

"Birth complication. Emergency surgery needed for a mother to stop the bleeding."

Hawker coordinated with the operator while the doctor and nurses in the room barreled out of there with the bed soaked in red. The man whose frantic asking about her wellbeing followed and hounded them for answers.

"Is my wife going to be okay?" he asked, tears streaming down his face.

"Doctor, operating room two," Hawker shouted, and then intercepted the distraught man. "Sir, you need to stay here with your daughter. Let the staff care for your wife."

"Is she going to be okay?!"

"I don't have an answer. They need to get her into surgery now if they're going to have a chance at saving her life. Let's go back in and check on your daughter. What's her name?"

"Jemm."

It was hard for Emma to watch, but she couldn't figure out if it was the woman who was going to die or the man's emotional breakdown which was getting to her. Maybe both?

Hawker led the man back to the room while the students stayed put. A few kids gossiped in whispers, but not her. Neither did Marcus. Out of the corner of her eye, she watched him, and he was above it all. Leaned against the wall, he appeared to stare off at nothing.

Twenty minutes passed, and nurses began returning to pick up their charges. Eventually, only Emma was left waiting. When the doctor returned to the room, she expected Hawker would come out. Instead, she heard the man wail, and she knew the worst had happened. Emma's gut sank. Jemm wasn't a day old, and she'd lost her mother.

Reality was that not everyone could be saved, and she knew it. But it was only now, in the midst of a tragedy, it resonated. When Hawker returned, he motioned for her to follow him back to his station.

"Have a seat," he said and pulled out a chair. "You look a little pale. Would you like some water?"

"Yes, please."

He was quick about it, and she barely noticed how fast she guzzled the water down. He took the paper cup from her and tossed it in the trash.

"That's one of the hardest things anyone can go through," he said. "Experiencing death, whether it's someone you know or a stranger, is horrible."

"I know it happens, and people are born and die every day, but all I can think about now is how that little girl is going to grow up without her mother."

"You're right, but they'll receive all of the support they'll need through Chas's social systems. The hospital is already taking care of setting up counselling, looking for someone to donate their breast milk, and caregivers will be assigned to help out with Jemm's needs."

Despite that they would be cared for, Emma couldn't help but wonder what her life would have been like if she'd have suffered such a tragedy. Would she still be the caring person she is? Or would death have hardened her? She supposed she could never know, nor did it matter then.

"Speaking of support; I would recommend talking to a counselor. While nothing can prepare you for things like this, you'll need to learn to work through them being in this field."

"I'll talk to my school about setting something up," she replied.

"Good. Would you like to continue?"

"Yes, I would."

♥

Chapter 16
Constructive, Destructive

All week long Emma, Rina, Skye, Chase, and Denis would have to stay after school for their conflict resolution class. When she entered the room, there was a middle-aged man there, his name in print on the board. 'Mr. Viceroy.'

"Please, take a seat," he said.

The other four entered and followed suit. Skye and Chase sat next to each other, Rina sat next to Emma, and Denis isolated himself away from all of them.

"My name is Mr. Viceroy, and I'm one of the school's psychologists. I'd like to jump into the heart of the matter. We already have statements about what happened, but now you've all had time to reflect, I'd like you all to tell me who, what, where, when, and how. No interruptions while another is speaking."

Nobody wanted to volunteer, and so Mr. Viceroy had to start them off. Everyone was rather guarded about recounting what happened, starting at the night of the Junior League tryouts. It took most of the hour just to get through the stories. The counselor took his time, listening and writing on a notepad.

"I want you all to go home tonight and think about the recollections you heard and compare them with what you saw. When you approach a complex social problem, it's best to break down the arguments and approach resolutions logically."

The five of them left, and no one said a word. Secretly, Emma hoped Denis would follow or come talk to her. Maybe acknowledge his manipulation of Doctor Elanda was wrong. But he didn't.

Instead, he walked with his head down and left the school before she and Rina did. Because the UFA was in the other direction, the train he got on wasn't theirs, and so the opportunity for him to make amends with her had come and gone for the day.

The home routine was normal, most of which she spent silently studying while Phyllip worked out in preparation for a fight. When she was caught up, it seemed like an opportune time for a diary entry.

It feels like everything that could go wrong in our group has. Sure, it was easier when it was only Rina and I, but I feel like not making new friends is a missed chance at new experiences.

I don't think it's reasonable for everyone to get along all of the time, but if it weren't for the conflict resolution class, I don't think they'd be seen near each other. It would be nice if we could work it out and go back to being a group of friends. How can that happen though? Acknowledgement of wrongs? Denis already acknowledged what happened with Chase and tried to correct it. It wasn't his fault that his father said no.

I guess if we can't figure this out, I'll have to decide if I want to keep being friends with them individually instead of as a group. In the end, I have to make sure I don't let any of this interfere with my studies.

I can't let Marcus beat me. He probably volunteers in the medical field already. Maybe I should have taken Denis's offer, even though it would have felt wrong.

The next day, classes were busy, and it made the time go by quickly. Before she knew it, the regular day was over, and it was time for the resolution session. When she came in, she found the others were already there, and an argument had begun.

"It must be nice being Denis *Lindali*, getting everything you want," Chase snapped.

"That's not constructive," Mr. Viceroy commented. "While you're entitled to feel upset, what we need to work on is how to resolve the problem without the usage of personal attacks."

"How can he?" Skye interjected. "When someone abuses their power, how is someone supposed to react?"

It seemed like Mr. Viceroy had no problem starting early since they were already in conflict, and she took her seat quietly.

"The power of words is an important concept. Long ago, we used brute force as a method of conflict resolution, and it usually ended in many deaths. Now, I understand Denis and Chase are both interested in being fighters for the UFA—"

"Not anymore," Chase interrupted. "Their organization is corrupt."

"But you *did* want to. That puts you two in a unique position because, as entertainers, your job would have been to fight others for a living. Do those fighters hold grudges against the other if they lose? Do they take their conflict out of the ring?"

Emma raised her hand, not really sure if it was the right thing in this more intimate setting.

"Emma?"

"My dad is also a fighter for the UFA. One of the rules is that outside of the ring there's not supposed to be grudges or negative feelings."

"Thank you," Mr. Viceroy said, and then looked to the other four. "Why do you think that is?"

"They're entertainers. Professionals," Rina replied. "They may bruise each other, or break bones, or whatever else, but in the end they're both there to earn a living. They respect one another."

"Respect. A perfect answer. Chase, do you feel Denis has respect for you?"

"No. I don't." He bared his teeth like an animal. "And I don't respect him or his dad."

"Come on, man," Denis huffed. "We were friends. My pops told me there was a reason, but he wouldn't explain. It's not my fault."

"Whatever. Blame your dad. Blame whoever you want. The fact is that I'm better than you! I'm faster! I beat you!"

"Chase, please calm down. We need to take this one step at a time. Let's work backwards and start from the fight that happened in school," Mr. Viceroy said with low, soothing voice. "Skye, in your words what started the fight in school?"

She looked down and away, embarrassed. It took her a moment to build the courage to speak, and when she did, it came out forceful.

"Chase was wronged, and I felt like I had to retaliate in some way."

"But what did Rina and Emma do that warranted your actions?"

Her voice got soft, and her face turned redder. "Nothing. It wasn't them. I was just mad."

"Would you say your actions showed respect for them in regard to the situation?"

"No…"

"It's not a secret that when we become emotional, we lose objectivity. What we're here to learn is how to regain control from our emotional state and resolve the issue in a constructive way. What do you all think are some ways we can do that?"

"It's hard not to react emotionally when someone is also so, maybe instead of reacting, they could step away," Emma said.

"That's a good first step, a level head, but walking away doesn't solve the problem itself."

Mr. Viceroy stood and approached the board. He uncapped a marker and began a list: calm communication; active listening; empathetic acknowledgement; building rapport; following up.

"Emma is on the right path. Calm communication. What would have been a good second step after stepping away for a breath?"

Everyone hesitated to answer for a moment, then Rina spoke.

"Talk to the other person, ask them why they were being hostile."

"Yes, but in calm communication, you must keep in mind it's not necessarily about what you say but how you say it. There's a difference between 'what's your problem?' and 'what did I do to upset you?'"

Mr. Viceroy continued, and Emma listened intently. Throughout their time, Chase became more closed off. He fidgeted in his seat and avoided eye contact. Emma wished Mr. Viceroy would figure out a way to get through to Chase so they could resolve this divide, but it was looking less likely.

On her way home, she played out scenarios in her mind's eye on how things could be approached between them. If they tried to resolve the problem on their own now, would they be successful? She doubted it, as Mr. Viceroy had more to cover with them.

Phyllip was making dinner, and she sat on a stool at the island counter.

"Hey, Dad."

"Hey, Em. How was school?"

"It was okay. I need to ask you something. It's about Denis."

He looked over his shoulder and nodded. "Shoot."

"Denis did something I think was inappropriate. He talked his dad into creating a volunteer position for me at the UFA's clinic, after Doctor Elanda specifically said there was no position. I got upset at him for abusing his father's position of power, and we haven't talked since. Have you heard anything at work about that?"

"No, I haven't."

"How would you deal with this?"

"Well, you can always approach him yourself and try to explain more in detail why you reacted that way. Your mom and I have a very solid line of communication with one another."

"That's what Mr. Viceroy was talking about today in our conflict resolution class. But Denis hasn't even tried to talk to me since I got upset."

"It takes two people to communicate. You can always try, but he may not be ready to express how he's feeling."

She nodded and helped her father finish preparing. They had a nice dinner, and they discussed his upcoming match. She thought, if anything, she might see Denis there and be able to talk with him.

The next day was calmer, even before the conflict resolution class. Emma received no harsh looks or cold shoulder from Skye. While she and Skye still weren't talking, and Denis and Chase weren't either, Van stood with Emma and Rina in the lunch line.

"Hey," he said meekly.

"Hi, Van. How are you?" Emma replied.

"I've been better. Since the Junior Tryouts, things have been kind of messed up. Even more so because you're all in that class after school. I've been going home alone, which is really weird for me."

"It'll be over soon. We only have a couple more days, and then Skye and Chase will be back to their normal schedule," Rina said.

"I kind of want things to go back to the way they were before the tryouts. Where we were one big group," he said.

"Me, too." Emma reached over and hugged him.

"I don't think it's going to work, though. Chase has been acting weird."

"What do you mean?" Emma asked.

He shrugged. The fearful look on his face and the sadness that hung above him gave off an ominous vibe.

Van went to sit with his friends while Emma and Rina went to their normal table. Every day, she wanted more for Denis to come sit with them again. He didn't, but she caught him looking over his shoulder at her, and she wanted to think it was a good sign. It was at least better than the day before, and the one before that.

When lunch was over, she got her wish. Denis approached and opened the door for her on the way out. Rather than say anything other than 'thank you,' and spoil the moment, she headed toward her classroom. He followed.

It seemed like his way of getting back in her good favor, and when she entered the nurse's office, she gave him a little wave.

When it came time to go to the conflict resolution class, she'd had more than a few minutes to reflect. Eager to learn from Mr. Viceroy, she entered and found everyone there except Chase. He'd been at lunch, so she anticipated he was close behind her.

"We'll wait a few minutes for Chase to get here," Mr. Viceroy said.

The clock ticked, and five minutes passed. It became clear Mr. Viceroy had no choice but to start without him.

"Today, I'd like to—"

The door to the room burst open, and a gust of wind blew in. Air swirled around the room like it was being hit by a tornado. Papers, books, and vacant desks were thrown about. Skye screamed. Denis stood up and fought the wind to get to Emma.

"Everyone, exit the building!" Mr. Viceroy yelled over the almost deafening wind.

Denis grabbed Emma and Rina's hands and pulled them toward the door, but it was as if the wind didn't want to let them go. They were pushed back to the center of the room. He tried again and, this time, they were all hurled into the desks.

When Emma was falling, she thought for sure she saw someone running. The sound of feet drummed against the floor like the humming of the train on the tracks. It became more intense before fizzling out. In the wake of the destruction of the room, Chase stood in the doorway, sneering.

"Chase! Stop!" Skye blurted.

"I told you, I'm better than you. Your *pops* is scared of my power. That's why he rejected me. He took away my future!" Chase yelled, staring Denis down. "All I wanted was to join the UFA. I held back at the tryouts so that *you* wouldn't get disqualified!"

They all returned to their feet, and Denis put himself in between Chase and the others. He put his hands up, palms out, to show he wasn't looking for a fight.

"Chase, whatever this is, there's no need for it," Mr. Viceroy said trying to calm him.

"Chase, don't do this," Skye pleaded. "You're better than this. Better than them. They see that now."

"*Everyone* is going to see it…"

She saw it this time. She knew what was happening, just not *how*. The blur. Chase moved so fast that their eyes couldn't perceive him. The wind kicked up, and the blur headed directly at Denis. It—Chase—connected, and Denis flew into the wall.

"Denis!" Emma called out and rushed to him.

When she looked behind her, Chase was grinning maliciously, standing where Denis had been. Denis was having trouble breathing, gasping like a fish out of water. He collapsed facedown.

Seeing he wasn't getting up, Chase towered there for a moment, and the ecstasy on his face dwindled.

"Chase! What did you do?" Skye screamed.

In a rush of air, he was gone from the classroom. Denis needed serious medical attention, and Emma began triage without a second thought.

She pointed at Mr. Viceroy and yelled, "Call emergency services!"

It took him a moment to snap out of his shock, but he ran over to a holo and began the call.

"Come help me get Denis onto his back!" she commanded.

Rina and Skye helped turn the now unconscious Denis over. Tilting his head back, Emma put her ear next to his nose to see if he was still breathing. It was so shallow she couldn't see his chest rise and fall, but she felt a little breath on the hairs on her ear.

Checking his pulse with her fingers to his neck, his heart was still beating, but it was faint.

Leaning over, she took a deep breath, and gently pushed the air into his lungs. Another breath, and again. She counted to ten and gave two more breaths. She needed to keep him alive until the first responders got there, then they'd save his life. It was only minutes before they burst through the door with a stretcher.

"What happened?" one of them asked.

"Chest trauma. Hard impact. Shallow breathing. Has a weak pulse," she replied. "He needs imaging done."

They fitted a mask over his face and switched on a machine attached to the stretcher. The machine breathed for him, and they wheeled him out of the room.

"Call my dad and have him get ahold of Mr. Lindali," Emma said to Rina before following the first responders out.

"His name is Denis Lindali. His father is Trevor Lindali, over at the UFA. Can he be transported there for medical treatment?"

"We have to take him to a nearby clinic to be stabilized first."

She gripped his hand as they rolled him from the school and up into their emergency vehicle. In the back, there was nothing she could do but think. How did Chase do that?

The odd movement at the Junior League tryout, where Chase seemed to speed up to tackle Denis came to her mind. At the time, she was sure she was seeing things, but now that was clearly out the window.

♥

Chapter 17
High Praise

Emma spent the night with Denis in Asta Memorial. Mr. Lindali had arrived shortly after she had and, though they were strangers, they were united in their worry for Denis. He spent his time coming and going, and there were a few times that she heard his voice raised out in the hall.

Phyllip and Gwendy stopped in to check on them, and she cried into her dad's chest. Explaining what happened proved impossible without getting choked up. Shock. Fear. Disbelief. It overwhelmed her into silence.

When he was stable, Denis was transferred to UFA's medical ward, and Emma continued to visit every day. With several fractured ribs and soft tissue damage, he was ordered to rest. His admission to the Junior League was postponed for six to eight weeks. He was furious when Doctor Elanda gave him the news, but Mr. Lindali had come down to calm him.

"Listen, kiddo, I know how much it means to you to begin training, but like any of my other fighters, your health is more important."

"I need to be better *now*. I haven't been to school in over a week. I've been poked, prodded, imaged, and monitored, and I'm going insane! I need to get out of the building."

Emma squeezed his hand, and he looked over at her. He sighed and rested his head on his pillow. Trevor sat and placed his hand on Denis's knee.

"I understand. But we also have to think about your safety. Chase hasn't been caught. The safest place for you right now is in this building, where there are hundreds of trained fighters who are on guard."

Denis resigned and closed his eyes. Trevor was right that it was safer here. Chase hadn't come back to school, and Skye passed on that his parents hadn't seen him since the day it happened.

Trevor gave him a quick pat and stood to leave. He motioned for Emma to follow. Out in the reception area, he turned around and smiled sadly.

"I know I already thanked you for saving his life, but I feel like I have to say it again."

"You don't. Really."

"What can you tell me about how this happened? Denis won't tell me anything. The school doesn't have any answers other than it was a student, Chase Ral Valrog. Nobody, including his parents, has seen him. I'm at a loss."

"I-I don't know how to explain it. It all happened so fast. Chase was so fast. He came in and started attacking Denis. We couldn't do anything."

He became quiet and stared off for a moment. It was clear that it weighed heavily on his mind. When he spoke again he changed the topic.

"I would like it if you reconsidered the offer to volunteer here."

"I feel really awkward about it. Doctor Elanda made it clear there wasn't a position set up for volunteers. And now since Denis brought it up, there could be. It feels...manipulative."

"I get it. You're hesitant because Denis is in a position to influence me, and you feel he pulled some strings in your favor."

She nodded. "Can I be honest with you?"

"Of course."

"After what happened with the Junior League tryouts, and this thing with the volunteer position, I feel like if I took the opportunity, I would be feeding a corruption."

Trevor didn't react negatively. In fact, he leaned in a little bit to listen closer. It helped put Emma at ease about speaking her mind.

"When I think of the UFA, I think of honorable people coming together to put on a performance. Everyone here, not just the fighters. But something is creeping in, tarnishing that view. Not bad people. Just bad decisions."

Trevor nodded and smiled softly at her.

"You are absolutely right, and because this is my establishment, these failings are my responsibility to fix. That being said, if Doctor Elanda and her staff were on board with it, not as and order, would you reconsider?"

If she asked for more kids to receive this privilege, would she be a hypocrite for using a position of power she's in to benefit others? It felt wrong to her if it were only her who got the opportunity.

"Can I make a recommendation?" she asked.

"Go ahead."

"What if it was a non-exclusive position? Not only a position for me but for other up-and-coming caregivers who want to get more hands-on experience?"

He nodded and extended his hand. She shook it.

"I will confer with Doctor Elanda about establishing a volunteer program. If she agrees, I would like for you to be the first. Your integrity is impeccable, and that's the type of character I admire."

She smiled and he turned to leave. After she stopped back into Denis's room to tell him she'd see him tomorrow, she headed to Phyllip's next fight a few floors away.

In the front row, she watched him in his ballet of fists and feet. Reflecting on the recent events, she wondered what was going to happen if someone did catch up to Chase. Would he be arrested? How would they deal with what he could do? It seemed so unreal that if she hadn't witnessed it herself, she probably wouldn't believe it.

Phyllip came out as the winner. She cheered for him and met him at the side of the stage as he was exiting.

"You need to keep your elbows up more, old man," she chided playfully. "He landed some blows on you that could have been mitigated."

"Don't retire me yet, Coach. I still have a few more years left in me." He laughed.

On the way home, she recounted Trevor's offer to her and her recommendation. Phyllip beamed with pride.

"You handled it amazingly. Standing up for your values can be an awkward thing when offered advantages in exchange. Mr. Lindali was one hundred percent correct that it was a powerful show of integrity. Doc. Elanda will see that, too."

Hearing her dad's praise made her smile.

The next day was the beginning of her weekend, and she lay in bed. Life had become beyond complicated in this new school year, and she wondered if it was an omen of her future.

A knock on her door startled her, and she sat up. Gwendy entered cautiously to see if Emma was awake, and when she saw she was, smiled.

"You have a call on the holo, Em," Gwendy said.

"Thanks, Mom."

Throwing on a long sleeve shirt and some baggy, comfortable pants, she headed over to the holo interface. Doctor Elanda was waiting.

"Good morning, Doctor."

"Good morning, Emma. I'm going to cut right to the heart of the matter. I've talked it over with Trevor, and while I initially did not think it would work, he has outlined a manageable plan for volunteers. I'm calling to see if you will accept the first volunteer position."

Knowing Doctor Elanda offered it willingly made her answer infinitely easier to give.

"Absolutely!"

"Because you attend school during the day, your scheduled shifts will be in the evenings. When can you start?"

"Today?"

"Good. Be here at sixteen hundred, promptly."

"Thank you! I will!"

The holo call ended, and she turned around to find her mom hovering in anticipation. They both squealed in delight, and Emma grabbed her mom's hands and jumped up and down.

"I'm going to be a volunteer nurse!" she practically yelled.

Gwendy put her finger up to her lips to quiet them both down, and Emma saw Phyllip wasn't up yet.

She couldn't contain the excitement, though. Before even eating breakfast, she called Rina and told her the news. She was excited, and they discussed going out to celebrate tomorrow.

There was still quite a lot of time left in the day before she needed to be there, so Emma sought to get things in order. She called Mrs. Grada first to let her know of the new volunteer opportunity, and it would take up her time from now on. Mrs. Grada understood and thanked Emma for her hard work.

When that was taken care of, she tried to get some schoolwork done. But no matter how hard she tried to stay focused, she was too excited. She pulled out her diary.

I really don't know how to describe these past few weeks. Everything has been turned upside-down. If I could have told myself at the beginning of the school year what was going to happen, I don't know if I would believe it.

Denis is getting better, and I'm glad. When I saw him hurt, I felt like my heart was going to stop. I don't know what that means, really. Was it just the shock of everything going on or something else? Nobody has an answer for why Chase could move like that. Mr. Viceroy tried to explain it away, but it was unconvincing.

Van isn't sure what to believe. I mean, how do you convince someone who wasn't there that a person moved so fast they disappeared from your vision? Of course, Van wouldn't be able to fathom that without seeing it.

This craziness isn't normal. How is it that I'm at the epicenter of all of this?

Phyllip still hadn't woken up, and Emma was a little sad she wouldn't get to update him about the opportunity before she left.

She paced on the train almost the whole ride there, and only after it arrived at the station nearest to the UFA tower did she think about the fact she was already going to be on her feet most of the night, and she should have sat during the ride.

Thirty minutes early, she was able to take her time heading up to the medical ward. When she arrived, Doctor Elanda was nowhere to be seen, but the receptionist welcomed her, smiling.

"Good evening, Emma. The doctor set aside some nursing clothes for you," the receptionist said. "Please, change into them, and we'll begin."

They were the same plain nurse's uniform most of the workers were wearing here, however she also received a name tag with the word 'Volunteer' under her name. She was ecstatic.

In the women's restroom was a row of lockers, and one of them had her name on it. She quickly changed into her uniform and deposited her regular clothes in the locker.

Returning to the waiting area, she again approached the receptionist, and there was a middle-aged man waiting. Before she could say anything, he extended his hand for a shake, and she accepted.

"Welcome. I'm Nurse Jordan. As our pilot volunteer, you will both be here to learn and help but also allow our staff to further define the volunteer role as we offer it to other young students. Your shifts will be four hours long."

Nurse Jordan gave her a tour. Some of it she'd become quite familiar with while visiting Denis, but he was soon showing her the staff only areas. Storage, medical devices, the digital medical history file system. It was all quite overwhelming at first, but Emma stayed strong and tried to take in as much as she could.

Jordan sat her down at a terminal and walked her through how to access medical histories of patients.

"One of our keys to success is ensuring we accurately log the health of each of our employees. Everyone from Mr. Lindali down to building maintenance personnel is kept on record. Now you're volunteering here, we're going to create an entry for you."

He was soft spoken, and his directions were easy to follow. Step-by-step, he helped her create her file. After inputting basic information, she was met with what felt like a thousand item questionnaire of any and all health issues she might have.

It took her an hour to finish the whole thing, which was a full recounting of her medical history. Jordan came back to check on her and saw she'd completed the task.

"Great, now you understand the basics of data entry we can move on. For now, you'll shadow me, and we'll work our way up to giving you opportunities to assist."

He led her to one of the patient rooms, and they both washed their hands before entering.

Inside was a fighter whom she recognized only by appearance. Stout, he couldn't have been more than an inch taller than her. He was fitter, though. His biceps were like small melons, and she knew he favored upper body strength to win his matches. The cast on his arm told her he probably hadn't won his last one.

"Hey, J," he greeted Jordan. "Time to get this thing off me."

"Good evening, Mick. It is that time isn't it?"

"Believe it. I'm dying to get back out there."

"After we remove the cast, we'll do a quick checkup, imaging, and I'll send you off with some muscle rehab exercises."

"Perfect," he said, then glanced at Emma. "You look familiar, girl. Where do I know you from?"

"I'm Emma Pureheart. You probably know my dad, Lifeshaver."

"Oh, yeah! Phyllip's girl! Man, you've grown! What're you doing here?"

While they talked, Jordan moved to the cabinets in the room and retrieved a small cast saw, a large pair of fabric scissors, and another tool she was unfamiliar with.

Keeping her eye contact with Mick, she stole a glance at Jordan prepping the tools by sterilizing them.

"I'm helping with a pilot volunteer program for caregivers here. It's going to be a great learning opportunity!"

"That's great. Good luck!"

Jordan came over and handed both Emma and Mick safety glasses. They adorned them, and Jordan put his on. Mick placed his arm up onto a side table to give Jordan a steady place to work, and she watched intently as he cut through the cast on both sides.

Her first reaction was to clench her back and arm muscles, as if she were the one cutting it off. She knew the saw would only cut rigid material, and if it touched skin, it would simply jiggle it. But there was an irrational fear that something would go wrong. It made her skin crawl.

Jordan was quickly done making the cut through the cast and used the unfamiliar tool to wedge in and spread the hardened shell apart. With enough room, he cut the fabric inside all the way down, and freed Mick's hand.

Mick opened and closed his fingers several times and moved his arm around freely. The relief on his face told Emma all she needed to know about his time in the cast.

"Extend your arm for me," Jordan requested.

He did, and Jordan looked over his skin. He waved for Emma to come closer, and she did.

"His skin is a little dry from the cast, but he hasn't had the cast on long enough I would anticipate seeing large scale peeling," he said and turned his attention to Mick. "If you do get some, that's okay. It won't be a problem unless you start seeing deep cracks. If that happens, please come in before your next follow-up."

Mick nodded, and Jordan continued his examination. He massaged the arm gently.

"Do you have any sharp pains currently?"

"No."

"Good. Let's go get that imaging done."

They headed out from the examination room and down the hall to the imaging department. Excited, she followed Jordan closely, and after he set Mick up for the imaging, they ducked behind a wall.

"Please, stay completely still," Jordan instructed. "Three. Two. One."

She expected a noise of some sort, maybe a click, but nothing. Still, on one of the screens in front of them appeared the image of the bones in Mick's arm.

They exited and headed back out into the reception area. Jordan gave Mick a soft rubber ball and walked him through exercises to regain his strength. Mick thanked them and was sent on his way.

Jordan kept it fairly light for the rest of the evening, allowing Emma to become more familiar with the operations. In her haste, she'd forgotten a pen and paper to take notes, and she made a mental note to bring them on her next day.

The shift flew by, and she hardly realized it was nearly time for her to go home. Before that, however, she wanted to see Denis. Though she'd been close by, there had been no opportunity.

"Would it be okay if I checked in on Denis?" she asked.

"Sure. I don't have anything else for you tonight. When you're done, you can head home, and I'll see you back in three days."

"Thanks!"

Practically skipping, she headed to Denis's room and knocked lightly. The light was dimmed, and there was no immediate answer. After a quick hand wash, she entered and saw he was asleep. At the side of his bed, she watched the monitors keeping track of his pulse and oxygen levels. They were normal.

Partially uncovered, she checked his skin temperature. He seemed a little cold, so she brought up his blanket to keep him warm. Where they were at now, after what had happened, she wasn't upset at him anymore. She just wanted him to get better.

Leaning over, she gave him a soft kiss on his forehead, and then left. After a quick change and good nights to the staff, she was headed home. The night was cold. Wind tore between the buildings, threatening to knock her over as she headed to the train station. It was even worse at the top of the skyscraper.

Relief came when the train rolled up, and the warm air rushed out as the door opened. When she sat, the fatigue hit her like a wave. Leaning her head against a pole, her eyes swapped their focus a number of times between her reflection on the glass and the city light's outside.

Her eyelids were heavy and closing them for even a moment caused her body to startle her. Fearing she'd missed her stop, her eyes darted to the location sign overhead. Still several stops to go.

Home, she was eager to get into bed. That small burst of energy wore off as she waited for the elevator to descend, and her body protested when she realized how far it was to her apartment.

Finally in the apartment, she gave a cursory hello to Phyllip before shuffling on to her room. In bed, fully clothed, she passed out.

♥

Chapter 18
It's a Date

Emma had been so busy with school, study group, and volunteering, she almost didn't have any time for a life. The path of a caregiver was intense but, because it was her passion, she wasn't yet feeling burnout. Every day was a new opportunity for her to grow.

Unfortunately, it also meant there were sacrifices. She only saw Rina on the morning train and in school. It felt like she was becoming disconnected from her best friend, especially when she needed her the most.

On the other end of the spectrum, because she was volunteering every few days at the UFA, she was getting more time with Denis. Whenever he wasn't training, or sparring in preparation for his first Junior League match, he would come hang out in the medical offices.

They mainly chatted when she was on a scheduled break, and he would bring her dinner from the staff kitchen every night. She was becoming fonder of him and looked forward to the time they had.

Together in the break room, they ate and discussed their day.

"So, when Plank came at me, I grabbed his arm, pulled him in, and launched him over my back."

"Do you think throws are going to be your signature? You seem to be favoring them lately."

"Yeah. After Chase knocked me out, I wanted to make sure I'd never be caught off guard like that again. Using someone's momentum against them will help me gain the upper hand."

"It may not be fair to yourself to use Chase as the reason. He has some ability I don't think anyone could have been prepared for. Rina told me she'd been looking for stories about others like him, and all she's finding is myths and folklore."

"He's a freak. Next time he comes around, I'll be ready."

Secretly, she hoped Chase ran away and wouldn't come back. There hadn't been any word that he'd been seen, and it made her uneasy. He hadn't been back home, according to authorities who investigated the assault. Skye sulked about school, depressed. Van had all but become a recluse. Emma felt sorry for them.

Despite Denis's bravado, Emma wasn't sure another encounter with Chase would end any different.

In the short amount of time she had to eat dinner, they finished, and talked some more. While he was resting his arms on the table, she reached over and put her hand on his. He blushed. She smiled.

"You want to go out sometime?" he asked.

"Yeah. What did you have in mind?"

"Nothing in particular. Just figured maybe we could go do something you like."

"I don't even know what I would find fun right now," she said and laughed. "I've been so consumed with studying, if I'm going to take a day off, I want to not think about anything."

"Okay. Leave it to me, then. I'll plan the date, and you can relax. You have free time in a couple days, yeah?"

It hit her like a brick. This wasn't just hanging out with him. It was going to be an actual *date*. What would she wear? Should she do something other than braid her hair? Makeup or natural? Now that it was real, she was getting nervous. She'd never been on a date.

"Y-yeah. The day after my next volunteer shift, I have a day off. What should I wear?"

"I'll plan and let you know," he said and took her tray. "I'll let you get back to work."

She nodded exuberantly and smiled. Back at her volunteer work, she was re-energized. The rest of the night, she practically danced through the medical facility while she was about her cleanup duties.

This feeling was new. She wanted to savor it for as long as it lasted. Infatuation? A crush? Love was discounted in her mind, at least for now. She felt it was too early for that. But whatever this was, it was nice.

At the end of the night, she headed home and spilled the details to her parents. It burst out of her, and she couldn't stop herself.

"Well, that means if he breaks your heart, I only have to wait a few years before I can retaliate in the ring," Phyllip joked.

Gwendy smacked his leg playfully.

"Don't you dare think of threatening that young man," she chided.

"I won't threaten him. He won't even see it coming."

The three of them laughed.

"Do you need an outfit, dear? I used to know this really good seamster back by where we used to live," Gwendy asked.

"No. I'm sure I have whatever I need. Thank you."

"I sure hope so. Otherwise, I might have to hide the card with all our credits on it," Phyllip said, grinning.

Gwendy slapped his leg a little bit harder this time and gave him a dirty look. It only enticed him to laugh even more.

Emma felt lucky to have the role models she did. They got along so well and seemed perfectly suited to one another. It made her feel sad for Rina, though. Between her parents splitting, and Emma not being able to spend as much time with her, she felt bad.

Her mood changed from happiness to guilt as she knew she would have to break the date to her. It was late though, and she had school the next day. She'd tell her on the train ride in.

Even though she got up early to mentally prepare what she'd say, Rina didn't take it well.

"What do you mean, '*a date?*'" she exclaimed.

"He asked me to go out with him. I don't know what he's planning though."

"He's using his clout again to get what he wants! It's no secret you're a prize to be won to him!"

"I don't see it that way. He likes me."

"He manipulated a situation to *get* you to like him. That's what he wants. He's vain!"

Emma wasn't sure how to respond. Defending Denis's supposed feelings didn't feel like it would get her anywhere. Rina's attitude wasn't fair, but she didn't want to get mad at her. She sighed.

"I want you to be excited for me. This is my first date."

"I'm sorry, but I can't. Denis is a user. If you can't see it, then I don't know what to tell you."

They sat quietly for the rest of the ride in, and Rina wasn't vocal for the rest of the day. Emma figured she'd give her time to let the idea sink in, and then approach the issue again.

After school, she was heading to the train to go to the library for one of her study sessions with AJ and Jakob when Denis approached her.

"Hey. So, I have it figured out for your day off. Dress casual, with a warm coat," he said and grinned from ear to ear.

"Okay!" She smiled back.

"Headed to the library?"

"Yeah. Tests coming up. Need to make sure I know the material inside and out."

"Good luck."

"Thanks."

She waved and jogged to the station. The study group was intense, and yet she found a few fleeting moments within the materials to wonder what Denis had planned.

"Emma? The five point triage scale from lowest priority to highest?" Jakob asked.

"Oh, uh. Non-urgent, semi-urgent, urgent, emergency, and resuscitation."

"Good. Stay with us. We're getting through it. Just a little bit more."

They covered many different subjects, most of which they knew the basics of inside and out. She was getting better at her communication skills, thanks to volunteering at the UFA, but still needed to work on in-the-moment problem solving.

The end of the study session came, and she felt a wave of relief.

The clock moved so slowly in her classes the next day, or at least it felt that way. She knew because she was waiting for something good to happen, her perception was skewed. Anticipation was killing her with every tick of the second hand. When the day was over, she rushed to the train.

After studying, she began planning what she'd wear. Sure, he said casual, but she didn't want to go too casual. Her typical overalls were not going to be acceptable, at least that's what she figured. Instead, she picked out a pair of snug denim pants, and a light blue T-shirt with a flowery lace collar. Those were set aside, along with her denim jacket.

With that out of the way, she had a little time before bed and fantasized about what the date was going to be like. Out in the family room, she sat down on the couch and watched Phyllip lift weights.

"Dad…" she started and wondered how to continue, "what was your and Mom's first date like?"

"Your mom, being the go-getter she is, decided for me we were going to take a trip to ride horses on a guided trail tour."

"Aww. That sounds romantic."

"It was. When we were done, we came back to the city, and went to a nice seafood restaurant."

"Did you date anyone before Mom?"

"Yeah, I had gone out with a few other girls. I didn't connect with them like I did with your mom, though."

"How did you know when you were in love?"

"It wasn't like those steamy romance novels your mom reads, where people fall head over heels at first sight. It was a gradual thing.

It built up over time until one day I realized I couldn't live without her in my life."

It still seemed dreamy to think about, that one day she might have someone she wouldn't be able to picture not being there. She was still young, so she didn't anticipate it would be Denis, but the idea of love was intoxicating in its own right.

The next day felt even slower. There was no school, but she still had to study, and then go volunteer. When she was moving, time slipped by fast, but any down time felt like an eternity. Her shift ended, and she had difficulty sleeping when she got home. She was too excited.

Finally, the day of the date was at hand. Her morning was spent showering, getting dressed, and putting on her makeup. Even though Denis had told her to dress casual, she wanted to do something different with her long hair other than the usual mega-braid.

"What do you think about a braid bun?" Gwendy offered.

"We have time. We could try it out, and if it doesn't look right, then we have time to change it."

It was a pleasant change, albeit a little heavy due to her long hair. Gwendy tucked the bun high, and it made Emma look a bit fancy. Admiring the look in a hand mirror, she decided it would work.

Denis arrived midafternoon, dressed casually. He offered her a single beautiful flower, a Vibrant Iris. Though the light from the apartment dulled it, the blue luminescence was still visible. She'd only ever seen them in pictures, and she wondered where he got one in the city. Rather than placing it in a vase, she hastily clipped the stem down and tucked it into her hair on the side of her head.

"It looks good. Really brings out your eyes," he complimented.

"Thank you!"

"Are you ready to go?"

She grabbed her jacket and threw it on. "Yes!"

"Mrs. Pureheart, if it's all right, I'm going to keep her out a little late, but I promise I'll bring her home safe."

"No problem, Denis. Have a great time, you two!"

He held his arm out for her, and she hooked hers through. Excited, she wanted to ask where they were going, but refused to so the surprise wasn't ruined.

She was confused though when Denis hit the down button in the elevator. At ground level, they exited the building, and he pulled away to open the rear door of an antique, well cared for vehicle. He motioned for her to get in.

Ground vehicles had become scarce when the train system had been developed to connect the entire city, and she'd never ridden in one. Until now. Inside, Denis shut the door behind her and climbed in the opposite door. In the front seat was someone to drive them.

"Pops bought this from an auction several years ago and had it restored. He only uses it when he goes out of town, but since this is our first date, he insisted we borrow it."

"Wanna get underway, Denis?" the man in front asked.

"Yeah. You have the address for the first place."

They accelerated, and their driver made his way south. The streets were somewhat busy with people on foot, but he was able to get by just fine. Forty-five minutes later, and half the city from where they started, the vehicle pulled up to a restaurant, *Your Tastes*. She'd never heard of it before.

Denis exited and came around to open her door. After she'd climbed out, he poked his head in to talk with the driver.

"Meet us back here in two hours or so."

The driver acknowledged with a nod, and Denis closed the door.

A greeter welcomed them, and Denis confirmed a reservation. As he spoke with the greeter, Emma couldn't help but notice this was no ordinary restaurant. Each table had a small kitchen, dishes, utensils, and a miniature fridge.

"Table number eight, Mr. Lindali," the greeter directed.

"Thank you."

Emma gave him a look as he led her to their table. Letting go, he motioned for her to sit on the bench seat against the wall. Taking her coat off, she set it on the seat and sat down.

He hung his coat up and retrieved an apron, a hair net, and some clear disposable gloves. It became apparent what was going on.

"So, I'm a terrible cook, but this restaurant makes it so even the most unskilled can do it," he said, smiling and donning the garments.

He handed her the instruction card so she could look it over. Creamy pasta with mussels and prawns, served with a side of fresh vegetables and a fruit medley. She handed it back. It sounded delicious, and she felt the whole thing was incredibly sweet.

With the instructions back in hand, he prepped ingredients.

"I wanted our first date to be interesting. Figured either we get a decent meal or I make a complete fool of myself despite foolproof instructions. Either way, should be fun, right?" he said and laughed.

She laughed along with him.

"Don't worry. Regardless of outcome, this will be recorded as a permanent record in my diary."

"Your diary, hmm? Got anything else about me in there?"

"Just everything."

"I hope not *everything* because then I might think you spy on me."

"You'll just have to wonder what's in there and never know."

The whole meal only took forty-five minutes to prepare because most of the ingredients were pre-measured, cleaned, cut, and ready to be assembled. The longest segment was cutting up the fruit for the medley. Emma estimated it would have normally taken hours to be ready to eat. But as Denis had said, even the unskilled in cooking could do it.

He dished her plate up and garnished it with chives. She waited for him to get his before taking a bite, and the white sauce mixed with the flavors of the sea was amazing.

Denis reached over to the mini-fridge and retrieved a bottle of sparkling cider.

"Since we're a few years too young to have a drink of wine, I asked them to supply some cider for us," he said with a smirk.

Picking up her glass, she offered it to him, and he obliged. Feeling a little cheesy and caught up in the romantic gesture of him cooking for her, she waited for him to fill his glass.

"To our first date," she said, offering her glass up in a toast.

He tapped her glass lightly. "The first of many?"

Blushing, she could only smile in response, and then took a drink.

After she savored the meal, they rested until they were approached by the greeter.

"Mr. Lindali, your driver has returned. Would you like me to tell them to park and wait?"

"No, thank you. We'll be heading out."

He stood and helped her up. They retrieved their coats, and he led her out arm-in-arm. The sun had set, and the street was lit up with storefront signs and lights from apartments above. Inside the vehicle, the driver started slowly making their way through the city again, but not toward her home.

"Isn't this the wrong way?"

"I have something else planned."

"Oh?"

"Can't tell you what it is yet, though. Hoping to surprise you."

Accepting that, she scooted closer to him and put her hand in his. He gripped back, and it gave her a tingly feeling.

The trip was longer than she expected. Though, what was she actually expecting? Where could he possibly be taking her so far away?

Emma grew nervous as they reached something completely unfamiliar to her. The city's edge. She'd never been outside of Chas before and only ever seen photos of beyond the giant urban jungle. Now, in front of her, the buildings were disappearing, and there were no lights beyond.

"Where are we going?" Emma asked.

"You said you wanted to not think about anything, so I thought we could do some stargazing."

The car breached into the dark unknown, following a road to a building off in the distance, barely lit up. When they got close enough, she could still only discern the shape of it but knew from putting away enough astronomy books it was an observatory.

The driver turned off his lights as he approached, and parked in an alcove, next to another vehicle. Denis did as he had before and jumped out to open her door. She took his hand, and they headed to the building. Inside the wide, double doors was a massive telescope.

Emma was awestruck at the size of it. Even though she'd seen pictures, they didn't do the construction justice. Breaking away from Denis, she quickly approached and began looking over everything and was startled when an older man turned in his seat to greet her. She screamed.

"Sorry. Didn't mean to startle you," he said.

She laughed at her embarrassment.

"It's okay."

"You must be Emma and Denis?"

"Yeah," Denis replied. "Thanks for allowing us to come out here."

"We usually only bring visitors out here every third week for demonstrations and stargazing, to avoid interruptions in our cosmic searches."

"I understand, and we appreciate you making an accommodation," Denis said.

"What would you like to see?"

Denis looked at her for an answer.

"I don't know. The universe is so vast. What are you pointed at right now?"

"I've been collecting images of the Vale Nebula, which is about fifteen light years from Salvoa."

He tinkered with some buttons and waved the two of them over to an eyepiece. Denis let Emma take the first look. She was astonished at the beauty, at the way it seemed to sparkle orange amongst its mostly yellow body. Looking over every inch, she wondered what made it the way it was. Denis took his turn but spent far less time than she did looking.

"It's beautiful," she said to the astronomer.

"It's a wonder, for sure. What else would you like to see?"

"I don't know anything about astronomy, really. Show us what you like?" Emma asked.

He nodded, slid his chair to a console nearby, and pushed several buttons. The whole platform they were on rotated, and the telescope adjusted. When it stopped, he looked into the viewfinder to adjust, and then moved aside.

They spent the night, looking at the astronomer's favorite celestial bodies. Valdu, a galaxy at the end of its life, with only a handful of systems left to be devoured by the center gravity well. Garimn, a trinary star system with a dozen variously sized planets. The Mixie nebula, where an assortment of colors swirled together and created a cosmic gradient.

By the time they were finished, it was incredibly late. Emma yawned and leaned her head on Denis.

"Thanks for doing this," Denis said to the astronomer.

"Yeah, yeah," he said and waved them off. "Get home safely. Make sure the door latches on your way out."

The two of them stood up, and Denis put his arm around her. Out into the darkness, the cityscape's lights had mostly gone out for the night. High in the sky, somewhere, were those magnificent things they'd just seen, and Emma stared up in wonder.

The Lindali's vehicle hummed to life and pulled up to let them in. The ride back was peaceful, and Denis walked her to her door. Outside, she turned to him and smiled.

"I had a really good time tonight. Thank you for taking me out," she said.

"No need to thank me. I did, too."

Feeling bold, and not wanting to miss another opportunity like in the library, she craned her neck up and kissed him softly on the lips. He pressed back a little. Her heart beat hard, and her head swam.

She broke away and sheepishly waved to him as she entered her apartment. After she closed the door, she practically bounded to her room to write in her diary.

I can't believe it! I had my first kiss!

♥

Chapter 19
Making the Effort

School, studying, volunteering, and dating. Her entire schedule was full. The disconnection from Rina felt weird, and it didn't help she kept bringing it up and sulking when they were together. Standing at their locker, they had a few minutes before the first class started.

"The library isn't the same without you there. It's different not being able to come chat with you about a book I'm reading or hang out."

"I know. I miss it, too. Maybe when my UFA volunteer rotation is over I'll be able to come back."

"You're just getting into your studies for being a caregiver. I don't think you'll have much free time at all in the next school year. I heard it's more intense."

"I can't imagine my every waking moment will be filled."

"If your current schedule is any sort of sign of what's to come, we probably won't be hanging out much outside school. Especially now that you're dating Denis..."

It seemed like Rina's words were meant to sting, and she felt bad. Rina was staying with her mom during the week and weekends with her dad. It was because her mom was closer to the school, and they didn't want to disrupt her life even more.

"I'm sorry," Emma said.

Rina was quiet and looked away. The bell rang, and they headed to language class where, despite the title, they focused far more on reading notable literature and proper writing techniques than speaking. The room was mostly silent and, therefore, gave Emma no opportunity to continue the conversation they'd been having.

As the day went on, it only got more awkward. Rina subtly hinted she felt like a third wheel. Though Emma was able to complete her assignments and tasks, it came at the cost of quality due to the preoccupation of feeling like a bad friend.

And it definitely didn't help when she got on the train with Denis to head to the UFA. She wanted to hang out with Rina for a bit, but she couldn't shirk her volunteer work. She silently decided to plan out time just for the two of them.

Denis was excited about getting to spar and train with some of the senior staff today, and she tried to be excited for him, but she obsessed about what to do to make things up to Rina.

The night dragged on, especially because there wasn't much to do except some filing and treating of minor scrapes. Denis wasn't able to make it down for dinner like normal so, instead, she took her break and watched him get thrown around by a more experienced fighter. She didn't feel too bad for him as all of the Junior Leaguers were in the same predicament.

By the time the night was over, she'd had enough time to think about how to make it up to Rina. They would have a girl's day, just the two of them. She had the idea to find out when one of her favorite authors would be in town, so they could go get an autographed copy of a book.

The timing had to be perfect. After researching on her downtimes for a week, she found when the author of *Experience the Rain* would be in Chas. It was still a month out, but it gave her plenty of time to arrange her schedule to make it happen.

Leading up to the surprise, Emma tried going the extra mile for Rina. Even as small of a gesture as going to Rina's house after school to study seemed to put Rina in a better place mentally. They studied separately but took enough breaks they could talk and hang out.

Rina put her current book down and seemed to stare off for a moment before saying anything.

"Do you think parallel universes exist?"

"I'm not sure. Why?"

"I'm reading this new book about some woman who can jump between these two universes, where it's the same world, but things are drastically different."

Emma shrugged. "I suppose it's an interesting idea, but that's probably all it is."

"I keep wondering if there's a universe out there where my parents stayed together…"

This struck Emma right in the heart. Her chest tightened, and all she could do was get up from her homework and hug Rina. Rina hugged back.

"I'm glad you're here," Rina said.

"Me, too. I'm sorry I haven't been around as much as usual."

"I get it. At some point, we have to start living our own lives. I just don't want us to grow apart."

"Never! We'll always be friends, no matter what!"

Rina smiled, and they returned to their activities. It turned out for Emma, studying at Rina's and taking micro-breaks, was actually helping her retain more knowledge. The monotony of staring at a book and taking notes seemed to have been holding her back. With the end of the school year fast approaching, she felt she would be more than ready to take Marcus Bones on in the competition.

Emma could hardly believe how fast the month passed. The day she was going to take Rina to meet the author had been completely planned out, and all with Rina having no clue about what was going on.

On the day of, Emma went to Rina's early in the morning. She'd stopped by a store on the way to grab apple pastries and fruit smoothies. When Rina answered the door, it was plain she'd just stumbled out of bed.

"Em?"

"Hey. I brought breakfast. Hurry and eat so you can go get dressed."

"Why?"

"Don't ask, just do."

Rina glanced sideways at her but took the breakfast and sat at the table. Emma devoured hers and went to pick out an outfit for Rina while she was still eating. Afterward, she spent an hour pampering her friend and getting her ready to go.

"I'm really confused right now. What is all this about?"

"I got you a blind date," Emma said.

"Shut up." Rina smacked playfully at her.

"It's a surprise. Don't ruin it by asking too many questions," Emma said while brushing Rina's hair.

On their way out the door, Emma scribbled a note for Mrs. Gladia, explaining that they went out and they'd be back in the early evening.

Though they made small talk, Emma knew what was really on Rina's mind. She wanted to know where they were going. Emma, however, had no intention of even hinting at their destination on the western edge of Chas. A large bookstore that featured many entertainers from all mediums. Even if Rina surmised where they were going, unless she knew about the signing, she'd never guess why.

Rina gave her another puzzled look when they switched trains, but Emma batted her eyelashes and shrugged. Flying along, they were both now in an area of Chas they hadn't ever been, and that made her glad she checked what stop they'd be getting off at ahead of time.

They exited and made their way to the bottom floor of a massive bookstore, packed full of people waiting to have books signed. It wasn't only Rina's favorite author who was there but several others all doing a group signing.

"What...?" Rina was speechless.

"'What' what?" Emma poked her.

"That's Evalyn Weaver! She wrote *Experience the Rain!*" Rina finally blurted it out, drawing attention to herself.

Rina blushed and looked down. She fidgeted nervously with her hands. Emma grabbed her and led her to the line formed to meet Evalyn and get an autographed book.

"How did you find out about this?"

"I did some research and wanted to surprise you. I know how hard things have been lately, and I wanted to give you a break."

Rina threw her arms around Emma's neck, and they hugged tightly. In line, it was an hour before they even got to the station with Evalyn's books on it for choosing.

"Which ones have you read?" Emma asked and picked up the book that gave her this idea.

"This is her newest one! I haven't read it yet because it's not at the library!"

Rina snatched up one titled *The Eve of Space Piracy*, and then contemplated it.

"I have some money, but I don't know—" Rina started, but Emma cut her off.

"Don't worry about it," she said, pulling out a card with credits on it. "I already talked to my mom and dad about getting you a present."

"Thank you! You're the best friend anyone could ask for!"

Despite Ms. Weaver being a woman of older age, she was well put together and projected herself. Her gray hair was pulled tight into a bun, her wire frame glasses balanced perfectly at the tip of her nose. But the exuberance in which her hand moved as she signed books made it clear she still felt youthful. Each book she handed back to the purchaser was delivered with a warm smile.

Rina gripped her book to be signed as if it were the last copy on Salvoa. At the register, Emma paid, and they moved up to being next in line. Immediately after the person in front of them moved out of the way, Ms. Weaver's eyes met Emma's, and the smile she'd been giving everyone felt like it was meant for her.

Rina bounded up and handed the book over.

"Evalyn, I have been a fan forever! I remember the first time reading your short stories! I absolutely had to read more from you. You're the reason I wanted to follow the entertainer career path!"

Ms. Weaver opened the book to the title page and looked between the two girls.

"I am so glad my stories have captured your heart, Miss…?"

"Rina. Rina Gladia."

"To Miss Rina Gladia. I hope my books continue to entertain and inspire you to create. All the best, Evalyn Weaver," she voiced as she wrote it, and then handed the book back.

"And how about you…Miss?"

"Emma. I only came to get a book for my friend. As you can tell, she's a fan, and I wanted to do something special for her."

"Well, aren't you a sweetheart!"

Emma felt like there was something familiar about her but chalked it up to her friendly attitude.

"Enjoy the book, dear," she said to Rina, and then waved for the next customer.

As they walked away, Rina practically squealed with glee. She gripped the book so hard Emma was sure she was going to warp it even against its hardback cover. She was glad she could make her best friend happy.

On the ride back, Rina couldn't help but poke around on the first few pages, and then slam the cover closed.

"If I start it now, I'll end up completely zoning you out. I don't want to do that."

Emma laughed.

They stopped off for a bite to eat at a burger shop, and Emma treated her there, too. After sitting down, Rina got teary-eyed.

"What did I do to deserve you?" Rina asked.

"We were made for each other." Emma reached over and held Rina's hand. "No matter how busy we get with our lives, I will always be there for you."

This made Rina laugh and cry at the same time.

They sat and talked for hours about everything and nothing without realizing how much time passed. It was like when they were younger. They didn't have to be doing anything. They could just *be*.

After the hearty meal, they got back on the train and continued on toward Rina's apartment. They entered one of those quiet, reflective moments and rested their heads against each other while watching the rooftops pass by.

The feeling of contentment faded, and Emma's mind wandered. She again split her attention between the past and the future. The end of the school year, and the competition, weren't too far off.

She wondered if the others in her year following the caregiver career path were also trying to beat Marcus, or if they had their own rivals. How many other actual people were trying to win? AJ, Jakob, and Vera? Everyone?

Win or lose, her parents would be proud of her. And she was already proud of herself for everything she'd accomplished so far in the year.

She dropped Rina off at her apartment and headed home to prepare for the upcoming school week and volunteer shifts. Instead, she picked up her diary.

Today was a success, and I think I put Rina's mind at ease. Friends to the end. I hope when things settle down between her parents, she'll be able to see that I genuinely like Denis and give him more of a chance.

I'm a little nervous about the end of the year. I want to win but, at the same time, I know it's only a special merit. It won't stop me from being a caregiver if I don't win. I'll still be able to become a first responder and a doctor as long as I keep putting in the effort.

Life has become busier than I expected. What does that mean for my future and how busy that'll be? Five years from now? Ten? Where will I be in my progress? Will I be married? So many things to plan for but can't actually plan them until I'm through schooling. I suppose it's one day at a time until life throws more things at me.

She took her braid out and got ready for bed. Her bedspread always felt amazing after a shower. It was like the comforter was giving her a hug. Only moments passed, and she was out.

♥

Chapter 20
Mending the Fracture

It was abrupt, and she wasn't expecting it. Skye appeared at Emma's locker as she was getting her books for the day. She looked like she hadn't been taking very good care of herself. Her hair was pulled back haphazardly, with stray strands going in many directions. Dark circles hung under her eyes.

"Hey," Skye said.

"Hey." Emma gave a curt wave.

"I'm sorry for everything. I thought I was doing right by Chase. I was defending him. But after what happened... I didn't know he would do that. I'm sorry Denis got hurt."

"He's better now." Emma wasn't sure where the conversation was going. "Any word from Chase?"

"That night after he attacked Denis he tried to get me to run away with him. He knew he would be in trouble if he was arrested." Skye looked down, tears forming. "I told him he needed to turn himself in and he got mad at me. He said that I didn't understand."

Emma wasn't sure how to respond. She thought about it for a moment, trying to form her words.

"I'm sorry, too, for how things happened. For what it's worth, Chase should have had the spot in the Junior League, and Denis tried to make it right."

"I know. I understand that now."

The conversation fell to the wayside, and Emma finished gathering her supplies. It wasn't until she closed her locker and was getting ready to head to class that Skye spoke again.

"Would it be okay if Van and I sat with you at lunch?"

Emma wanted to say yes, as she felt Skye deserved another chance, and Van was an innocent bystander in all this, but she wasn't going to make the decision on her own.

"I'm going to have to check with Rina and Denis. I can't speak for them, and it's kind of a group decision."

Skye nodded. "Just let them know I'm really sorry for how I acted."

Emma returned the nod and headed to Language class. She was ahead, having finished an essay early which was due at the end of the week. In the free time she was given, she and Rina passed notes back and forth.

Skye came to my locker before class. She asked if she and Van could sit with us again. She apologized to me, and said she was sorry for how she acted.

Absolutely not her. Van is welcome. But not her.

I think it would be a good idea to at least hear her apology before deciding. I feel like she deserves a second chance.

I don't like her. She was always pushing her way in between us. And after what she and Chase did...

She didn't know things would happen like that. She didn't know he could even do that. Please, hear her out? If you think it's not working, then we can call it off.

Have you asked Denis about this yet?

Not yet. I wanted to talk to you first.

Rina gave Emma a sideways glance, and then a reluctant sigh to say she would allow it. Emma knew it would be a strained situation, and any little conflict, perceived or real, would likely end it. With Rina on board, all she needed now was to catch Denis in the hall before lunch and ask him.

It wasn't hard. She had his schedule memorized and found him between classes.

"I don't know. What do you think?" Denis asked.

"I think we should give her another chance."

"And she hasn't heard from Chase?"

Emma shook her head. "Not since that day."

Denis shrugged.

"If that's what you want to do, then I'll support it. If Chase shows up, though, I can't say I won't confront him."

"You shouldn't. He might hurt you again."

Denis gave her a look that said he was planning something, but he didn't give away what was in his head. She gave him a hug, a quick kiss on the cheek, and they headed to their classes.

It made her a little happy Rina and Denis agreed to allow Skye and Van back to the lunch table. It wasn't fair to punish Van, and if Skye was heartfelt in an apology to them then they could work on putting things back together. She would get the chance to tell Skye in their math class coming up next. When she entered the classroom, Skye was already seated. Emma smiled at her, and when she approached, she gave her the news.

"I talked to them. They're reluctant, but they are willing to hear you out at lunch."

Skye smiled weakly, and her shoulders relaxed from a hunched position. Skye looked away, but Emma could still see the side of her eye, and it looked like she had a tear. Allowing her to come back was the right thing to do, she was sure of it.

At lunch, Emma, Rina, and Denis followed their routine of standing in line together. Upon sitting down at the table, Skye and Van approached. Van sat down with a weak smile to the three.

Skye was hesitant. She set her tray down, and it looked almost like she was going to cry. Emma couldn't tell whether from happiness or sadness.

"I'm sorry for the way I acted," Skye said, looking between Denis and Rina.

They gave her their attention, but neither said anything.

"I was wrong to attack you like I did, and there's no excuse for it. All I can do is apologize and try to make it up to you. As for Chase, I had no idea he would hurt you like that."

She sat down, and it seemed like she wasn't going to get a response from the others. But Rina spoke up.

"It's going to take some time, but I think we can move past it, so long as you don't have any more contact with him. I won't lie, some of the things you do irritate me, but we can try to be friends again."

"Yeah, and I don't blame you for what Chase did. A person's actions are their own, and he'll have to own up to what he did sooner or later," Denis added.

Skye looked down and nodded. Van was visibly uncomfortable for a few moments but relaxed again.

"You all want to do anything this weekend?" Van asked.

"I have a lot of studying to do," Emma said.

"I have some stage planning and lighting work to do with some classmates," Rina answered.

"Got Junior League practice."

Van frowned but persisted.

"There's nothing worse in life than all work and no play. It's bad for your mental health."

Emma was reluctant to revise her earlier answer because there was so much left she wanted to cover before it was too late. But she also knew he was right, too. If she did nothing but study from now until the competition, she might finally burn herself out. If she went along, Rina and Denis might, too.

"What did you have in mind?" Emma asked.

Van grinned triumphantly.

"Switch-Ball. I have a group I play with every weekend, and we're looking for some new players."

"He's been begging me to go for months now," Skye said. "Except he knows I'm not into sports."

"We're not competitive. We play to have a fun time."

Emma had only ever heard of Switch-Ball in passing. What she did know about it was how it got its namesake; every time a ball was passed, it must switch between hands and feet.

"I'm going to need a break from studying at some point. Might as well be to burn off some energy," Emma said, agreeing to play.

"Great!" Van replied.

As she'd thought, both Rina and Denis followed her lead, and Skye was the last on board. With the five of them, they had half a team. Van assured them there were more than enough people to fill three teams, enough for each team to have people rotate out.

In less than a day, things had become more amicable between them. Whether they could hold it together remained to be seen, but Emma had hopes they could move past the unpleasantness they'd all been a part of before.

The rest of the week seemed to fly by, and Emma found herself looking forward to going out. She'd looked up some of the game's rules during one of her trips to the school library to make sure she knew what to expect.

She knew for certain she wanted to be on the support line, but she could only guess if she'd be better with her hands than her feet based on what she was currently training for.

They met at a local park several blocks from the school, and Van took the time to introduce them to the other boys and girls who came to play. The ages seemed to vary, but Emma reached the conclusion none of them were over twenty.

Breaking into groups, Van pulled them aside to some benches where others were gathering.

"I'm hoping to get more people into playing, so I brought my friends from school. Nikkie, can you help figure out where everyone should be placed?"

A muscular young woman stepped up. She looked intimidating but spoke with a soft voice.

"What are all of your strengths?" she asked.

"I'm good at supporting people," Emma replied right away so there was no chance she'd get put on the front line.

"Good with hands or feet?"

"Hands, I think."

Moving down the line, Nikkie pointed to each of the newcomers.

"Front line, hands," Rina said.

"Front Line. And I guess feet." Denis shrugged.

"Support, hands," Skye replied.

"Okay. We'll start you two off." Nikkie pointed to Rina and Emma. "The others can sit until we switch. Are you familiar with the rules?"

"I read up on the game a little, but I definitely don't know anything beyond the basics," Emma replied.

"We'll be starting in ten minutes or so. Van, give them the rundown and make sure to go over fouls and penalties so we keep possession of the ball."

He nodded excitedly and turned to them. He was succinct in his explanation. It almost felt like she was missing some information, but the simplified version was that support line set up shots, and front line attempted to score. Kicked balls were scored through the top of the goal, and thrown balls were scored through the bottom; anything else was not considered a point, and the ball would be turned over to the protector to put back into play.

After a quick huddle with the rest of their team to discuss positions and strategies, they assumed the starting position mid-field to see who would get first possession. Their team won the coin flip, and Emma was placed on the far left with the instruction that, when the play began, to run a little ahead, receive, and pass the ball.

She was nervous. She'd never been into sports, and she worried about making a mistake. Pushing down the fear of embarrassing herself, she moved forward on the field, but still close. The ball was being passed back and forth between the team members. Throw. Kick. Throw. Kick. Emma's turn.

The ball came at her with great force and, instinctively, she put her hands up and out to protect herself. The ball bounced off her hands and fell to the grass. The person assigned to guarding her tried to retrieve the ball before her, but she threw herself on it.

Standing back up, ball in hand, she scanned for an open teammate to pass it to. Pulling her arms behind her head, she readied the ball to be lobbed at the nearest teammate. When she let it fly, the boy was clearly not expecting it.

At first, he put his hands out to catch but seemed to realize he would get a penalty and let it fall. He did what he could to keep the ball away from his opponent by kicking it but ended up turning over the ball to the other team.

"Sorry!" Emma exclaimed.

Nikkie came and clapped her on the shoulder. "Don't worry about it. We're here to have fun. No pressure."

The game went on, and Emma found herself getting into the spirit. There were still mistakes, and she turned over the ball to the other team more than once, but no one complained.

When it was her turn to rest, she cheered from the sidelines any time one of her friends made a good play. Denis was quick to score a few points after Skye set up the shots. The protector tried to deflect, but Denis's aim to an opening was impeccable.

Emma had no illusions. The mending would still require time, but it felt to her like this was a positive start.

They rotated players a few more times, and everyone got their chance on the field. After watching others' tactics, Emma felt a little more confident and passed the ball better than before. In the end, their team still lost, but she couldn't help but walk off the field with a smile on her face.

Denis stood up and handed her a towel.

"You've got some sweat on your forehead."

"Thanks," she said and wiped it away.

"This wasn't an *awful* experience," Skye told Van, smirking. "I suppose I'll have to give it another try."

"If you'd have just listened to me last year, we could have been doing this every weekend." Van laughed.

"Don't push your luck." Skye playfully punched him in the arm.

The five of them departed but, rather than head home, Skye convinced them to come to her mother's dessert shop for some fresh pastries. When they entered, Mrs. Torrie greeted them.

"Oh, ho! Brought your friends to pilfer my goods, did you?" she said with a laugh.

"Yes, ma'am!"

"All right. One each. I don't want phone calls from your parents accusing me of spoiling your dinners." She grinned.

They picked out their favorites and sat at one of the tables. They ate, talked about the game, and hung out until Emma realized it was far later than she anticipated being out. After a 'thank you' to Mrs. Torrie, and farewells to her friends, she hopped on the nearest train and headed home.

It took some time to get her study material out because she was preoccupied with the day's events. It put her head in the clouds, and it felt like things were going to get better.

♥

Chapter 21
Irrevocable Actions

Rina bounded up to Emma at lunch, a twinkle in her eye and an ear-to-ear grin on her face.

"Guess what!"

"What?"

"For our finals, my teacher gave us a choice of projects based on our year's work. The group chose to write screenplays! We'll all write one and submit them. The teacher is going to choose one to have a limited production!"

"That's amazing! What are you going to write?"

"I'm going to adapt a scene from the book you got me! It's about this fiery, red-headed, loud-mouthed woman who causes a ton of problems in the galaxy. She's also inspirational."

"Wow!"

"I have two weeks to get a script done. Then, they'll judge the scripts. After that, it'll be rehearsals, prop making, and then showtime!"

Denis was also on the entertainer path, and she wondered what his options had been.

"So, what's the scene?"

"I'm debating between a couple. There's one where Eve breaks into a mining facility to steal this special crystal to use it for a power source for her ship. The other is where she's fleeing the galactic police, and they punch their ship through an asteroid."

"Both of those sound like they'd be great scenes, but that also sounds like a lot of work and props."

"I'll be interpreting it with minimalism in mind. Keep the sets small and let the audience use their imagination for filling in the details."

"You sound like you have it figured out."

Rina had been pouring her attention into her craft more those days, and Emma knew it wasn't just because of the nearing finals. With the divorce proceedings speeding up, Rina was looking for any avenue to not be at home right now. The time she'd been spending at Rina's for study sessions moved to her apartment.

The students had submitted their manuscripts. The deliberations took two days, and Rina was a mess the whole time. When it came to the announcement, Emma was there with her. They held hands, and the decision came down. Rina had won first place. They squealed and jumped up and down in excitement.

"I'll make sure everyone is there to see it! No matter what!" Emma told her.

Wanting to celebrate, Emma thought about hosting a party after the school year ended. Partially for Rina, and partially for everyone else as a congratulations for their first year.

Planning a party was actually hard for her to keep to herself, though. Volunteering, study group, and Rina coming over every other day kept getting in the way. After a week of almost nothing decided for the party, she figured she was in over her head if she kept going it alone. She needed to recruit others.

"Skye," she said as she sat down in math class. "I need help!"

"Sure! Anything you need!"

"I'm glad you said that. Rina's working on a play for her final, and I was wanting to organize a party to congratulate her."

"That sounds like a great idea. You're a good friend, y'know?"

That made her cheeks redden. She wasn't expecting a compliment.

"Thank you."

One down, two friends to go. Then, she also had to coordinate both her and Rina's parents in coming, too. Life was sure to try and get in the way, but Emma was determined.

Denis was just as easy to convince, considering there was no convincing needed. She caught him in the hall between class, and he explained he'd already be working on the props, and he would also be doing the rigging of the lights during the performance.

"That's a great idea. Do you think we could do it for the whole group, though? A lot of other students will be putting in a huge effort."

"I had already thought about it being a party for all of us, but we could definitely invite everyone else in the production. I do want to make sure there's a little part of it specifically for Rina, though. With her parents separating..."

"No problem. We'll do something special for her. I'll ask Pops if I can borrow a few guys for setup and breakdown of the party stuff, too."

Throwing her arms around his neck, she gave him a quick kiss on the lips.

"You're the best!"

She approached Van with the idea, and while he was on board, the thought of a party for everyone made him sad.

"I feel bad. Chase was supposed to be here with us."

"I know. I wish things had happened differently. But we can focus on the friendships we have now. That's what's important."

He gave a sad smile and nodded.

"Can we do something special for Skye? She isn't showing it, but Chase being absent is affecting her more than she's letting on."

Emma nodded despite being overwhelmed. It was supposed to be a small party, and now it was multifaceted.

Another week passed. Skye helped Emma plan something special for Rina. Van and Denis helped plan something special for Skye. Emma's life was a runaway train. Her time to sleep was the only reprieve from being on the go.

The final days of the school year arrived for Chas Elite Academy. End of year at this school was different from her previous one. Instead of having classes up until the last day of the last week, students were allowed a week before their final projects or tests to take the time to self-study, prepare, or do whatever it was they needed to do.

To Emma, the year seemed to have flown by, and she was doing everything she could to *not* study right now. She was already overloaded with everything she'd learned, and all the book smarts in the world wouldn't help her with the practical portion.

Skye's group final, a fifty story model skyscraper built to withstand major tectonic shifts, was already completed. It was also the first of her class to be displayed at the builder's finals.

When Emma stopped by to look at it, Skye pointed *it* out. Her name, in tiny handwriting, hidden inside one of the many windows.

"I may not be an artist, but just like that, I'll make sure my name spreads throughout the city. Maybe even all of Salvoa!"

True to what she'd said earlier in the year, it was like a small inside joke between them. They laughed together until an abrupt vacuum of the air in the room took their breath from them. As they had seen exactly once before, a phenomenon entered the room at an impossible speed. There was no time for reactions.

The scale model building Skye and her group had worked hard on was in a million pieces, blown across the room.

"That's what you get for betraying me!" Chase screamed at the top of his lungs.

The blur disappeared, and everyone there, teachers included, were left in disbelief and devastation.

Skye stood there, eyes wet with unshed tears, at the absolute betrayal Chase had just dumped upon them. He had gone beyond a petty argument, beyond a single attack against someone he perceived as an enemy. He was now in the territory of tearing down even those whom he was close to.

"I..." Skye started but couldn't continue.

Everyone was in shock, and nobody said a word. Her group members also felt the loss of their hard work, but none could properly express themselves. One boy broke down and cried while another consoled him.

Skye went from upset to angry in a flash. Her fists clenched. Her face reddened. Tears streamed down her cheeks. She let out a scream of rage and slammed her fists on the table. A teacher approached but jumped back when Skye yelled.

"I'm going to KILL HIM!"

Emma did the only thing she could think to do at that moment. Throwing her arms around Skye, she hugged her tight and buried her head into Skye's collar. Skye pushed away.

"We need to warn the others. If he's willing to do this to you, then the rest of the group are at risk," Emma said.

Skye closed her eyes, took a deep breath, and let out a sigh. The teacher approached again.

"What…was that?" They were bewildered.

Surely, rumors of what happened with Chase before had spread, but the idea someone could move so fast was fantastical. It made sense they wouldn't immediately put it together.

"Chase Ral Valrog destroyed our project," Skye said.

"What do you mean? Who is that?"

Skye shook her head.

"We don't have time to explain." Skye turned to Emma. "Van has a cooking presentation later today."

"And Rina and Denis are working on their class production."

"We should split up to cover both."

Emma nodded, and they hurried out of the room. The theater was on the other side of the school and, no doubt, Chase would get there first if he was heading there. However, she still had to try. A fast walk turned into a jog, into a run.

By the commotion coming from behind the doors, Emma could tell it was too late. Before she reached the door, it burst open. Startled, she jumped back and tripped over her own feet. For a brief second, she saw Chase's face, twisted into a grimace. Then, he was gone.

Denis and Rina came running out after him, and she screamed at the top of her lungs.

"You filthy, wretched, lizard-faced under-dweller!"

Slammed lockers and a thrown garbage can didn't change the fact that Chase was long gone. Denis helped Emma to her feet.

"Did he hurt you?"

"No. He barely missed me. I was coming to warn you. He just destroyed Skye's group final."

"That subhuman, fetid piece of trash obliterated two weeks' worth of props!" Rina paced about, kicking more lockers and cursing Chase's name.

Emma had never seen her so angry, and she was stunned into silence for a moment. Denis saw Emma was unsure how to calm her down, and so he put his hand gently on Rina's shoulder. She stopped, and it gave Emma an opening. She hugged her friend as tight as she could. Rina burst into tears.

The sobbing couldn't be controlled. Her tears quickly soaked Emma's shoulder, and it was ten minutes before she slowed down. In that time, the rest of the class, and teacher, had exited into the hall. They were dumbfounded, unsure of how to handle what they'd seen. Denis spoke up.

"A student, Chase Ral Valrog, did this to us. Don't ask how, because I'm sure you won't believe me anyway. But this was his fault! He did this!"

His declaration didn't help. Chase, for all anyone could tell, wasn't in the room. Emma figured they'd likely seen the same blur, and possibly a whirlwind of set pieces being trashed. Unless they knew what they were looking for, they'd have never seen his face.

Rina calmed, and the three of them came together.

"Chase needs to be stopped," Denis said.

"How do we stop him? He's faster and stronger than any of us," Emma replied. "We need to get law enforcement involved."

"There's no way he'll come if he knows they'll be there. Or if he sees them. He's a coward. We have to set a trap. Something that will keep him until local authorities figure out what to do with him..." Rina said weakly.

"Let's find Skye and Van, and then maybe we can come up with something," Emma suggested.

Rina and Denis nodded. It wasn't long before finding them, and not in a good way. As the three were coming down the hall, Skye was jogging alongside a gurney, where Van was laid out. His face was bloodied, and his jaw contorted. They rushed over.

"What happened?!" Emma cried out.

"Chase broke his jaw while he was presenting." The fire in Skye's voice told Emma she was going to want revenge. "I'll *never* forgive him."

Chase's actions were escalating, and it made Emma fearful of what was going to happen to *her*. She was the last one left who had an important end-of-year assignment. As if she didn't already have enough stress hoping she'd do well in the competition, now she had to worry about a vengeful, powered menace.

They followed the gurney out to the first response vehicle, where Van was lifted in. There wasn't enough room for all of them, and they were directed to Asta Memorial. The vehicle wasn't a block away before Emma spoke.

"He's coming for me next..." she blurted and hyperventilated.

"I won't let that happen." Denis laid his hand on her shoulder to reassure her.

"No matter what, we'll stop him before he hurts you," Rina said.

Skye was silent, but she looked at the three of them and nodded in agreement. None of it made Emma feel any better. Chase was doing things to them to keep them from completing their finals. If Chase would break his friend's jaw to keep him from presenting, did that mean he would break her fingers to keep her from her final?

She scared herself with the thoughts of all the ways he could hurt her. It made her stomach hurt, and she felt nauseated. Could he be reasoned with? Talked down? She wasn't a therapist, but she was going to be a caregiver. What if she could use some of the basic listening skills and mediation techniques from the conflict resolution class to talk him down?

"We need a way to stop him," Rina said. "But how can we stand up to him?"

"I don't know. But we should go to the hospital and make sure Chase doesn't come back to hurt Van more," Skye suggested.

They all agreed. Skipping out on the rest of the school day, they rode the train to Asta Memorial. Inside the massive hospital, they headed for reception.

"I'm looking for Vanguard Creed. He was brought here with a broken jaw," Skye said.

"Relation to Mr. Creed?"

"We are his friends from school. We're worried for him," Emma said.

Nodding, she pointed to the sign-in sheet on the counter. After each of them printed their name and contact information, the receptionist punched some buttons, and looked at her monitor.

"Mr. Creed is currently being attended to. I can't provide details, but when he's finished, he'll be moved to the recovery ward on floor fifteen," they said and pointed to their left.

"Thank you," Skye replied.

They entered a side hallway and found a bank of elevators. The mood was somber while they waited for one to open. Emma figured that if he was in surgery, it might be a while before he got to the recovery room. She resolved to look for a holo to call her parents as soon as she could.

On the fifteenth floor, they arrived at a second reception desk, and they were instructed to wait in the waiting area. Off to the side, there was an area for people to make calls, and she jumped on the first one. Phyllip answered at home.

"Hey, Dad. I'm at the hospital, waiting for a friend to be released to recovery. A kid from school hurt him pretty bad."

"I'm so sorry to hear that, Em. What happened?"

She explained Chase and his superhuman ability to move fast. It sounded impossible even as she was saying it, but something told her that he wouldn't think she was crazy. He listened intently to the very end. When she said that she was the only one remaining who hadn't been attacked his demeanor changed. His brows furrowed and his mouth clenched.

"I'm going to talk to Mr. Lindali, and I'll start recruiting fighters to help protect you and your friends."

She nodded, and they ended the call.

Back in the waiting area, the other three sat silently. Skye with her head in her hands, Denis with his head laid back, and Rina staring off. Emma wasn't content in waiting for her dad to come to the rescue.

They needed a plan, but how were they supposed to take Chase down?

♥

Chapter 22
Desperation

After trying to call Van's family and receiving no response, they sat around the waiting area and talked.

"We have to do something. We can't let him hurt anyone else. He's coming for Emma next, but after that, where will he stop?" Rina said.

Skye shook her head. "He's stubborn. It will keep getting worse and worse."

"We have to find a way to take him down. He's fast, but there has to be something we can do. Use his own momentum against him?" Denis suggested.

"Maybe. But then what?" Rina rested her chin on clasped hands.

"That won't stop him for long though." Skye rubbed her face. "He'll be back on his feet in no time, and then we start over."

"I know an investigator. Cris Prentis. She might be able to help us out," Rina suggested.

It all seemed like a long shot to Emma. If her dad could get some of the UFA fighters on board, she'd feel a little more hopeful of the outcome. But, even then, she wondered if Chase could be subdued.

Rina headed to the bank of holos. They could all overhear the conversation between her and Investigator Prentis.

"Rina, is everything okay?"

"Cris, I need help. There was an attack today at school. One of our school mates destroyed a bunch of our stuff and broke our friend's jaw."

"I'm not really the right person for this kind of situation. I can—"

"Please. I don't know who else to call right now, and I don't think a detective from Public Services would believe me."

"Why not?"

Rina explained, and it was quiet for a moment.

"Are you joking?" Investigator Prentis asked.

"No!" Rina became defensive. "Why would I make something like that up?"

"I know things have been hard with your parents divorcing— "

"That's not it, at all!"

Emma went to stand and come to her rescue, but Denis beat her to it, and he was at the holo in a heartbeat.

"Hello, Investigator. My name is Denis Lindali. My father is the owner of the UFA. If I hadn't seen it myself, or know the person, I might not believe it either, but what Rina told you is true. Chase has already put two people in the hospital, and if we don't stop him now, it's going to escalate."

Baffled by the insistence of a third party that this was all true, Investigator Prentis appeared to be at a loss.

"I'm not sure how I would even help you with this problem. I'm in the family services department, not violent crime."

"We need a way to contain him. Something to stop him from building speed and momentum," Denis said.

"Please. You're the only one I know who can help us. Emma is in danger!" Rina pleaded.

"Let me call an investigator from the violent crimes division and send them over. Where are you at?" Investigator Prentis asked.

"We're at Asta Memorial, waiting for our friend to get out of surgery. Floor fifteen." Denis said.

"I am going to make some calls. Give me a little time."

They ended the call. Coming back to the chairs, Rina did something out of character.

"Thank you for doing that," Rina said to Denis with a sad smile.

He shrugged. "We're friends. We back each other up."

They continued discussing ideas for how to slow or stop Chase completely. In the middle of their discussions, the elevator opened, and they all instinctively looked. An older man and woman exited, and frantically came to the reception counter. Skye jumped up and ran to them.

"I'm so sorry," Skye said and burst into tears.

"Skye? What happened?" the older woman asked.

"Chase broke his jaw."

"Why would Chase do that?" the man asked.

"He's out of control. He's attacking all of us because we're friends." Skye motioned behind her to the rest of the group.

"I'm calling Public Services. That boy is going to answer for his actions," the man said.

"We already did. An investigator should be on their way to help us figure out how to apprehend Chase," Rina said.

Skye somberly introduced the others to Van's grandparents, and the pleasantries felt empty. They all took a seat again, but the kids sat apart from the adults to continue their planning in hushed voices.

"I think we should let the authorities handle catching him," Skye said.

"They're not in any better position than we are, are they? They won't even get close before he hurts them," Denis whispered. "He needs to be caught by surprise."

"I don't like this," Emma told them. "How do we stop him?"

"We'll keep working on the how. For now we need to do some working out. Practice throws. If we can react fact enough, use his own speed against him, we have a chance to stop him."

"Emma and I don't have the same strength you and Rina do. You've had the benefit of the weight room at school all year." Skye leaned in.

Denis put his hand on Skye's shoulder.

"It's all right. You don't need a lot of muscle to use someone's momentum against them. We can practice basic techniques. After Van's in recovery, we should head to the UFA to practice."

"What about after we take him down, though? Can we tie him up or something?" Emma asked.

"I have a better idea," Denis said. "We'll grab a syringe of Sleep Serum from the medical facility at the UFA."

"How?" Emma asked.

"Doctor Elanda is going to give it to us."

Emma wasn't sure it would be that easy, but she trusted Denis.

"Take him down, knock him out, lock him up." Skye's voice shook with uncertainty.

After a while, both Investigator Prentis and another person exited the elevators onto their floor. They looked lost for a moment before Rina leapt up and waved her over. She and her male counterpart approached.

"This is Investigator Lars. He was already assigned to the case of finding Chase Ral Valrog. We linked up when I was trying to get in contact with the lead of the violent crimes division. Mr. Lindali wanted charges pressed after his son was attacked and Lars was the person assigned to the case."

"That's me. I'm Denis Lindali." He stuck his hand out for the inspectors, and they shook hands.

"Tell me in your words what happened," Investigator Lars said.

The four explained what had happened, including the impossible ability of moving faster than the eye could see. Lars took notes and, to Emma's confusion, didn't interrupt or question.

"We need to capture him. He's targeted all of us already, except for Emma. We need something to contain him. A small, portable cell to contain him. Is that something Public Services can do?" Denis asked.

"It's possible. Your father has provided us with some information, and we've been coordinating in an attempt to find and contain him. Unfortunately he has eluded us for now."

"We think there's an opportunity coming to take him by surprise," Emma said with hesitation in her voice. "I don't like it, but it might be the only chance we have."

Before she could tell them, Van's grandparents approached and interjected themselves. The kids became quiet.

"Excuse me, are you the investigator they called?" Mr. Creed asked.

"Yes, sir. And you are?" Investigator Lars extended his hand for a shake.

"Eddie Creed." He shook Lars's hand.

"Mr. Lars, I want that boy, Chase, locked up," he said fervently.

The elevator dinged again, and Van was wheeled into the area on a bed. The hospital staff turned down a hallway and placed him in room thirteen.

The investigators held back while Van's grandparents and Emma's group approached quickly. Before the doctor could close the door to Van's room, Mr. and Mrs. Creed were inside.

"What's your relation to Mr. Creed?" the doctor asked.

"We're his grandparents," Mrs. Creed said. "Is he going to be okay?"

"He's going to have a long recovery. Do you know what happened to him?"

"He was attacked by a classmate."

The doctor moved aside, and what they all saw was horrifying. Van's face was black and blue, and his jaw was wired shut.

"He's going to be on a liquid diet while he heals, and there's a good chance he'll have issues in the future. We did what we could to reconstruct his lower jaw. I need to speak with you in private." The doctor pointed to Van's grandparents.

"Excuse me, I'm Investigator Lars. I'm from the violent crimes investigation division, and am assigned to Van's case. Would it be okay if I sat in?"

Mr. and Mrs. Creed nodded in approval. The kids exited and headed to the elevators with Investigator Prentis.

"Let's head over to the UFA," Denis said. "We can practice, and Emma can grab Sleep Serum."

"What are you planning?" Prentis stood in front of the elevator doors as they opened.

"We have to be ready for him. I hope that Inspector Lars can come up with something to help, but I'm not going to put all my hope in law enforcement being able to capture him. I'm taking the girls over to the UFA to practice defensive techniques," Denis said while standing tall.

Investigator Prentis wrote down Lars's contact information and handed it off to Denis.

"You need to call right away if you see or hear from Chase at all."

The group nodded and headed out of the hospital. The train ride over to the UFA tower was more animated than normal because Denis had already started showing them the basics of grabs and throws.

When they arrived at the UFA tower, they entered through the back like usual, and they all headed up to the medical facility. Despite the odd looks the group got wandering through, Denis led the way to Doctor Elanda's back office. He knocked, and she answered.

"Come."

They entered, and Doctor Elanda's initial look was of contempt at the group entering her office, at least until she saw Emma.

"What can I do for you?"

"Doc, we need your help," Denis said.

She set down some papers she was reviewing and gave her full attention. Denis explained their situation. Doctor Elanda was unfazed.

Turning around, she retrieved files from one of the cabinets. Laying them on the desk, she opened the folders. One was Chase's medical evaluation and file.

"We knew Chase was special at the Junior League tryouts. He was too fast. The judges flagged it and it's why he was disqualified."

"You knew?!" Denis accused.

"He's not the first, either." Doctor Elanda opened two more files and opened them. Samuel and Samson.

Their unique way of communicating, and uncanny ability to be in tune with one another, turned out to be an actual power. Telepathic communication.

"I knew it!" Rina yelled out.

"They were retired because they could read each other's minds?" Denis asked.

Doctor Elanda nodded. "After deliberation between Mr. Lindali, judges, and medical staff, it was decided the twins would retire, and all others with special abilities would be denied to preserve the fairness of the fight. And there have been others."

"Why didn't my pops tell me any of this?"

"You would have learned eventually, when you were a bit older and more involved in the business. People with superhuman abilities are rare, and covered up as hoaxes."

"We need Sleep Serum to help catch Chase," Emma blurted. "He's hurting people. He's going to hurt me. But he also needs help. He needs to be seen by specialists."

Doctor Elanda sighed and shook her head.

"Sleep Serum is a powerful drug. Accidental overdose and you could kill him."

"We don't have a choice," Rina said. "If law enforcement can't stop him and he gets to Emma he could kill *her*."

"She's right. He feels betrayed and alone. He's lashing out and we need to help him. But we can't do that unless we stop him," Skye begged.

"It goes against my better judgment," Doctor Elanda said and sighed. "but if you're positive he's coming for you next, Emma, then it seems you'll have the best opportunity to administer. We're going to go over everything about Sleep Serum, though."

While Denis took the others to practice on the next floor up, Doctor Elanda and Emma spent time going over safe handling of needles, dosing, injection sites for quickest absorption, and what to expect.

"His metabolism is sped up. He's going to process the compound fast, so the law enforcement you're working with is going to need to restrain him quickly."

"What if he recovers before they can?" Emma asked.

"A second dose of Sleep Serum this potent would kill him. They'll need to have a second tranquilizer available and dart him while he's slowed."

Doctor Elanda provided her the capped needle with the serum, and Emma thanked her on her way out.

Her emotions were on overload, with anxiety at the charge of it all. There was a part of her that wanted to laugh nervously at the absurdity of the situation, and another part wanted to cry out of fear of what he would do to her if she failed.

When she found the others, Denis was coaching while Rina and Skye practiced. He saw her and picked up on her unease. Leaving the other two, he met her halfway up the stairs and put his hand in hers. He smiled to try and ease the tension.

Rather than saying anything, she leaned up and kissed him. The others would do whatever they could, but she knew her own safety was on her.

♥

Chapter 23
Test Subject

The day of her clinical skills final and the competition was finally upon them, and it started off with abruptly startling awake. Emma had been sweating profusely in her sleep from a nightmare, and the bed was gross. Groaning in disgust, she got up to start her morning. Whatever the bad dream was about had already faded back to the nothingness from where it came.

She felt exhausted and mentally sluggish. Her shower didn't help much. The day wasn't starting as she'd hoped. Still, she made every effort to not let looming dread take over. After she'd readied herself, she checked on the Sleep Serum. Cap was still intact, the plunger hadn't been accidentally pressed, and there were no air bubbles.

At breakfast, she discussed the plan with her parents.

"I spoke to Mr. Lindali, and he's sending over several fighters, including myself, to help subdue him," Phyllip said.

"He knows who all of you are. Following UFA fighters was a hobby for him. If he sees you or anyone else from the UFA, it might scare him off." Emma frowned. "We'd lose our element of surprise."

"I don't want you getting hurt," Phyllip replied and crossed his arms.

"I know, but you won't always be able to protect me. If he sees you and postpones his attack, he could hurt me later when you're not around and when I'm not ready. At least I'll be able to have some chance today. And law enforcement officers are going to be standing by, hidden."

Phyllip grumbled, and Gwendy rubbed his shoulders to soothe him.

"I don't like it either," she said, "but Emma's right."

Rina showed up to escort her, per usual. On her way out, Emma gave her parents strong hugs.

"I love you," she said.

"Love you, too," they replied in unison.

The whole train ride to school, Rina was adamant about being nearby.

"He got the better of us because we weren't expecting him. He's in for a rude awakening this time."

At the school they disembarked and headed toward the colosseum. Emma looked around. Though she knew the investigator was close with reinforcements, they were nowhere to be seen. That was a good thing.

Inside the colosseum, Rina disappeared before Emma even realized it. Rina, Denis, and Skye had agreed to meet up and form a strategy to stick close to her, so she anticipated they were doing it now.

She awed at the setup for the competition. There were twenty numbered makeshift hospital rooms. Each had ugly pea green curtains, hospital beds, and full-body mannequins in various poses. Nearby were supply cabinets and many different machines and instruments she'd seen within the UFA doctor's office.

Joining her fellow first year participants off to the side, she took a place next to Vera, AJ, and Jakob. There were quiet murmurs amongst the group while Doctor Mansworth reviewed paperwork. Finally, he looked up, counted heads, and began checking off a list on his clipboard.

"Students, this is both your final, and a competition. As I informed you at the beginning of the year, you will be performing a series of tasks related to the treatment of patients. Each station will be proctored by someone from your senior caregiver class. They are there to assist you as you direct them but will not provide any answers. When you have provided care, they will score you and direct you to your next table. At the end, I will tally all the scores and declare the winner.

"In the unlikely event of a tie, there will be a tie-breaker question to settle the score. As contradictory to the real world as it may seem, you may only rely on what you've learned this year and the patient chart on each of the tables. No notes, no asking for help. Any signs of cheating, and you will be disqualified and have to re-take this class."

Looking at his clipboard, he called names and designated numbers. One by one, each student was assigned. Emma was given station twelve. He gave them the signal to disperse.

"Good luck!" Emma told her study partners.

"You, too!" AJ and Jakob replied.

Counting up through the stations, she came to hers, where a mannequin had its arm over its eyes.

Doctor Mansworth's voice came over a loudspeaker, "Remember, this is simulating real life medical problems. Treat accurate, treat fast, and don't kill your patient. You may begin!"

Emma grabbed up her clipboard and flipped it over. The patient's chart stated they've been suffering chronic migraines for the past month, using Cure-All to help mitigate the pain.

This was an easy one. Migraines could be triggered by many things, but there was a surefire medicine she knew would help; a prescribed medication called Free-Mind. The side effects would be rebound headaches if not managed right, but it could be addressed after a patient was in recovery.

Heading quickly to the nearby cabinet, she opened it to a well-stocked and organized supply. Searching through the medicine bottles, she found the Free-Mind but also searched around for something she could use to elevate the patient's head and cover their eyes with.

After propping the mannequin's head up, she brought the bottle of Free-Mind, a glass for water, a small towel, and a cooling pack. Turning to her proctor, she addressed them as if they were the nurse and she were the doctor.

"Chronic migraines can be related to a number of different ailments, including dehydration. Our first course of action will be to address the migraine as a symptom. They should drink a full glass of water and take one dose of Free-Mind.

"Then, with their head elevated, we'll place the towel and cooling pack on their head to help them relax and subdue the pulsating they're likely feeling.

"Lastly, given that the migraines have been going on for over a month, it would be good to get scans of their head to see if a cause can be found. We need to set that up once the Free-Mind has activated."

The proctor took notes and looked up, waiting to see if she had anything else to add. When she didn't say anything, they spoke.

"Is that your final answer?"

She nodded with confidence, and the proctor made one more note.

"Your next station will be number two. Please, wait for the doctor to call for the switch."

While she waited, the proctor reset the station to its original setting. Ten more minutes passed, and Doctor Mansworth called time, but not to switch. He appeared in her station, collected the proctor's sheet, and moved on.

"Move to your next station!" he called out.

The students quickly shuffled, and not a word was spoken.

The mannequin at station two was in a seated position, with one arm limp and the other arm positioned to hold it. The order to begin was given, and she picked up the clipboard. Dislocated shoulder.

So far, the competition seemed simple enough, but she wondered how it would affect everyone else. Doctor Mansworth seemed sure it would be unlikely there'd be a tie.

She got right to work in getting ready to set the patient's shoulder. The steps would be easy enough; set, immobilize, ice, and prepare for imaging. She instructed her proctor in assisting, and they laid the mannequin down and rolled the shoulder back into its socket.

It was only the beginning of the competition, but she wondered when Chase would make his appearance. The syringe was ready, but could she draw it fast enough?

Like the previous station, she finished, was given her next station number, and waited for the doctor to issue the command. Station seventeen. She didn't need the clipboard for this one as the mannequin's hands were at its throat in the universal sign for choking.

As soon as the clock started, she moved around back of the mannequin and gave it five blows between the shoulder blades with the heel of her hand. This was a little awkward for her, because of her small stature versus the taller mannequin. It was even worse when she wrapped her small arms around it to give abdominal thrusts.

After the second round of blows and thrusts, she was surprised when something actually popped out of the mannequin's mouth. It was a wadded up paper ball. Grabbing it, she returned it to the proctor, who took it and wrote notes on her sheet.

A few more stations completed, and her anxiety built steadily, and it wasn't because she'd messed up by not immobilizing a mannequin's neck after a *fall*.

When was he coming? Was he coming at all? Would she be able to stick him and plunge the syringe fast enough? Pressure felt like it was building around her, almost as if she knew his attack would be soon. She'd never had extrasensory perception, but something in her gut felt wrong.

The next station, number five, was ingestion of a toxic cleaning chemical. After a quick read of the chart, she moved to the mannequin while the proctor watched.

"Can you hear me?" she said to the mannequin. "Are you conscious?"

"They're unconscious," the proctor replied.

"Has there been any sign of seizures?"

"Negative."

Grabbing some bottled water they had nearby, she turned the mannequin on its side and began flushing its mouth out.

"Do we know what chemical—"

The familiar thunder crack sound was the herald to her fear. She slid her hand into her pocket and popped the cap off the needle, taking great care not to stab herself. She continued what she was doing, pretending to be too engrossed in her exam to notice. Because the students were separated by curtains, it was her hope she might be able to anticipate him coming by the movements.

It would only take him seconds to search all of the stations, though, so she didn't have much of a window.

She heard the first *woosh* on the next row over and turned her head slightly. There! The curtain moved to her right. Syringe in hand, she was ready. Before she could pull it out, though, a series of events unfolded.

Chase was there, right on top of her, but so were Denis and Rina. From the shadows in between the stations, they anticipated his angle of attack and leapt out. Rina was the one to get a hand on him. It distracted him just enough that Denis got the tackle, and the momentum sent the three tumbling several feet from Emma.

Startled screams and yells were let out by the student body nearby, and students scattered while the three wrestled. Denis pinned Chase's legs, and Rina grabbed his arms.

"Hurry!" Rina shouted at Emma.

Skye appeared and threw her weight onto Chase's torso to keep him from moving too much. Emma sprinted to try and sedate him but, despite being held by three people, Chase still got the upper hand. He wedged his knees between him and Denis, and then pushed.

Whatever power allowed him to run fast also appeared to give him incredible lower body strength. Denis flew in Emma's direction, and he landed on top of her. He threw the other two off and, in the blink of an eye, stood over Denis and Emma.

"You can't win against me! I am faster and stronger! You, your dad, the UFA, and everything you care about is going to crumble!"

Denis struggled to get up off Emma, but Chase kicked him back down. Emma could hardly breathe, let alone move to get close enough to jab Chase.

"What I've done to you idiots during your finals is only the beginning!"

Denis shifted to the right a little, and Emma hoped it meant what she thought. He quickly rolled off her, and she swung around to insert the needle into Chase's leg. She was too slow. He disappeared from sight, and before the other students could escape, he began assaulting them. Doctor Mansworth saw what was happening and attempted to protect the students behind him.

Denis helped Emma up. Skye and Rina ran over, and they prepared to try again.

"I'll taunt him, see if I can get him to come over. Hide and be ready," Denis said to Emma.

Denis, Rina, and Skye spread out in the pathway while Emma ducked behind a turned over table.

"Chase!" Denis yelled. "These people didn't do anything to you. I lied! I'm the one who told them to disqualify you from the UFA!"

"You'll never amount to anything!" Rina followed up. "You'd have never made it in the UFA anyway!"

"You are a lousy friend and a horrible person!" Skye screamed. "I hate you!"

Emma peeked out long enough to see that did it. The blur turned from the side of the colosseum to the center where Denis stood. Ducking back, she prepared to leap out the moment she saw the air cut.

Before she could, though, there was a distant noise. Something she'd never heard before. A high discharge of air from up in the stands. Chase stumbled, and Denis used his forearm to catch his neck and throw him to the ground.

Denis, Rina, and Skye leapt on top of him again, and Emma wasted no time. The needle of the syringe was pushed into his neck while he struggled, and she depressed the plunger, giving him the full dose of Sleep Serum.

"What did you do?! Get off me! Get...off!" Chase's voice slurred while he screamed.

They continued to hold him down until the fight had left him. His eyes rolled back and, for the moment, he was out.

Law enforcement flooded in from the sides and stands of the colosseum, including Investigator Lars. They rushed down to ground level and cuffed Chase's wrists and ankles. Rolling him over revealed a dart stuck into his backside.

"Are you all okay?" Investigator Lars asked.

The three girls nodded, and Denis acted as their spokesperson.

"Bruised but okay," Denis said.

"Now what?" Emma asked.

"We've devised a temporary holding cell to shackle his feet in place. If he can't use his legs, we're hoping he can't escape. Not sure how the law is going to interpret this one, but at least for now he won't harm anyone else."

The terror was over. She was safe, as was everyone else, relatively. Though Chase had managed to assault a number of people, few were carried out on stretchers. Doctor Mansworth stood off to the side and directed people in triaging. Emma put her hand into Denis's and headed toward the doctor. She felt like she owed him an explanation.

"Doctor Mansworth, I'm sorry I couldn't tell you earlier," Emma apologized. "We knew Chase was going to attack today, and we had to have the element of surprise."

"Is this what the other teachers and students have been going on about? How can he do that?"

Emma shrugged.

"We don't really know. I feel bad because he's probably going to become a medical subject."

The consequences of capturing him, with his extraordinary ability, was that his life was functionally over. His freedoms were now forfeit. What would ultimately become of him? Would the people try to figure out the secret to his ability? What would the ethics be in this process?

As Emma mulled over the future, Investigator Prentis and Detective Lars bid farewell, and Doctor Mansworth addressed the students. His voice was subdued. Emma had never seen him like this; at a loss.

"In the wake of the events here, the competition is on hold until we ensure everyone is healthy and can get all this cleared up and reset. Anyone willing and able to stick around to help, please do. Just clear the field. Bring everything to the side."

Those who hadn't been taken to be checked out by medical professionals stayed. Even Marcus, whom she would have figured was too arrogant to *demean* himself with physical labor helped.

Cleaning up took hours, but they finally got everything pulled to the side and semi-organized. Doctor Mansworth thanked them for their efforts and dismissed them. It was early evening, and the sun was already touching the top of the nearby buildings on its way down.

The four friends made their way to the train station outside the school. Thoughts of Chase's fate plagued Emma's mind, and their silent company was a slight comfort to her. Whether or not they did the right thing in assisting with his apprehension ran through her mind. She knew he couldn't be allowed to terrorize and hurt people but, at the same time, his fate was partially her fault. It felt like she sentenced him to death.

The ride home was unpleasant, and it didn't get any better when she got there, and her friends said their goodbyes. Gwendy was at work, but Phyllip was there and wanted to know how it went. Emma rehashed everything and confided her guilt to him.

He hugged her tightly, and because he was twice her size, he engulfed her. She finally felt safe enough to let out the emotions she had pent up. Her tears left darkened patches on his shirt. Exhausted, she eventually felt herself drifting.

Phyllip lifted her and brought her to her room. He laid her down, covered her up, and kissed her forehead.

"It's all going to be okay, Em."

♥

Chapter 24
An End and a Beginning

It had been two weeks since the attack. Except for Van, who was given a passing grade due to extenuating circumstances, the students who had their final projects destroyed were given the opportunity to redo everything.

Emma cheered her friends on, and when it came time to go to the play Rina had won the honor of writing and directing, she made sure there were front row seats reserved for the most important people; Rina's and Emma's parents, Mr. Lindali, and seats for Skye and Van. The play was a success, and at the closing curtain, Emma leapt up and cheered. She didn't care she was being louder than everyone else.

From there, she was the last to get a redo opportunity. In the downtime waiting for the competition and between studies, she'd had time to reflect on everything. Emma was thankful they were able to stop him, but his unknown fate still weighed heavily on her. This brought her to a conclusion; her idea of becoming a first responder receded in place of a passion. Transhuman biology and genetics.

Of course, her drive to help people was still there, but now it was focused. She had to know what made Chase special. And there were others out there like him. What could she learn? Was this a mutation? Were the abilities induced by something?

She'd need all the information Doctor Elanda had on the others if she was going to help them, or potentially save others from them.

What if there were someone with a more devastating power than Chase? If she could learn the what and why behind these special abilities, could she prevent a future calamity? Could a neutralization process be developed so Chase could have a normal life?

The call for the makeup final and competition was finally given. Because the school year had ended, and the other students had been let out for their end of year break, Doctor Mansworth was forced to call upon school staff to set up the stations once more, and then act as the proctors.

She stood again with AJ, Jakob, and Vera, and they engaged in small talk until Doctor Mansworth was ready to begin.

"Barring any further interruptions or disasters, today will conclude the competition. A winner will be declared, you will be given your final grades, and then you'll be officially dismissed for your end of year break."

As he'd done previously, the doctor called out names and station numbers. Emma's first assignment was station nine. The signal was given to begin, and she went directly to the clipboard and reviewed the information.

One after the next, she completed the care for each of the stations. Back spasm, fainting, unresponsiveness, hamstring strain. It all seemed easy enough because of her extracurricular training, and she felt she was a top contender for the competition.

When she got to station eighteen, her confidence had peaked. Reading the chart, the patient had inhaled water and was unconscious. Immediately, she checked for breathing, and then a pulse.

"They're not breathing, and there's no pulse," the teacher acting as proctor stated.

Emma checked the mouth for fluid, tilted the head back, and gave a couple breaths before starting chest compressions. For a minute, she went back and forth, and then turned to the proctor.

"Call for first responders. I'll continue trying to revive them," she directed.

The proctor nodded and made notes on their scoring sheet.

Emma went through the motions again. Breaths and compressions. Then, the proctor questioned her.

"First responders haven't arrived yet, and the person revives, what's your next steps?"

It caught her off guard as the other proctors hadn't asked follow-up questions.

"Um…we roll them onto their side, into the recovery position."

The proctor seemed to be waiting for something else, but it was slipping her mind. Did she need to check their oxygen levels? Check their responsiveness? It was slipping through her grasp, and her confidence level declined. What was she missing?

"Time!" Doctor Mansworth called through the loudspeaker.

The proctor wrote down on her scoring sheet, and then pointed to the right.

"Station nineteen is your next stop."

Heading there, she crossed paths with Marcus. He held his head high, and an air of superiority swirled around him. Even though they ended up going to neighboring stations from one another, he didn't even acknowledge her presence. He was snooty but, at the same time, she respected his dedication.

While she was sure he was going to make an incredible and technically minded doctor, he wasn't going to win any personality contests. It felt like this competition was his chance to shine. Emma wasn't going to purposely pull back and let him have the win, but after everything she'd been through this year, the silent rivalry she held with him felt like wasted effort.

Instead, she chose to forget about trying to beat him and do her best to treat the patients.

Approaching the sitting mannequin, the hands were blotched with red ink. The chart gave the diagnosis; second degree burns.

"First, we need to run cool water over his hands," she said and helped the mannequin up to a sink in her station area.

There was no running water, so pretend had to be enough. While her patient was at the sink, she grabbed the supplies she would need to continue treatment. Because she didn't have enough time to allow for the full water-cooling, she announced to the proctor her thoughts.

"We don't have enough time in the test to allow for it, but under normal circumstances, the patient would need to cool their hands for fifteen minutes."

The proctor acknowledged and wrote on her sheet.

After administering a dose of Cure-All, she applied Burn-Heal antibiotic cream to the blisters, covered the hands with sterile gauze, and wrapped them with bandages. There was time to spare, and she helped the proctor reset the station for the next student.

At the end of it all, she was exhausted. She'd treated everything from vomiting to a broken leg. But it was over, and she'd done her best. They had to wait around for Doctor Mansworth to go through all of the sheets and score.

"How do you think you did?" Emma asked her three clinical skills classmates.

"I definitely messed up on the harder things," AJ said. "I hope it's enough for a passing grade."

"I'm pretty sure no one flunks out. You'll just get a different set of classes next year than the rest of us," Vera said with a smirk.

They laughed. It was a rare moment where Vera's arrogant attitude was pushed aside for a more jovial one.

"I did well," Jakob said. "All that extra studying really came in handy, and I followed your example and picked up volunteer shifts at a hospital," he said to Emma. "What about you?"

"I did okay, but I definitely made mistakes. I got overconfident and slipped up."

"I'm sure you did fine," he replied.

After another ten minutes, Doctor Mansworth called them all over. Their scores were posted, and the winner of the competition was exactly who she thought it would be, with ninety-nine points. Marcus. Jakob took second with ninety-eight, and Emma tied for third at ninety-five with another student.

It was okay. She didn't win the competition, but nothing could replace the experiences she'd had this year. It also couldn't change the realization of wanting to specialize in something she'd never even given a thought to before.

"Congratulations!" Emma told Jakob.

"Thanks. I didn't win, though."

"You still did great! We all did."

Several students congratulated Marcus personally, including Emma. Even if she didn't like him, it felt right to acknowledge his execution of knowledge and skills.

The day came to an end, and Emma could now feel relieved until the next school year. With two months off before her next classes started, and her volunteering at the UFA ending, she was free to begin researching how to get where she wanted to go with her chosen career path.

The ride home on the train was serene. The weight of anxiety had been lifted, for now, and she enjoyed watching the sun set. The hum of the train was almost enough to put her to sleep.

Arriving at her stop, she wasn't in a hurry to disembark. The seat had grown warm, and it was comfortable. But her parents would be waiting to hear the news, and she'd have to call Rina and Denis on the holo to let them know, too.

At the apartment door, she was pleasantly surprised when she opened it to see a large 'Congratulations' banner. Waiting for her were her friends and parents, who clapped for her as she entered.

Her smile felt like it stretched from ear to ear. She was torn on who to hug first, and so she decided it was easier to start with her mom and work her way across the room.

"We didn't get to have the party you were planning for us, so we all pitched in to throw you one instead," Skye said.

"Thank you, everyone. This means a lot to me."

"How did you do in the competition, honey?" Gwendy asked.

"I tied for third, but it's okay. I've decided I know what I want to do with my career."

"What do you mean?" Rina asked. "Did you change your mind on being a first responder?"

"Mmhmm. I'm going to dedicate my life to understanding why Chase has his ability and maybe a way to help him."

Conveniently, she left out the part where she hoped to find a way for him to live a normal life not incarcerated. She figured it would be easier for them to digest this way, considering the harm he'd done.

"There are others out there like Chase," Emma continued. "Others who may be burdened by an ability they didn't ask for. I want to help them and prevent future incidents by powered people."

"I have no doubt we can get Doctor Elanda to help us," Denis said.

"Us?" she questioned.

"Of course. We're in this together." He grabbed her hand.

Not to be left out, Rina threw her hand on top of theirs.

"Count me in."

"And me." Skye added her hand.

Van grunted through his wired jaw and put his hand on the pile.

"Well then, what do we call our group?" Emma asked.

"After you, of course. Pureheart," Skye said with a wink.

"No. Thanks. I don't need a big ego," Emma replied.

They all laughed and broke their hand-stack.

Phyllip and Gwendy served up a cake, ordered from Mrs. Torrie. Throughout the evening, they talked about the year, and all of the problems they'd had, which now seemed trivial compared to the grand scheme of things. Van mumbled through his wired jaw, and despite the severity of the injury, he managed to make a joke of it by miming out what he was trying to say.

They all took turns playing the game and laughing. Skye played dumb and insisted to everyone he was asking for cake, then proceeded to smear frosting on Van's lips.

Emma felt alive with wonder, amongst these people whom she loved. If this was just the beginning, what else did her life have in store?

♥

<u>Epilogue:</u>
<u>What the Future Holds</u>

"We're running out of time," Rina says and taps her foot while Emma peers through a microscope.

Taking a quick glance at the clock, she notes she still has an hour before she has to be there.

"I'm fine. Still have time. This sample won't analyze itself!"

Rina grabs her shoulder, stands her up straight, and glares.

"Just because *you* don't want any makeup doesn't mean *I* don't. Let's get going so I can look good."

Emma sighs and relents.

"Fine. I wanted to see the compound work firsthand, but I'll set the machine to record and watch the playback. I guess I'll at least get to view the 3-D model of it."

Having won, Rina pulls her along, and they head out from the lab.

On the train, Emma feels differently about the ride than she has before. As far back as she can remember, she and Rina shared a bench and stared out the window at Chas. Having grown, she sees the city in a different light. The world had opened up to her after she'd graduated, and now it was changing again.

The decorations in Asta Park could be seen blocks away. *Of course,* Denis had spared no expense. Rina nudges her and points at the obvious. She giggles with giddiness for her friend.

"Remember how much you used to hate him?" Emma laughs.

"Used to? I still hate him! He's such a slave driver!"

"Where does he have you scouting next?"

"Some frozen tundra city to the north. Temra, I think it's called."

"Good. Maybe the next candidate you come across will hold the key."

They exit the train, and head to the park. The sun warms her neck, and she closes her eyes for a moment while walking.

Entering the tent designated for the bride, the dress she'd picked out is having its final alterations done by the seamstress. The woman spots Emma and smiles warmly at her. She pushes graying, curly locks from her face and waves Emma over.

"Come in, dear. I need you to try it on so I can make sure I got it right."

Rina pushes her, and she's quick to get out of her doctor's coat and scrubs and into the elegant masterpiece. Fancy dresses weren't her normal style, but she fell in love with the seamstress's personality and the skill she had in creating unique garments.

"Come, Emma darling," the old woman says and waves her over.

A tri-fold mirror gives Emma a full picture of how the dress looks on her. It's sleek, with a very small train.

"It's wonderful," Emma tells her.

"I'm glad you like it, dear. I've had this dress in my mind for many years, waiting for someone very special."

Spinning around a few more times, looking over her shoulder, she admires it. Rina pokes at her.

"All right, missy. Almost time to make him Mr. Pureheart."

The duo heads to the makeup area, where Skye was already having hers applied.

"It's about time you showed up!"

"Sorry! I was engrossed in work."

"Figures," she smirks. "How's Chase?"

Rina sits, and a second makeup artist begins applying light touches.

"He's doing well in therapy, and the medicine he is on is proving effective in controlling his emotional disorder. They've also been letting him exert enough energy to keep his power from building up too high and breaking down his body. He's content with that. Though, we're hoping for a breakthrough in neutralizing it completely so he can live a normal life."

"That's good. He's going to be in a weird place with no career though if you can get him back to normal."

"Denis has already offered him a position in the company, and he accepted."

"I'm glad. I should really get out to see him sometime soon."

"He'd really like that."

After the women, minus Emma, had their makeup applied, they head to the reception tent, where Denis is checking over everything. He sees Emma, and his eyes light up. He pulls on his suit jacket to get rid of any wrinkles and runs his hand through his dyed black hair.

"You look amazing, honey," he tells her as he strides over.

"As do you!"

Emma pushes up on her tiptoes, throws her arms around his neck, and kisses him briefly. He puts his arms around her waist.

"All of the guests have arrived, and the officiant is ready to begin whenever you are. You ready?"

"I am!"

Emma peeks out from the curtains to the make-shift, sunlit courtyard. An innumerous amount of people are either seated or standing to the sides, waiting for the processional to begin, a sign for the both of them to show how many people support their marriage. Colleagues, UFA fighters, friends, family. Everyone was there for them.

Those in the processional take their places, and a light music begins playing to signal the start. Family first, Phyllip and Gwendy walk down and to the left of the stage. Trevor follows and breaks to the right. Rina and Skye are next and walk the aisle throwing flower petals on the ground, splitting the stage when they get there. Van and Jakob each carry a pillow with a ring tied to it and do the same when they reach the end.

Finally, Emma and Denis begin their walk. All eyes are on them as people turn in their seats and, at the stage, the people who matter most beam with happiness.

When they reach the end, they step up and Emma glances at Denis. He gives her a warm smile, and then nods to the man who is their officiant to begin. The salt-and-pepper bearded man makes a gentle wave to the band, who trails the music off. The officiant speaks, and projects his voice well enough that he needs no speaker.

"Today, we are gathered here to witness the joining of two lives into one: Emma Pureheart and Denis Lindali. From the beginning, it seems their lives were destined to intertwine, and they have made the choice to devote themselves to one another for the rest of their lives. As you've watched them grow up, you supported them individually and as a couple. You felt the love they have for each other.

"Denis Lindali, do you have your vow prepared?" the officiant asks.

He nods.

"Emma, from the first time I laid eyes on you, I knew I wanted to be with you forever. Every comfort had been guaranteed me in my life, but it wasn't until I met you that I knew, without your love, it would never be enough. Only through you am I whole, and I am honored you would take me as your husband."

Tears came to Emma's eyes. Happiness overwhelms her.

"Emma Pureheart, do you have your vow prepared?"

She nods.

"Denis, before we met, I hadn't thought about dating, love, or marriage. Of course, we were still in career school so that was to be expected!" She pauses as the congregation laughs. "But as we encountered challenges together, we grew closer. I think fondly of our first date, out at the observatory, looking up to the skies. I remember thinking then that, though everything was so vast and overwhelming, you grounded me. You made me feel like I was the center of the universe, and I still feel that way. I am honored you would take me as your wife."

The officiant nods and smiles.

"The finest vows I've ever heard," he says and looks to either side, to the fathers. "Please, present the rings."

Phyllip and Trevor step toward Van and Jakob to remove the rings from the pillows and present them to their children. Denis and Emma take them and exchange them by placing them on each other's hands.

"With the power of the duties charged to me, I declare you husband and wife in front of all witnesses here. May you live long, and love deeply. I present to all, Mr. and Mrs. Pureheart!"

The audience erupts into applause, cheers, and whistles. Emma reaches up and kisses her husband deeply, and he pulls her in tight. They hold the embrace for what seems like forever. The sound dies down around them, and when she pulls away, she's caught off guard.

Everyone around them has stopped moving. They're completely frozen in place.

"What's going on?" Emma asks, her voice threatening to crack in fear.

Denis looks around, also frightened. "I don't know."

"I know this is a little disconcerting, but don't be afraid," the officiant speaks, clearly not affected.

The seamstress approaches from the side and takes a place right next to the officiant.

"What is this?" Emma's voice quivers.

"I've frozen time for everyone but the four of us. We're *special* individuals, as you call those with powers. We call ourselves Alkosians."

"What do you mean to do to us?" Denis asks.

"Emma, dear. It's been so long," the seamstress says. "An entire lifetime for us. We wanted to give you a gift, a gift I promised you a long time ago."

The seamstress hands her a bulged envelope. Emma opens it and finds a necklace with a pinkish-purple, heart-shaped crystal as the centerpiece. There's also a letter, familiar in that it once scared her so completely she panicked. That same panic fills her again.

"Who are you?!" Emma cries out.

"Why are you doing this?" Denis steps up to defend her.

"Denis, once upon a time, in another life, I wronged you," the officiant says. "I made the decision to help you be a better person this time around. Of course, I had no way of knowing you two would still find each other."

"You're not making any sense!" he replies.

"I can change that. I can give you sight beyond what you know. Lives you never lived. I can show you wonders, which will guide you on your journey to finding and understanding Alkosians. Once I give it, you will not be the same. You will know of a timeline which no longer exists, and the people you did not become," the seamstress says gently. "And I will only give it to you if you consent."

Emma is beyond confused, as is Denis. It all sounded like nonsense, but the reality was that one of them clearly has powers, and maybe something that could help Chase and the others like him. Did she want to risk never finding a way to help them by denying this freely offered knowledge? Looking to Denis, she wonders what he's thinking. He looks at her, and it's clear he wants direction also.

"What would this knowledge cost?" Denis asks.

"Nothing material," the woman says.

"It won't hurt us?" Emma asks.

"It won't hurt," he tells them.

Emma looks to Denis one more time.

"What do you think?"

"Our whole goal was to find others and try to help them," he replies. "If they have something that can help us, then I think we should go for it."

She nods to him, and then to the older couple. Without any more words, the seamstress steps forward, places Emma and Denis's heads gently together and kisses their foreheads.

It's gradual. Images in their mind's eyes come first, and they show Emma and Denis in another life as viewed through the seamstress and officiant's eyes. They'd existed in an alternate timeline and were completely different people. Things were similar, yet vastly dissimilar to what they'd lived so far.

And then came the knowledge of the vraditi, the tarak. The Alkosians. The knowledge of the crystals, and the influence they have on the biology of humankind. The answer to Chase's power was there, in the crystal-heart necklace she gripped.

"I..." Emma starts and trips up on the thought of her parents' deaths in the other timeline. She finds her voice again when the pieces come together. "You're the one in the photos. You and...Evalyn? Wait, the author?"

"The same. Evalyn has been watching over you. Just as I have someone watching over Eve in her time," Rain says.

"You're strangers but also familiar. I felt it when I held the letter and when I saw the photo in Trevor's office," she says.

"You won't have the same feelings I did when Rain brought my alternate timeline soul and memories to me," Ami tells her. "But what you're describing is what we call a time-echo. In another life, our fates were intertwined, and that bleeds over."

"I was a...terror...in that other life," Denis says.

"Yes, but *you* are not that person." Rain places his hand on Denis's shoulder. "When I reset the timeline, I became a paradox. I knew of the things that would happen and changed them so you wouldn't follow the same path. You two still have a lot to accomplish, but one day in your future, after you've achieved much, I will return to offer you another new opportunity."

"What happens now?" Emma asks. "What do we do?"

"That's up to you to figure out," Rain replies. "I only made changes at the beginning, and let life take its course up until now. Your destinies are still your own."

It's clear as mud to Emma but, armed with the new information about people with powers, she had hope she could find a way to give Chase his life back.

"I'm going to restart time. For continuity, I need you to return to kissing so your audience doesn't see something they shouldn't."

Ami walks off stage and returns to where she came from. Emma and Denis return to the embrace they were in before and, with that, the noise of the crowd returns. They break away from one another and turn to the crowd, hands intertwined, and Rain places his hands on their shoulders.

Emma and Denis look at one another with uncertainty, now armed with a knowledge that will greatly assist them in the pursuit of helping people with *alkos*.

Together they bow to everyone, and they break from the stage to go to their reception, enjoy their newlywed status, and eat their magnificent cake.

♥

~~~~Emma's journey is only beginning!~~~~

About The Author

Thomas W. Everson thinks you're awesome for reading his book(s). The love of entertaining is what inspires him most to write. He uses influences from many different places, people, and events, in the hopes that readers will relate in some way and lose themselves in the story.

His passion outside of writing is enjoying time with his wife and son, where they read books and comics, watch movies, and play video games together. Beyond the fantastical, he is also very enthusiastic about real life astronautics.

9 780986 412073